THE
MARCUS
DEVICE

THE MARCUS DEVICE

A NOVEL BY **Ib Melchior**

HARPER & ROW, PUBLISHERS

NEW YORK

Cambridge
Hagerstown
Philadelphia
San Francisco

1817

London
Mexico City
São Paulo
Sydney

B-2

FIRST EDITION

Designer: Sidney Feinberg

Library of Congress Cataloging in Publication Data

Melchior, Ib.
  The Marcus device.
  I. Title.
PZ4.M51457Mar [PS3563.E435] 813'.5'4 79-2654
ISBN 0-06-013038-5

80 81 82 83 84 10 9 8 7 6 5 4 3 2 1

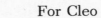

For Cleo

Acknowledgments

I should like to express my appreciation for the valuable assistance in my research given me by:

The United States Air Force
USAF Flight Test Center, Edwards Air Force Base
Death Valley National Monument Rangers
Elliott L. Markoff, M.D., Ph.D.,
   Associate Clinical Professor of Psychiatry,
   University of Southern California
Haus Am Checkpoint Charlie, West Berlin

The vastly intricate human mind is encased in a space some seven-inches wide, but is still vulnerable. Although we possess much knowledge of it—it is still largely a wilderness, a seven-inch wilderness. . . .

COL. ROBERT J. SOKOL, M.D., PH.D.
Chief, Psychiatric Division
97 General Hospital, AUS,
in *Of Minds And Men*

The USAF devices and equipment described in the story are in fact undergoing development and testing and are not figments of the author's imagination. The medical diagnoses and conditions are psychiatrically and neurosurgically authentic.

I.M.

PHASE I

1

He could hear their heavy, hobnailed boots pounding down the cobblestone street in pursuit. There must be at least six of them, he thought. The steady tramp hammered on his ears and reverberated in his battered mind. His breath came in convulsive gulps, and a sharp sting in his side knifed through him with every step. But he forced himself to go on.

A few steps ahead of him he could make out the shadowy form of Willi as he followed his friend down the dark and empty street of the little Bavarian village.

There was a nightmare unreality to the whole thing. He had an eerie feeling of being outside himself, watching his own struggle, caught in the trap he had set for himself. Why had he ever thought they could succeed in escaping?

He ran. Ahead, the square, cupola-topped church tower disappeared into the overcast night sky. Next to him, almost brushing his side as he hugged the shadows of the buildings, Christ labored under the cross on his way to Golgotha, and the Virgin Mary looked down on him benevolently—fresco paintings that adorned nearly every house in Oberammergau.

HOTEL ALTE POST, he read as he raced by. High on the wall, Christ hung on the cross. The houses thinned out. The streets were utterly deserted. Wartime Oberammergau had retreated into itself. A wire fence stretched before them. They ran on. Unseen—but inexorably heard—their pursuers were gaining. The massive building dead ahead of him began to take form. He knew what it was. The Passion Play Theater. The huge open-air stage where the Passion Play was performed once every decade.

He followed Willi as his friend entered the auditorium area. Desperately he tried to keep up as he clambered onto the great stage, open to the majestic Bavarian mountains beyond, dominated by the looming Kofel Mountain. He raced across the expanse of the stage.

He didn't see it in the dark. It was only an old plank left lying in the open. His running step hit the edge. His ankle twisted under him, buckled—and he fell, hitting the floor hard.

From the stage floor he saw Willi running for the wooded hills beyond—being quickly swallowed by the blackness.

He struggled to his feet. Pain lanced up through his leg. He knew he could not follow his friend. Frantically he looked around. There. In the wings. An open door . . .

He stumbled toward it. Perhaps. Perhaps the pursuers would follow Willi.

He slipped through the door. For a moment he leaned against the wall, trying to quiet his breath and his racing heart. He could hear the pursuers pound through the auditorium toward the stage. . . .

A flight of stairs led to the area below the stage. Painfully he hobbled down. . . .

Corridors. Turns. Right. Left. He limped on. . . . Doors. Some open. Some locked. He lost himself, his sense of direction—of time—as he hobbled on. . . .

He found himself in a large, high-ceilinged room. Row upon row of racks filled with costumes on hangers. Biblical costumes for the Passion Play. Used only once every ten years. The robes of priests and Pharisees; the simple garments of Hebrew men and women; the togas and tunics of Roman nobles and soldiers. He brushed between them, breathing their musty smell.

Through another door. Another room. Props. All kinds of props. Crude wooden furniture—the benches for the Last Supper—sharing space with Roman shields, swords and spears, helmets and standards—the tools of war.

He stopped. Spent. He sank down behind a rough-hewn cart with huge wheels.

And he heard it.

The dull thumps of heavy boots on the wooden floor. He sobbed. He knew he could run no more.

The beam from the flashlight struck him in the face. He blinked—but remained huddled on the floor.

There were three of them. Black-clad SS men, their red swastika armbands looking like bloody wounds; the silver death's-heads gleaming in evil mockery from their black caps. All three were carrying Schmeisser submachine guns.

"You!" one of them growled. "Get up."

Holding on to the cart, he pulled himself to his feet.

"Where is the other *Scheisskerl?*" the SS man snapped.

He shook his head.

"Who is he?" the man demanded. "His name?"

Wearily he looked at the SS men who stood glowering over him. He said nothing.

Suddenly one of the men jabbed a gun butt into his back in a crushing blow. A ball of livid pain exploded and spat fire through his entire body. He fell to his knees. Tears of agony burned his eyes, blinding him.

"His name?" the SS man barked.

"Krebbs." He forced the word from his lips. It did not matter. They would find out soon anyway. "Wilhelm—Krebbs. . . . Dr. Wilhelm Krebbs."

The SS man placed the gun muzzle under his chin and lifted up his head. "You," he growled. "Your name?"

"Marcus," he whispered, his voice hoarse with despair. "Dr. Theodor Marcus."

The three SS men came to attention as a young officer strode into the room. Arms akimbo, legs spread slightly apart, his trim black uniform strangely at odds with the colorful Biblical robes, he stood looking at the man huddled on the floor.

A thin smile played on his lips. He took a small object from his pocket and began to flip it into the air, catching it as he contemplated the captive.

Marcus followed the little oblong metal object as it rose and fell with hypnotic rhythm. He shivered, dread turning his blood cold. He knew what the young SS officer was playing with. The identification disk of the Gestapo . . .

The officer glanced at one of the SS men with an inquiring look and nodded toward the man on the floor.

The soldier snapped to attention. "Dr. Theodor Marcus, *Herr*

Obersturmführer," he called. "The other one, a Dr. Wilhelm Krebbs, got away."

The young Gestapo officer nodded. He returned his eyes to Marcus.

"Dr. Marcus," he said. He flashed him a quick smile which stretched his lips while his eyes remained cold. Gestapo Deputy Chief Heydrich himself had once told him that under certain conditions a smile was far more frightening than a frown. He had never forgotten. "Dr. Marcus, I am *SS Obersturmführer* Gerhardt Scharff." He paused. He smiled. "Gestapo.

"I have three questions for you, *Herr Doktor*. Three." Another quick smile. "I shall expect an immediate answer to each one."

Leisurely he took out a cigarette and lit it with a lighter on which the lightning insignia of the SS was prominent. He took a luxurious drag.

"Now, Dr. Marcus," he said evenly, "these are my questions. First—who else besides you and Krebbs is trying to escape? Secondly—who helped you? And thirdly—what were your plans?"

Marcus stared at the young Gestapo officer. Inside he shriveled up in dread. There *were* no others. Only he and Willi. No one had helped. And they'd had no plans—except to get away. He suddenly realized how utterly naïve they'd been. But how? Oh, Josef-Maria, how could he convince this Gestapo Lieutenant of that?

He stared at him, not knowing what to do.

"First," the young Lieutenant said. "Who else is trying to escape?"

"There were only Willi—Dr. Krebbs—and me," he whispered, fear constricting his throat.

Scharff did not change his expression. Slowly he nodded. "Secondly. Who helped you?" he asked pleasantly.

"No one helped us, *Herr Obersturmführer*," Marcus breathed.

"So," the SS officer said. "And last—your plans?"

"We—we had no real plans," Marcus stammered. "We—we just wanted to—to get away."

Scharff smiled at him. He took a deep puff on his cigarette. Slowly he brought out his lighter. He turned to the soldiers. "Strip him!" he ordered curtly.

At once the soldiers hauled Marcus to his feet. They tore his jacket off and ripped his shirt until he stood trembling, naked to the waist.

Scharff nodded toward the cart. "On the wheel," he said.

Two of the SS men slammed Marcus against the huge cartwheel; the other grabbed a bridle from a hook and ripped it apart. With the straps they tied Marcus to the wheel, his arms stretched out and lashed to the top of the rim. His legs buckled under him. He could neither stand nor kneel. He hung against the spokes.

Scharff contemplated him. If the man knew anything, he, Scharff, would have to get it from him. Now. While the pursuit was fresh. There was no time for a—eh, proper interrogation. He would have to improvise. He was good at it. He flipped the tinder wheel on his SS lighter. A flame flared up at once.

"Now, Dr. Marcus," Scharff said almost kindly, "has your memory improved?" He smiled at him.

Marcus stared at the lighter. He was stiff with terror. He shook his head in desperation. "Please, *Herr Obersturmführer*. There was no one else. I am telling you the truth. No one . . . "

Scharff suddenly stretched out his arm. The flame from the lighter touched the hair on Marcus' chest—and it flared up, shriveling into black curls as it burned.

Marcus screamed. The flash-fire seared his chest. The sickening stench of burning hair assailed his nostrils and made him retch.

"Well, *Herr Doktor?*" Scharff asked pleasantly.

Marcus stared at him in horror. "Please," he whispered hoarsely. "Please. There—was—no one. . . . Please. I swear . . . "

Scharff sighed. With deliberate care he tapped the ash from his cigarette. He inspected the glowing tip. Slowly he inched it toward Marcus' chest.

Marcus strained against the wheel, trying to shrink away from the fiery point.

Suddenly Scharff jabbed it lightly on his hairless, already blistered skin.

Pain shot through him. He cried out.

"Who else, Dr. Marcus?" The question was asked in a low, almost silken voice. "Who else?"

Marcus shook his head, too terrified to speak. Again Scharff touched the burning cigarette to his skin.

"Who helped?"

Marcus was petrified. He made no reply. He only whimpered softly in abject fear.

Suddenly Scharff jabbed the glowing cigarette at him and ground it into his skin.

A searing flash of agony shot through him.

He screamed.

The sweet stench of burning flesh reached him. He gagged. He heaved—and the vomit spewed from his mouth. It ran down his chest, acid in the fresh wounds.

"Your plans?" Scharff demanded.

"We—had no plans. Oh, Josef-Maria, we—had—no—plans. . . ." He collapsed, hanging in limp agony, crucified on the wagon wheel.

Meticulously Scharff tapped another cigarette from his pack and lit it. He gave the petrified Marcus one of his special smiles.

"There is one specific little spot," he said affably. "A spot that is especially sensitive. It is usually regarded as being particularly—eh, effective in persuading females to remember, Dr. Marcus. Reserved for them. I think you will find it interesting to experience that it is equally effective—equally sensitive— on a male." He smiled. "I am, of course, referring to the nipple."

Marcus stared at the burning cigarette. It filled his world. His mind whirled in a turmoil of anguish. Why would the man not believe him? There had *been* no one else! There *were* no others. Only he and Willi. There was nothing to tell.

"Once more, *Herr Doktor,*" Scharff said softly. "I ask you once more." He held the fiery cigarette tip close to one of the terrified man's nipples. Marcus could feel it distend in the heat.

"Who—else?"

Marcus pulled his chin rigidly into his chest. His bulging eyes stared down at the glowing red ember so close to him.

"No—no one," he croaked.

Scharff jabbed the burning cigarette end into his nipple, gouging and grinding it into the tender flesh.

Marcus screamed.

A fiery shock seared through him. He arched against the wheel, the leather straps cutting into his arms. A million white-hot needles burned into his chest. Through a world of cotton he heard a dreaded sound. The click of the lighter being flipped.

Oh, Jesus God! No more! No more . . .

And he heard the voice of the Gestapo Lieutenant.

"Who, Dr. Marcus? Who?"

He felt the searing tip touch his already inflamed nipple. Agony shot through him. Agony he could not bear. And the voice—

"Manfried? Dr. Manfried?"

"Yes!" he screamed. "Yes!"

Again the fiery touch.

"Wertheim?"

"Yes!"

"Schaufuss?"

"Yes!"

"The—director?"

"Yes! Oh, Mother of God—yes!"

And he shrieked. A hideous sound that threatened to tear his throat asunder. Slowly, bit by bit, Scharff bored the fiery cigarette ember into the tortured flesh of the nipple, charring it, prolonging the agony as long as possible.

He ground it out.

"You are a fool, Dr. Marcus," he said contemptuously. "And a liar. I do not like being lied to."

He flipped the dead cigarette away.

"Take him down," he snapped at the SS men.

They cut the leather straps. Marcus fell to the floor. He lay whimpering, adrift on a sea of pain . . . of anguish—and self-contempt.

Scharff lit another cigarette. This one to be enjoyed in the conventional way. Scornfully he looked at the heap of sniveling humanity sprawled at his feet. It had been a waste of time. And of cigarettes. And not *ersatz*. Real ones! The idiot had been telling the truth. The two of them—Krebbs and Marcus— *had* been alone.

"Take him back," he ordered.

The SS men dragged Marcus to his feet.

Scharff gave him one of his special smiles.

"I suggest you do not try anything like this again," he said. He blew a puff of smoke into his face.

"I shall not forget you—*Herr Doktor Theodor Marcus!*"

PHASE II

1

Vandenberg Air Force Base, California
June 18, 1979

His mouth was dry, his palms clammy. They always were at this time. It was his personal reaction to the mounting tension; the only factor he could predict with unfailing certainty. From the dais of the Project Director he watched the projected image on the big color-television screen on the far wall of the control room. The huge Titan III rocket stood poised for flight on the launching pad, wafting impatient whiffs of vapor into the morning air. He was acutely aware of the steady countdown droning from the PA system:

"—minus five—four—"

He stopped breathing.

"—three—two—one—"

His eyes were riveted on the screen. Suddenly a fist of fire slammed from the base of the giant rocket. He could feel the raw power shake his very bones.

"Ignition . . . Lift-off. We have lift-off. . . . Plus two—three—"

He did not relax. Not yet. He followed the fiery flight of the rocket as it streaked toward space. It was a good launch. On the screen the rocket was slowly shrinking into a tiny point of brightness dancing in the blue sky.

The telephone on the desk next to his right arm rang. It startled him. He picked it up.

"Marcus," he said crisply. He listened. "Thank you, General, it *was* a beautiful launch. All should go well." Again he listened. He glanced toward the large, lighted clock on the wall. "Yes, General Ryan, I can be at Edwards Air Force Base late this afternoon. . . . Yes, your office."

He replaced the receiver. For a moment he sat in thought. He had a good idea why the General had summoned him from Vandenberg on the Pacific to the Mojave Desert flight test center 150 miles inland. He felt a surge of excitement. At last . . .

He returned his attention to the activities in the huge control room spread out below him: Technicians seated at many stations before a labyrinthine array of control panels and consoles; the vastly intricate machinery of space exploration; the orderly, measured chaos of a major launch. He never tired of it.

Dr. Theodor Marcus, Project Director, sat back in his chair. For the next several minutes he could do nothing but wait. He allowed his mind to sift back. Back to another time. Another place. Peenemünde. The rocket research center of the Third Reich. He savored the remembered excitement of those days of experimentation—the Stone Age of space exploration, as it were. Those minutes of almost unbearable tension. *Die Peenemünde Minuten,* they'd called them. No different to him from the Vandenberg minutes now—even after all these years, he thought. Both seemed so much longer than sixty seconds.

He smiled to himself. He had been a young scientist then. Twenty-seven. Eager. Dedicated. Thrilled to be working with men such as Wernher von Braun and Walter Dornberger— pioneers in man's greatest adventure; fired with the excitement of exploring new realms of science—and pushing to the outer limits of his awareness the realization of the deadly uses to which their work would be dedicated.

His thoughts went back to that fateful launch thirty-seven years ago almost to the day. June 13, 1942. The launch that had catapulted him into his life's work . . .

. . . At noon on that bright, clear day in June—after the bitter disappointment of one unsuccessful launch attempt— von Braun, the Technical Director of the entire Peenemünde Rocket Research Center, was ready once again, pointedly aware that success *had* to be achieved this time. Adolf Hitler himself had ordered it.

Until a few minutes before zero hour, he, Theodor Marcus, and his friend and colleague Dr. Wilhelm Krebbs had been with the launch personnel down in the blockhouse shelter near Test Stand VII. He remembered how awed and proud he'd been as he observed the hectic countdown activities in the firing command post. At their stations throughout the room, technicians were busy taking readings from a myriad measuring instruments. Tension was mounting steadily as the seconds ticked by. He smiled to himself. It had been a child's toy in comparison with the computer-dominated miracles of today's launch taking place before him. Only the tension was the same.

Then he and Wilhelm had joined von Braun and the Center's commanding officer, Colonel Walter Dornberger, himself a top rocket research scientist, and the official military observation party assembled on the flat roof of the camouflaged Measurement House. It was an impressive gathering: the armament chiefs of the three branches of the armed forces, Field Marshal Erhard Milch of the Luftwaffe, General Friedrich Fromm of the Wehrmacht and Admiral Karl Witzell, headed by the Armamanet Minister of the Reich himself, Dr. Albert Speer. Standing at the protective brick parapet, each with ten-power binoculars to follow the flight of the rocket, the men were watching the launch site in the distance.

He and Wilhelm had watched, too, excited and keyed up. *They could not—must not—fail!* The firing table of Test Stand VII was located in a clearing surrounded by tall pines, safe from air reconnaissance except a direct overflight. The missile stood in the center and beside it a gigantic scaffolding on wheels equipped to service the rocket. It had been an A-4 rocket. Only later did it get the name V-2, when Hitler—after the proved vulnerability of the V-1, the buzz bomb, adopted the A-4 as his second *Vergeltungs* weapon—weapon of reprisal—against the Allies.

It was the most imposing sight he'd ever seen. Painted black and white, its fins in different colors for easy tracking, the rocket, forty-six feet tall, towered immobile on the firing table, hidden in the clearing in the dense pine forest—ready to streak seventy miles into space and reach a speed greater than sound. Never before had this been accomplished. Never . . .

He had watched von Braun. He knew the enormous pressures on the man. Secretly he agreed with his superior's dream of developing rockets to conquer space. But he kept it to himself. The *Führer* wanted weapons of destruction. And he knew of Dr. Dornberger's warning: "Don't talk of space flight! The *Führer* may think we are dreamers and cut off our funds." And he knew only too well that long ears were among them, extending all the way back to Hitler himself.

He had been brought back to full alertness by the loudspeaker mounted on the observation roof:

"X minus one!"

He tensed with anticipation. Each second seemed eternal. He started involuntarily as a tracking shell whooshed into the sky, its tail of green smoke slowly spreading over Test Stand VII. He was aware of the final countdown seconds being called off over the loudspeaker, the tinny voice coming as if from miles away. And then:

"Ignition!"

Great clouds of vapor and smoke exploded from the rocket exhaust nozzle. Fire and sparks bounced off the blast deflectors and washed over the concrete launching platform in red-hued billows of turbulence. An awesome roar reached him, pressing on his eardrums with fingers of monstrous power.

"Preliminary stage!" the loudspeaker announced.

The blast of sparks and smoke fused to a livid jet of flame. Cable ends, bits of grass and dirt, pieces of wood shot through the air—and slowly, steadily gathering speed, the rocket rose from the firing table and shrieked into the sky as the loudspeaker triumphantly called:

"The rocket has lifted!"

Spellbound, he followed the flight. The jet of fiery gases spewing from the rocket's stern was clear and sharp, a column of thundering power. He was only vaguely aware of the loudspeaker monotonously counting off the seconds of flight: twelve—thirteen—fourteen—

And the rocket broke through the sonic barrier. He was wildly elated. The misgivings of many who had predicted that the missile would be torn asunder by this unknown transonic phenomenon had proved false. Jubilantly he joined the others at the observation post in their exultation. And still the rocket soared as the seconds went by: forty-two—forty-three—forty-four—

Suddenly the rocket lurched to one side as if struck by the fist of an invisible giant. It began to wobble, and a cloud of white vapor spurted from it. Immediately the monstrous missile reversed and with a rapidly swelling howl it plunged to earth.

Instinctively he sought refuge behind the protective parapet. Within seconds the rocket struck, crashing into the forest less than half a mile away. The explosion rattled the building on which he crouched.

He was shaken. Grim and gray-faced, the observers stared toward the column of smoke rising over the pines in the distance.

Colonel Dornberger was the first to collect himself. "We shall try again," he said quietly.

He sighed. The rocket had crashed—but they had proved their point. The V-2 would fly.

It had been the guidance system that failed. And it was then that the realization had struck him: a faultless guidance system was all-important. You can have the most powerful weapon, the most sophisticated space probe—they would be useless unless they could reach their targets; unless they were controlled by a perfect guidance system. Power and guidance: the two must work in perfect coaction. He had never forgotten. . . .

With von Braun and the other rocket scientists he had been evacuated to Oberammergau in Bavaria by the SS during the final weeks of the war, there to await the disposition of the *Führer.* They had been under guard. He'd had no illusions as to what the "disposition" would be if the *Führer* feared they and their special knowledge would fall into the hands of the advancing Americans. He knew that *SS Obergruppenführer* Hans Kammler had direct orders from Hitler to use his SS troops at nearby Innsbruck to kill them all. With a cold feeling he still vividly remembered the abortive escape attempt he and Willi Krebbs had made. Ever since, he'd had that often painful trouble with his right kidney. The memory of that night dominated his occasional nightmares. The burn scars on his chest had long healed—but not the ones branded on his mind. He would always carry with him the bitter knowledge that he had been willing to say and do anything to avoid the pain inflicted on him by the young Gestapo officer. He never did go near a beach or a swimming pool. He was ashamed of his mutilated chest. Somehow he felt that anyone seeing it would also see his weakness. But the scars were there—a constant reminder of something he would rather forget.

Willi had gotten away. He himself had not. He sometimes wondered what had become of his friend and colleague. He'd had no word from him—or about him—since.

Their SS guards had disappeared soon after learning of the suicide of Adolf Hitler. With his colleagues he had surrendered to the Americans in the little resort town of Garmisch-Parten-kirchen in the Bavarian Alps. He had agreed wholeheartedly with von Braun, who had said: "It is our obligation to mankind to place our rocket knowledge in the right hands." There had been little doubt where that would be.

In September he had arrived with the others in Boston, and had at once been sent to the Aberdeen Proving Grounds in the state of Maryland. His only regret was that Wilhelm could not have been among the scientists selected by the Americans.

His job at Aberdeen had been the beginning of a long-lasting and fruitful collaboration, leading to his position at Vandenberg—and his scheduled meeting with General Clifford Ryan at Edwards Air Force Base later in the day.

The labor of his life could be divided into two diametrically opposed eras, he mused wryly. The time spent developing the science of rocketry for his native country, for the Third Reich . . . and the time spent in his adopted country working with his fellow scientists there.

Time is not an hourglass, he thought. You cannot reverse its flow.

But—you can replace the sand. . . .

2

Edwards Air Force Base

Dr. Marcus stood looking out the open window in the office of the Flight Test Commander, General Clifford Ryan. The General had been delayed and Marcus was alone. Below him lay the huge Air Force installation. The late-afternoon sun cast long ocher shadows, the air coming in through the window was warm and dry.

Edwards Air Force Base occupied over 300,000 acres of desert and dry lakes, including the great Rogers Dry Lake, east of Mojave. A military camp since 1933, it was not until World War II that the unique possibilities of the area as an aircraft testing site were recognized. From the window Marcus could see the vast expanse of Rogers Dry Lake, the forty-four-square-mile heart of the Flight Test Center.

Nature had provided man with the perfect, self-maintaining test-flight landing field, usable a full ten months of the year. Cracked into a crazy-quilt pattern when dry, the surface of the lake was like fine talcum powder, a mixture of clay and silt that, when baked by the sun, was able to support the landings of even the heaviest aircraft. Every year the entire lake was resurfaced—by nature. During the couple of months in the winter when it rained, a few inches of water collected on the lake bed. The winds, blowing the water back and forth, smoothed out the lake surface, and when it dried in the sun, the landing site had been efficiently resurfaced. It was an ideal situation, Marcus thought. Where else but in California could you get such service from nature? A thirteen-mile runway—so perfectly flat that measurements revealed only an eighteen-inch curvature in 30,000 feet.

Marcus was thoroughly familiar with the history of the Base. In 1942, the year that he had been working with von Braun and Willi Krebbs testing Hitler's V-2 rocket at Peenemünde, the north end of Rogers Dry Lake had been selected as the testing ground of the U.S. Air Force's first jet airplane, the super-secret XP-59A.

The south end of the lake was used for bombing practice, and here a realistic 650-foot model of a Japanese Navy heavy cruiser had been built. Named the *Muroc-Maru*, it was used for strafing and skip-bombing practice. From far away the shimmering heat waves across the sunburned, dry lake bed made it look as if a real battleship were afloat in the middle of the desert. Many a passing motorist had been hard pressed trying to explain that one.

Eight years later the Base, until then known as "Muroc," was renamed Edwards Air Force Base in honor of Captain Glen W. Edwards of Lincoln, California, who had been killed in the crash of an experimental Flying Wing aircraft during a test flight. Since then nearly all of the Air Force's new aircraft had been tested at Edwards. And in 1947 Captain Chuck Yeager, piloting the Bell X-1, broke the once-feared sound barrier for the first time.

The door to the office opened and General Ryan walked in.

"Sorry to have kept you waiting, Marcus," he said. He walked straight to his desk. "Sit down." He looked at the scientist. "I suppose you can guess why you're here."

Marcus nodded. "The XM-9?"

"Right. Tomorrow."

Marcus looked startled. "Tomorrow!"

Ryan nodded. "0800." He gave the scientist a little smile. "Sorry you weren't notified sooner. The old need-to-know crap."

Marcus returned the smile. "Even my own baby," he observed ruefully. But he was well aware of the secrecy and security that surrounded the project—and of his own protection.

"We're mounting a test flight of the F-15. Iron out a few bugs in the latest modifications. Classified. Major Darby will be the pilot."

Marcus brightened. "Darby. Excellent. I know him."

"The plane will carry your XM-9, Marcus. . . . Darby is, as you know, totally familiar with it. He will employ it."

Marcus was obviously excited. "At maximum output?"

"Yes. All out. We'll need you in the control room."

"Of course, of course. . . . Eh, Major Darby—may I talk with him?"

"Tomorrow morning. Before he suits up." Ryan stood up. The interview was obviously at an end. "Darby is home now. Taking it easy for tomorrow. Hopefully getting a good night's rest."

Marcus walked from the General's office. He was as excited and exhilarated as a child on Christmas morning. It showed in his pleasure-creased face and in his jaunty walk as he hurried down the corridor, even the ache in his kidney forgotten. He believed in enthusiasm; he believed in showing it. He was unable to understand the younger generation who considered it "cool" to be devoid of emotion—or, at least, never to show it.

Tomorrow. Tomorrow would demonstrate whether his work of the last ten years would bear fruit. Tomorrow might well turn out to be a great step for him, the most important day of his life.

Perhaps also a great step for his adopted country . . .

3

The remodeling of the pool at the Officers Club had been finished only a week before and the Base personnel hadn't yet resumed the habit of spending the warm evenings there. Randi Darby liked it that way. They had the entire pool and barbecue area to themselves. It was especially nice tonight, she thought. They were finally getting together with a good friend of Tom's who had arrived at Edwards a short time before. To take over Base Security Operations, Tom had told her. He'd been at the Flight Test Center for almost four weeks getting acclimatized, and—according to her husband—already acted as if he'd spent half his life there. And although Tom had spent a good deal of time with his friend, this was the first chance they'd all had to get together. She'd enjoyed lining up a date for him.

Using a leisurely sidestroke, she let her sleek, sun-gilded body glide through the water. It was refreshing and cool, compared to the warm evening air. With easy grace she hoisted herself up onto the rim of the lighted pool. She shook the water from her blond hair and looked toward two young people dancing slowly on the wooden deck to the soft music of a portable stereo. Paul was a good-looking man, she thought. But she hadn't made up her mind yet if she really *liked* him. Something about him was—grating her. It was different from the fighter-jock self-esteem she was used to in the exclusive fraternity of Air Force test pilots stationed at Edwards, the dome of the world. He seemed a little too—macho. Perhaps when she got to know him better.

"Paul!" she called. "Judy! How about a dip before the hamburgers are done? Cool you off."

Captain Paul Jarman grinned at the bikini-clad girl in his arms. He pulled her to him. "Who wants to cool off?"

A faint shadow flitted across Randi's face. She threw a quick glance toward the barbecue.

At the barbecue Tom Darby began to flip the batch of hamburgers sizzling over the hot charcoal. Over his swim trunks he wore a white barbecue apron with a comic-book version of an F-15 fighter plane stenciled on it in red and blue. He turned toward the others at the pool.

"You can start the countdown, guys," he called cheerfully. "Minus five minutes."

Randi stood up. With a towel she began to pat herself dry. It was going to be a good evening, she told herself. A lovely evening. It was.

Paul and Judy walked over to Tom. Judy looked wide-eyed at the hamburgers on the grill, licked by quick flames from the glowing coals below as little droplets of fat dripped down.

"They've got holes in them," she exclaimed in surprise. "Like doughnuts."

"Major Darby's famous Holy-Burgers," Paul exclaimed. "I've heard about them. Renowned throughout the Air Force! Outranks the Colonel's Chicken any day!"

"But—why the holes?" Judy wanted to know.

Tom looked at her in mock surprise. "You don't know?" he said incredulously.

"No."

"Well, let me enlighten you, Judy, my love." He was enjoying himself. "It's computed scientifically. You see, the flavor is vastly enhanced when the heated air from the charcoal flows through the hole." He made the scientific mumbo-jumbo sound almost believable. "The—eh—convex eddy patterns of the vortex are inversely proportioned to the air density and compressibility—"

"Cut the crap and cook the burgers!" Paul cut in.

"Yes, sir! Since you put it that way." Tom turned the hamburgers. He gave Judy a confidential wink. "It's a very sound aerodynamic principle," he said. "Makes for a hell of a hamburger."

Judy was impressed. "Really?" She was not sure if she should take him seriously.

Randi had joined them. "Don't encourage him, Judy," she said, smiling. "He'll have them flying in a moment."

"Actually," Tom confided, "hamburgers are my only culinary accomplishment. Randi does all the rest." He gave her an affectionate pat on the rear. "Great cook."

"Sure," Randi laughed. "I'm no fool. The way to a man's heart is, after all, through his stomach." She patted Tom on his F-15. "Especially if you tell him how flat it is!"

"It's a fact," Tom insisted. "B.R.—before Randi—I used to cook for myself." He made a final turning of the sizzling burgers on the grill. "Believe me, my cooking tasted like a misprint in a Mongolian cookbook. I even had to give my garbage disposal Alka-Seltzer."

They groaned in unison.

They all helped stack the dirty dishes in the basket Randi and Tom had brought them in. It had been a nice evening. They had enjoyed Tom's Holy-Burgers—and each other's company. All the burgers had disappeared, along with a large pitcher of lemonade, handfuls of potato chips, a jar of dill pickles and gobs of relish and ketchup. All very successful. Even the ketchup bottle had been cooperative.

Randi, as usual, had her reservations about her husband's special hamburgers. The holes made them too well done for her liking. She'd never told him. He got such a kick out of making them. She had wondered how he'd gotten into the habit of cooking them that way. To be—different? It *was* a strange practice for someone who loved steak tartare . . .

They were having a last swim before calling it a day. Randi was sitting at the pool's edge, swishing her feet in the water and watching Tom and Paul swimming the length of the pool with powerful, rhythmic strokes. Judy came over and sat down beside her. She looked toward the men.

"I don't think I could ever get used to it," she said.

"To what?" Randi asked.

"Having a husband doing such a dangerous job. Never knowing . . ."

A forbidden phrase pressed briefly for recognition in Randi's mind: *shooting dice with death.* She shut it out. The pilots themselves could banter it about. The wives could not think it.

"I don't think anyone ever gets used to it," she said. "But I wouldn't want to change it. It's really wonderful for Tom."

"What do you mean?"

"He's doing something he really wants to do. It challenges him. It's exciting. And important. What more can you ask?" She looked at her husband churning through the water. "I—envy him that sometimes. . . ."

She knew Tom could not live without flying. It was part of him. It was a part she had accepted. His father had been a flyer, too. On February 25 in 1944—during "Big Week"—the Fifteenth Air Force, based in Italy, had roared across the Alps to attack the huge Messerschmitt factories in Regensburg in Bavaria. In his P-51 Mustang fighter Tom's father had flown bomber escort. He had not returned. That was something Tom's mother had had to accept.

Perhaps the son—in his own way—was making up. . . .

Judy's eyes followed the two men plowing through the water together. "Is it true Paul once saved Tom's life?" she asked.

Randi nodded. "It's true."

Judy looked toward Paul, hero-worship in her eyes. "Gee," she said in awe. "Isn't it exciting? What happened?"

"I don't really know all of it," Randi said. "Tom—doesn't like to talk about Vietnam."

"Was that where it happened?"

"Yes." Randi sat still for a while. "It was in 1971," she said. "Tom was a fighter pilot. He—he'd been shot down. Over North Vietnam. Paul got him out."

"Gee!" Judy said, impressed. "He's a real hero."

Randi nodded. "I guess so." She slid into the water and let the velvety coolness wash away her memories of a difficult time as she lay luxuriously on her back, keeping afloat with little hand and foot motions.

Suddenly she felt two powerful hands grab her waist and lift her up out of the water—to let her fall back down, dunking herself in the splash.

Tom caught her as she resurfaced, sputtering and laughing.

"You louse!" she said fervently.

He grinned at her with affection. "You looked entirely too sybaritic."

Together they climbed out of the pool. Tom took a large towel and wrapped it around his wife. She began to rub herself dry.

"Here," he offered, "let me help." He started to pat her.

Gently she disengaged herself. "That's all right," she said. She gave him a wan little smile. "I can dry myself."

"Can I just do the good parts?" he asked mischievously.

She looked at him, suddenly sober. "I—I don't think so, Tom," she said quietly. . . .

The evening had come to an end.

Together they walked to the cars.

"Thanks, Tom, old cock." Paul slapped his friend on the arm. "Those Holy-Burgers really took off."

"Really good," Judy chimed in. "For sure."

Paul gave Randi a peck on the cheek. "Good night, doll," he said. "I'm glad Tom picked himself a winner. Take care."

Randi looked at him. She had the feeling it was probably

the closest he'd ever get to complimenting a woman. "Good night, Paul," she said. "I'm glad finally to have gotten to know you."

They watched Paul and Judy drive off. Randi turned to her husband. "I hope I picked the right date for him," she said. "What did you think of her?"

"Judy? I'm madly in love with her."

"She really is nice."

"So, how did you like Paul?" Tom asked.

"I—liked him," Randi said. There was reservation in her voice. "He's very—masculine, isn't he?"

Tom grinned. "Right on!"

"You remember that old movie we saw at the Base theater the other night?" Randi asked. *"The Devil's Brigade,* I think it was called. There was a character in it—the one Jeremy Slate played. A real rough, he-man kind of character. Paul reminds me of him."

Tom laughed. "He'd love you," he said.

Randi looked at him. "Judy wanted to know how he saved your life," she said. "I could only tell her generalities. Someday I'd like to know the whole story."

Tom looked at her—without seeing her.

He was suddenly back in the jungle. Nine years ago. Was it that long? It seemed . . . It seemed . . . He could still hear the staccato crackle of the small-arms fire coming from the jungle as he huddled in the tall grass. It had been one of his first missions. He was still green. The SAM had crippled his Corsair II fighter, and warning lights had lit up the cockpit. He'd pulled the "D" ring between his knees with both hands and felt the cold, sharp blast of a 500-knot slipstream strike him as he blasted away from the sick bird . . .

. . . He saw his plane hit and explode in an orange-red fireball. It was sight he was never to forget. He saw the pillar of black smoke shooting up into the air—an ominous beacon to announce his arrival to enemy troops for miles around.

He felt unbearably exposed and vulnerable as he drifted with the wind, hanging in his chute, somewhere over enemy territory. He pulled out his survival radio. He could see his wingman circle high above.

"Cardinal Flight," he called. "This is Cardinal Three. I'm in my chute and OK."

The answer came immediately.

"Rog, Cardinal Three. This is Cardinal Four. I have you in sight. I see no activity below."

He stuffed the radio back into his vest and concentrated on his descent. Below was a large open area surrounded by jungle. He pulled on his risers and steered away from the trees.

When he hit the ground in the tall grass, he knew with cold certainty that anyone showing up for him would be Gomers— for he had punched out over North Vietnam far from any friendlies. Incongruously, he had wondered what joker first had come up with the nickname Gomers for enemy troops. Somehow it didn't sound nearly menacing enough.

He struggled out of his chute harness and pulled his survival radio from his vest. High above he could see his wingman still circling the area.

"Cardinal Four," he called. "This is Cardinal Three. I'm down."

"Roger, Cardinal Three." The answer came at once. "Cardinal Flight is at bingo fuel. We've got to leave. The Sandies are on the way. Sandy One will be on in a few minutes. Keep yourself together."

"Rog, Cardinal Four," he said. He knew his voice was too shrill. He didn't care. Images of reported atrocities against POWs flitted through his mind. He fought to shut them out. He had a damned good chance of falling into enemy hands; checking in at the Hanoi Hilton. Where the customers were always wrong.

And the price was high. . . .

He checked his crash kit and his pistol.

And waited. . . .

It was less than seven minutes, but it had seemed enough time to mobilize an entire North Vietnam division. His survival radio sputtered.

"Hello, Cardinal Three," a voice could be heard through the crackle and static on his radio. "This is Sandy One. Do you read?"

"Rog, Sandy One," he responded at once. "Cardinal Three. Read you five by. How far out are you?"

"Cardinal. Sandy. We're about ten minutes out. We've got a Jolly Green standing by. How about a hold-down?"

"Rog."

He flipped the switch to beeper, giving the Sandy a chance to get a direction fix on his position. He felt better. With the prop-driven, potently armed advance members of the rescue party coming in, he felt less alone. And there *had* been no enemy activity. So far.

He kept scanning the jungle for the first sign of the enemy. And the sky above for the Sandies. He knew they'd come. Both parties.

The radio crackled. "Cardinal. Sandy. We're coming in. Give us another hold-down."

"Rog, Sandy, Cardinal's holding," he said. He flipped the switch. He watched the sky. And he saw them rapidly coming up in the distance. Two beautiful A1E Skyraiders. The Sandies were arriving.

"Cardinal Three," the radio sputtered. "Sandy One. We're going to make a few low passes around you. Let us know if you hear any firing."

"Roger, Sandy."

Tensely he watched the jungle around him. And listened. It was not a new trick. The Gomers would lie in hiding around a downed flier and wait for the rescue mission. Only then would they open up—hoping to get both the rescuers and their subject. It was a trap used often before.

Suddenly the two prop fighters came roaring low over the treetops. Banking, jinking, they streaked along the jungle edge. Again and again. Checking the area for enemy troops.

All was quiet.

"Cardinal Three," the radio crackled. "We're going to put some Willie Pete in to mark the way."

"Rog, Sandy."

The two planes passed low over the clearing. The white-phosphorus smoke rockets went off with a whoosh. The smoke billowed up.

"Cardinal, we're going out now to meet the Jolly Green. They'll be here in a few minutes. Sit tight."

He saw the two Sandies disappear over the treetops.

He listened. And watched.

He strained to see into the distant sky, willing the HH-53 helicopter to appear.

And he heard it, the distinctive *whop, whop, whop, whop* of the big chopper. The Jolly Green . . .

"Cardinal Three." It was a new voice on the radio. "This is Jolly Green. We're coming in pretty good. We know where you are. Pop a red smoke."

"Rog, Jolly Green. Smoke."

He pulled the end of his smoke flare. A dense cloud of orange smoke drifted up on the wind.

"Rog, Cardinal. We got your smoke."

He could see the chopper coming in over the jungle edge about 100 yards from him.

"Cardinal. Jolly," the radio sputtered. "Hold with it. We're coming in."

The hovering chopper moved closer to his smoke. It started to descend.

Suddenly, from the jungle edge, a din of small-arms fire erupted. And machine-gun fire. The rescue helicopter banked sharply and pulled up with a roar of power, pursued by intensive ground fire. The Gomers had been waiting.

"Shit!" the radio spat. "The bastards are playing games again. We got to get out. Too much damned firepower down there." There was a pause, filled with static and anxiety. Then—urgently: "Cardinal. Sandy. Hold on for a few more minutes. We'll have to soften the bastards up."

Oh, sweet Jesus—more eternal minutes.

"Rog, Sandy," he said bleakly. He looked up at the Jolly Green hovering and dancing out of the range of the Gomer ground fire. "I'll—"

Suddenly a bullet slammed into the ground inches from his

knee. He jumped. Another—and another.

"Sandy! Sandy!" he shouted. "I'm under fire! I've got to take cover." His eyes flew over the area. "That hillock," he rasped. "With the brush. I'll make for it." He caught his breath. He hoped the adrenalin surging through him didn't garble the transmission. "The one nearest the smoke," he finished.

Bent low, clutching his pistol in one hand, his radio in the other, he began a broken-field run toward the clump of jungle brush. He was almost there. He veered sharply around a stand of thick grass. He stepped into a small, hidden hole and his left foot buckled under him. He crashed to the ground. He managed to hold on to his pistol, but his radio went flying from his grip into the grass. He did not see where it landed. He got up. Bullets were reaching for him, getting closer. Desperately his eyes searched for the radio, his only link with his rescuers. He did not see it. A bullet hissed through the tall grass close to his head—the whispering sound of death. He ducked. He ran on. His foot shot waves of pain through him with every step. He heard the whoosh of a rocket being fired by one of the Sandies. Almost at once it exploded into its jungle-edge target with an ear-rending blast. The force of the sledgehammer detonation struck him in the back and slammed him forward as he dove into the brush on the hillock. The machine-gun fire stopped.

But the small-arms fire was all around him.

He stared into the tall grass. He knew what was coming. It was not long. From the jungle edge he could see the furtive dark shapes of the North Vietnamese troops making their move toward him.

Anxiously he glanced up. In the distance over the jungle the two Sandies were banking, turning to hurtle toward the clearing.

He thought he saw movement in the grass. He fired. Answering rifle fire rattled through the foliage around him. Despair flooded him. He was hopelessly pinned down. Alone. How long could he expect to hold off the infiltrating enemy—with only a .38? His nerves were stretched to their ultimate tautness.

The Sandies came roaring low overhead, strafing the ground

with a hail of 20-mm. explosive and incendiary cannon shells. Rockets thudded into the jungle to explode in fiery destruction. Again the Sandies wheeled and came streaking back, pounding a continuous stream of fire down upon the enemy troops.

But still the Gomers were inexorably closing in on him.

Another few minutes?

Hell—there were none left.

He'd had it.

Suddenly a powerful whirring sound captured his awareness. The Jolly Green was whirling down from above, coming fast, headed straight for his cover. He could make out a figure standing crouched in the doorway—and he saw the gunner spraying the grass below with machine-gun fire. The chopper came to within fifty—thirty—ten feet above him. Abruptly it pulled up, banked steeply and came to a hovering stop for a bare moment. A man leaped out and crashed into the brush behind him. In the same instant the chopper shot away, fleeing a hail of small-arms fire.

The man came thrashing through the brush. He shrugged out of a pair of M-16 automatic rifles slung over his shoulder. He threw one to Tom.

"Here, old cock, use this!" He hit the ground next to Tom. "Better'n that popgun." He fired into the tall grass. "The Sandies'll have the Gomers cleaned out in a few minutes. You and I can hold the fuckers off that long." He fired again. "Name's Paul."

Side by side they lay in the dirt, firing at any movement in the grass, listening to the enemy bullets rustling through the brush, probing for them.

And all around them raged the battle. . . .

Gradually the Gomer fire died down—until only sporadic shots met the strafing Sandies, and the troops closing in on the two men seemed to have withdrawn.

Once more the Jolly Green descended toward the clearing. Quickly it came to rest on the ground near the brush-covered hillock. Tom and Paul broke cover and zigzagged toward the chopper, dodging scattered fire.

Rough hands hauled them aboard, and the Jolly Green

lurched up into the air and whirled away out over the jungle—passing over Tom's blazing Corsair on the ground as it flared up in a dying burst of pyrotechnics.

Not until Tom sat huddled on the floor of the chopper, staring at the man who'd risked his life to save him, did he realize he'd fouled his pants.

It was a simple realization. It mattered not at all. . . .

He focused on Randi. "You know most of it already," he said quietly. But he knew she didn't. "Paul was the leader of a Combat Mobility Team in Nam. He put his neck on the block for me. He didn't have to. Got me out of a tight situation." He looked away. "He'll tell you about it. Someday."

"Why is he transferring to Edwards?" Randi asked.

"Being in charge of Security Operations gives him a chance to be promoted to major."

"I hope he makes it."

"He will. He's damned good."

Randi sighed. "I suppose so." She glanced at her husband. "You think he liked Judy?"

"You can bet on it."

"Wouldn't it be fun—if they got serious?"

Tom laughed. "Paul? Serious? You must be joshing."

"Well—I think she'd make a lovely Air Force wife," Randi said.

There was a strangely wistful tone in her voice.

4

The house occupied by Randi and Tom Darby on Doolittle Drive in Housing Area G was only a few minutes' drive from the Officers Club. It was a pleasant one-story contemporary building with two large trees on the front lawn. A faint light could be seen coming from a window in the rear bedroom.

Randi was lying, her back to the empty side of the bed, staring into the semi-darkness of the room. Only the little lamp on the nightstand on Tom's side was on. She lay perfectly still.

Waiting. She heard her husband come into the room; she felt the bed sag as he sat down on it, heard the familiar, faint squeak. Oh, God—she *knew* how she would react. She knew she could not help it.

Her wide-open eyes were getting used to the dim light. Without really seeing them, she looked at the framed photographs standing on the dresser. There they were, just married, coming out of the AFB Chapel, running the gauntlet of laughing friends. It had been at Eglin. In Florida. Tom had just been promoted to first lieutenant. . . . And the photo of Tom grinning broadly, posing in his pressure suit before the lifting body mated to the B-52. It had been Tom's second day as a major. . . .

She felt his hand softly touching her back. She stiffened. Oh, Tom—please don't. Please—don't. . . . She felt his hand slowly, sensuously trace a gentle caress down the curve of her back. She lay tensely unresponsive—eyes wide, gazing in anguish into the dimness of the room.

She felt him lean over her and kiss her naked shoulder, her neck, her ear. And she stayed unmoving, unyielding in her misery.

"Honey," he whispered softly, close to her ear. "Honey . . ."

She did not respond. She could not respond—her every muscle so taut, she ached. Oh, Tom—I can't . . . I can't . . . I can't . . .

She screwed her eyes tightly shut, squeezing two tears from the corners. She did not move.

Tom sat back, defeated. He looked at the tense form of his wife beside him, his eyes filled with helplessness and hurt, the frustration a dull ache in his loins.

"It's all right, Randi," he said quietly. "It's all right. . . ." Bleak and wretched, he gazed at his wife, deep concern furrowing his face.

He opened the drawer in the nightstand, rummaged for a cigarette. He'd quit smoking months ago, but there had to be an old pack somewhere. He was not really aware of his actions. It was—something to do.

He found a pack, pulled out a half-crushed cigarette and

put it in his mouth. For a moment he sat perfectly still, staring in front of him. Then he removed the cigarette and put it—unlit—in an ashtray on the nightstand. Abruptly he got up from the bed and left the room, closing the door quietly behind him.

Randi turned toward the door. Her face was drawn and wan, her eyes haunted. She was about to call after him. She could not. From the room beyond came the faint sounds of a TV show. Johnny Carson, she thought dismally. There was always Johnny Carson—with those celebrities, famous only for being famous. . . .

Tom sat, still tense, in his favorite chair in front of the TV set, watching the mindless show; not seeing it, not hearing it. He'd spent too many hours in that damned chair in front of that damned set. . . .

He was aware of Randi quietly entering the room behind him. He did not acknowledge her until she came over and sat down on the sofa, one bare foot drawn up under her, the other dangling over the edge. Her sheer nightgown only enhanced her loveliness—and he ached.

She looked forlorn and hurt. Her voice was small.

"Tom," she said. "Please understand. . . ."

He switched the sound off the set with his remote control. He looked at her.

"I love you, Rand," he said quietly.

"And I love you. You know that." She searched for words, for understanding. "It's—I just can't help it." She hugged herself miserably. "I don't feel like I used to. Everything's—different now."

"It doesn't have to be." Tom looked earnestly at his wife. "We have to live in the future—not the past."

Randi stared bleakly at the TV set. "I—I don't have anything left," she whispered. "Not after what happened."

"I know what happened," Tom said, his voice tired. "But it's over. Dammit, it's over! How long do you want us to go on like this? I want you, Rand. What do you expect me to do?"

"I want you to understand."

"It's been months."

"I can't help it." She suddenly flared. "It's not my fault!"

"What the hell are you saying, Randi?" Tom was unable to keep his frustration out of his voice. "It's *my* fault?"

"I didn't say that."

"But you mean it, don't you?"

"No. I don't." She looked down at her bare foot. "I don't know what I mean."

"Let's not argue." Tom's voice was flat, numb. "We're both tired. Why don't you go back to bed? I'll be there in a few minutes." He returned his unheeding attention to the silent set.

She stood up. For a moment she stood watching her husband—wanting to reach out to him, but unable to breach the wall that had come between them. Slowly, defeatedly, she walked toward the door. She turned.

"Tom," she said. "I—"

Tom turned toward her expectantly. She struggled—but there were no words.

"Good night," she said.

She left the room.

For a moment Tom sat in stony silence. Then he flipped the sound on the TV set back on. . . .

Randi crawled into bed. She sat against the headboard, hugging her knees drawn up to her chin.

She searched her nightstand for a cigarette. She found none. She crawled across the bed to her husband's side and picked up the cigarette from the ashtray. She lit it. She stared at it without seeing it—and stubbed it out in the ashtray without having taken a single puff.

Her eyes fell on Tom's uniform jacket hanging over the back of a chair next to the bed. Slowly, absent-mindedly, she reached out her hand and touched the silver wings above the pocket.

Suddenly she grabbed the jacket, tore it from the chair and flung it savagely to the floor.

She buried her face in her hands.

And wept. . . .

PHASE III

DAY ONE

1

He was sitting in the calibration chair. He was already wearing his green flying suit, and his helmet-clad head was held immobile in the chair head-rest. He always expected to be asked to "open wide" when he sat in that contraption.

Two white-uniformed non-com technicians were mounting the Eye Movement Guided Sight on the two slender holding arms protruding from his bright red helmet. The little sighting device itself sat directly in front of his eyes just above his line of vision—like a weird sort of rearview mirror. Tom still hadn't gotten over being intimidated by the thing. It was strictly *Star Wars* stuff to him. A sighting device that read the movements of his eyeballs, instantly locked the plane's weapons system onto whatever target he'd be looking at—ready for him to blast it with a touch of his finger on the trigger button. The EMG Sight was truly sci-fi inspired. He felt excited. Coupled with the XM-9, mounted on the F-15 fighter, the plane should be damned near invincible. They'd told him he'd be packing enough power in his eyeballs to blast through Fort Knox! It would not be long before he'd find out just how much this new device of Dr. Marcus' could do. They'd set up a series of experimental targets on the test firing range at China Lake up north. Judging from the cloak-and-dagger secrecy they'd handled the whole thing with, you'd think old Marcus had invented Doomsday itself.

One of the technicians plugged the slender umbilical from the sight into the computerized simulator box on the floor next to the calibration chair.

"Okay, Major," he said, "you're plugged in. Look at Target A, please. On your left."

Moving only his eyeballs, Tom stared at the designated target, *A*, on the far left on the wall in front of him—close to the limits of his peripheral vision. Beneath the target letter someone had tagged up an ancient photograph of a 1906 six-decker-wing prop plane. A poor target for the XM-9, he thought. The picture at Target G at the opposite end was more in keeping with the whole thing, an elaborate flying saucer straight out of *Close Encounters.* Personally, he liked E. The girl in the bikini was just his type. And she looked awful friendly.

"Target G, please," the technician said. "On your far right."

Tom shifted his eyes. *Blam!,* you space critters. Take that—and that—and that! He grinned to himself. How things do turn out. As a kid he'd devoured science-fiction stories. Azimov. Heinlein. Siodmak. All the greats. Now it was real. And he was part of it.

The technicians were busy with the calibrations and adjustments, an exacting and precise procedure. The door to the calibration room opened and Paul stuck his head in.

"Don't move!" he called.

"Verrry funny!" Tom grinned.

"You're a lucky bastard," Paul said enviously. "You know that?"

Without moving his head, Tom replied, "Luck? Expertise, my boy. Expertise."

"Who's flying chase?"

"Barnes. Manning himself is flying Chase One."

Paul whistled, obviously impressed. "Hea-vy!"

"Guess he wants to see first hand how she handles at maximum performance—with the new enhancement modifications," Tom said. And witness the first maximum-output test of the XM-9, he thought. But he kept his mouth shut. He knew only a handful of people were in the know about the Marcus device, much less that it was about to undergo its first all-out test.

"Look at Target E, sir," the technician instructed.

"With pleasure," Tom agreed. "And I do mean pleasure."

"See you in the equipment room," Paul called.

"Right." Tom was eyeballing the bikini-clad girl. Some dish. A shadow flitted across his face.

"Target B, sir."

He looked away.

The flight-equipment room was one of the neatest and cleanest places on the base. Row upon row of multicolored flying helmets, each in its individual cubbyhole; orderly lines of olive-green compact parachutes hanging from their special racks. Everything in its proper place.

Accompanied by one of the non-com technicians, Tom entered the room. He was wearing his red helmet, the umbilical from the sight hooked onto his flying suit, ready to be plugged into the aircraft. While the technician busied himself with a log, Paul helped Tom into his chute.

"Got your Buck Rogers eyes all fixed up?" he asked.

"You bet," Tom confirmed. "Calibrated to hit the eye of a mosquito in evasive maneuvers at a thousand paces." He shrugged into the chute harness. "Whoever did coin the phrase: 'If looks could kill'?" He grinned.

Paul groaned. "Had to be a woman," he said.

A quick frown flitted across Tom's face. Paul shot his friend a sidelong glance. "Tom," he said quietly, "is—is everything okay?"

Tom looked up quickly. Perhaps a little too quickly. "Sure," he said. "Why not?"

"Hey!" Paul said earnestly. "Tom. You and I've been buddies a long time. You know what I'm talking about. That—that bummer you and Randi were handed. I know it wasn't an easy trip. How—how is everything now with you guys?"

Tom's face clouded over briefly. "Fine, Paul . . . fine," he said, his voice flat. He stopped, certain it was obvious he was lying. Soberly he went on. "Oh, hell, Paul, nothing's changed." He sighed, unaware that he did. "I'm really worried. Randi can't seem to get herself together. Ever since that damned— accident I can't seem to reach her." He looked at Paul. "If only I'd been *there* . . . If only—"

Paul interrupted him. "Tom—"

"I could have *done* something, dammit!"

Paul looked at his friend earnestly. "Don't you go blaming yourself, old cock. No way."

Tom nodded almost imperceptibly. "Yeah. I know. Only—"

From the door the non-com called, "All set, sir."

Paul slapped Tom on the shoulder. "Go turn some of that good jet fuel into noise, old buddy."

Tom gave him a thumbs-up sign and grinned. "Rog on the noise."

Dr. Theodor Marcus had those clammy hands and that dry mouth again as he sat in the test-flight control room at Edwards watching the maze of telemetry dials, gauges and meters registering a steady volume of information from the aircraft streaking through the California sky at more than the speed of sound.

So far the F-15 had performed flawlessly under Major Darby's expert handling. Every one of the upgrading changes in its capabilities had proved eminently successful. Marcus had been listening to the radio communications between the chase planes and the test plane and the instructions from Control One. In a few moments the test he, Marcus, was waiting for would begin. In a few moments he would experience the culmination of his life's work. Or—

Or—he would not. . . .

He glanced at the Test Flight Director, Control One. He knew the man, but he could never remember his name. A highly competent officer. Control One would do.

He tried to calm himself. He always did. It never worked. He had once read about an opera star—was it Flagstad?—who was always petrified before every entrance, then performed brilliantly. Every launch, every test was like that for him— until it began. Did he have greater reason for anxiety in this case?

The XM-9 required a great deal of instantaneous, confined energy at the point of activation. The plane. A surge of enormous power. Always a potential for problems. It worked in

static test. It worked well. But—in flight—there *were*
variables. . . .

He dismissed it from his mind.

Tom felt as if he were riding a cloud, although he knew it
to be a cloud that packed one hell of a wallop. More of a wallop
than the supreme power locked up in the blackest thunder-
cloud.

The F-15 was one of his favorite aircraft. Of all the fighter
planes he'd flown, he liked it best. Perhaps because it was un-
compromised. The F-15 Eagle was strictly U.S. hardware; a
high-performance, extremely maneuverable fighter—more so
now than ever with the new enhancement factors he'd just
tested.

Now he was ready for the big one.

He was flying at a cruising altitude of 40,000 feet, about
100 miles north of Edwards. He'd make his turn and start his
XM-9 test run. It would take him fifteen minutes to complete
the series. He made a visual check for his two chase planes.
Barnes in the T-38. Manning in another F-15. They were both
with him.

"Control," he said. "This is Eagle One. Forty seconds out
on XM-9 system wet run."

His earphones crackled. "Roger, Eagle One. We read you."

Manning came in. "Tom—this is Chase One. You're looking
good. You've got a real sweetheart there."

A pang flitted through Tom's mind.

Randi . . .

"Roger, Chase One," he said.

In the control room Marcus listened to the interchange. He
wiped his hands on his trouser legs. Only seconds to go. His
"Flagstad Syndrome" was at its peak.

"Any signs of stress?" It was Control One.

Tom's voice came over the PA system. "Negative."

The Flight Director was studying some telemetry indicators.
"Eagle One. Looks like you need to come right about five
degrees. You're drifting a little."

"Roger."

"Your flight angle is good. You're holding about fifty feet left of track at the moment."

"Roger. Correcting."

"Helmet umbilical connected, Tom? Lanyard okay?"

"OK."

"OK. Thirty seconds to firing."

"Roger. Thirty seconds."

The interchange between Control One and Tom was at the same time both tense and thoroughly controlled—delivered with almost exaggerated calm.

"Telemetry switch."

"On."

"Calibration switch."

"On."

"Pressure—Tank One."

"Tank One—normal."

"Pressure—Tank Two."

"Tank Two—normal."

"Minus fifteen seconds. Master arm—maximum output."

"On."

"Laser-enable switch."

"On."

"Ready to fire. Minus five—" Even the voice of Control One was taut. "—four—three—"

Marcus stopped breathing. His eyes were riveted to the indicators before him.

From his chase plane to the right of Tom's F-15, Manning glued his eyes to the test plane. He heard the countdown on his earphones.

"—two—one—"

In the test-plane cockpit Tom's thumb on the firing button tightened.

"Fire!"

Instantly there was a small explosion, and a blast of smoke coughed from Tom's plane. The fighter shuddered violently, rolled over and began to plunge toward earth.

"Tom! . . . *Tom!*" Manning called. "Can you read me? . . . Tom!"

In the control room Marcus stared in horror at the instrument panel. Every one of the telemetry indicators reporting on the test plane had gone dead the instant the command to fire had been given!

Manning wheeled his chase plane over, trying to follow the plummeting F-15 down.

"Tom!" he screamed into his helmet mike. "Punch out! . . . You're coming apart! Get out! Eject!"

Tom's plane was out of control. Trailing a long plume of smoke, fire and metal debris, spinning wildly, it hurtled down, the radio dead.

Manning stayed. The ground seemed to be rushing up to meet him. His altimeter needle spun as if twirled by a madman.

Suddenly he saw the cockpit canopy tear from the stricken F-15—and the ejection seat explode from the plane.

Within seconds the plane struck. The explosion was a fiery spasm of disintegration, scattering wreckage for hundreds of feet. A huge black mushroom cloud of smoke and dust rose from the main impact crater.

Above it a single white-and-orange parachute was floating down toward the rocky ground below—ragged silk billowing from several torn panels.

Manning pulled up. He could follow no farther. As he climbed, he saw the chute land among huge, rugged boulders.

"Control!" he said hoarsely. "This is Chase One . . . Dick. He's down okay. In the Sierra foothills. Near Mount Whitney. Some torn panels. I show him 322 at 64 off China Lake."

In the control room Marcus was staring at the PA speaker. He felt drained. Cold. He listened to the acknowledgment.

"Roger. Copy. Chopper's on the way."

2

The office of Colonel Jonathan Howell, Commander, 6517 Test Wing, in the Flight Test Center Headquarters Building was, in appearance, very much like the make-up of the man himself.

Orderly, functional, uncluttered—the large wall map of the Base and the symmetrical stacks of papers on his desk testified to that; a career Air Force officer whose life was his work—indicated by the prominently placed pictures of the latest U.S. Air Force planes, and the operational charts mounted on the wall over a row of uniform filing cabinets.

Howell stood at his desk, grim-faced, looking out the window. In the distance the disturbing sound of a siren could be heard. In his hand he gripped a telephone, his knuckles showing white.

"The choppers are already on the way to the crash site," he said. His voice was tense, but with controlled authority. "Yes—we know the exact spot. . . . Right. . . . And medical—now. I want Major Ward with the rescue party. And notify the Inyo National Forest Rangers. . . . Right. . . . I want to be kept fully informed."

He hung up. For a moment he stood frowning, gazing out the window. The siren had stopped. He picked up the phone again.

"Get me Captain Paul Jarman," he said.

Randi enjoyed a morning swim. It was still cool enough to be invigorating. She'd always loved the water. During a couple of her summer vacations from college she'd been an Aquamaid in the spectacular water-skiing show at Cypress Gardens only forty miles from Tampa, her home town. She'd loved skimming across the water in her lemon-yellow bathing suit, holding a bright red, wind-whipped flag aloft.

She dove gracefully into the water and easily swam the length of the pool. It was obvious she was in top physical condition—any way one would care to make the evaluation. She made a competition turn, pushing off from the poolside, and swam back. She climbed out and joined a small group of young women sitting at the pool's edge. She was about to make a comment when one of the women looked up, past her, with a suddenly sobering face. The others quickly followed her gaze, falling silent. Randi turned.

In the door to the clubhouse stood Paul. He looked stiff and grim. Randi's heart sank for an icy, adrenal instant. She saw in Paul that—that certain person. He—for it was always a man—he who had been chosen to deliver the final news, to pronounce the widow of the day in person. Always in person. That certain, special person, the messenger of death, bringing news about a husband whose life had been snuffed out in an instant, whose young body was now "burned beyond recognition"; a concept so hideous she had deliberately refused to visualize it.

And now—there stood Paul.

That certain person?

Paul started toward the group. The women watched him approach, apprehension darkening their faces as each of them was touched by a gust of her own special fears. Randi rose to meet him.

"Hi, Paul," she called. She was aware of her voice sounding forced . . . of the others watching her intently. "What're you doing here this time of day? Got time for a dip?" she asked, automatically tiptoeing around the dreaded subject, wearing the obligatory blinkers.

Her voice trailed off as Paul came up to her. "It's—Tom, isn't it?" she said, her voice husky.

Paul nodded.

"Tell me."

"He's down," he said. He looked at her earnestly. "That's all we know."

"Wait for me."

She ran for the dressing rooms.

Paul looked after her. He lifted his face and gazed up into the clear blue sky.

Sometimes. Sometimes its beauty was marred. . . .

3

Raising a whirling cloud of fine sand, the Air Force rescue helicopter skillfully set down in one of the few boulder-free, level spots among the outlandish stones and rock formations.

Major Quentin Ward jumped from the craft. All around him loomed gnarled and weather-sculptured rocks. A hell of a place to come down in a chute, he thought. This particular stretch of the Sierra foothills was called the Alabama Hills, he knew. But he had no idea why. Looked nothing like what he remembered of Alabama. In the distance the snow-covered peaks of Mount Whitney towered majestically.

Two men followed Ward from the helicopter. One of them a master sergeant, a big black bruiser of a man who had a well-earned reputation as an amateur boxer. Heavyweight. Name of Freddy Hays. The other, Airman First Class Norbert Wilson. They joined the Major.

Hays pointed up into the bizarre, oddly shaped rocks. "Up there, sir. A little ways," he said. "That's where we spotted the chute."

"Right." Ward nodded. "Let's go find it. Spread out."

The three men separated and began to climb up among the misshapen rocks.

Ward rather enjoyed himself. It was a perfect day. The sun was warm on his back as he made his way up among the boulders; the air was fresh and smog-free. Ward was a career officer, USAF Medical Corps. A search-and-rescue mission was a welcome diversion from Base duties, especially when chances of serious problems or injuries were minimal. And he fully expected to find Tom Darby perhaps shaken up—certainly chagrined—but OK. After all, he had ejected without trouble.

Ward paused and looked out over the crazily jumbled, boulder-crowded landscape stretched out before him. Like a bit of an alien planet—misplaced, he thought. One of the Jupiter moons . . .

Off to his right Sergeant Hays called out: "Over here, Major! The chute!" He pointed. "Up there!"

Ward changed the direction of his climb. He joined Hays and Wilson, who stood on a ridge, looking down a little slope. He followed their gaze and his mood changed abruptly. At the bottom of the slope was the parachute—a great expanse of crumpled orange and white. Tom Darby was nowhere to be seen, but in the center under the chute an ominous bulge caught his eye. Without words the three men hurried down. At once Hays and Wilson pulled the chute away from the motionless bulge beneath it. They stared. On the sandy ground lay a large, oblong boulder.

Ward sighed with relief—relief at once troubled by a greater enigma. Where was Darby?

Hays held the empty chute harness toward him. "Look, sir," he said. He pointed to a small pouch snapped onto the webbing of one of the risers. "He can't be hurt. He hasn't touched his medical kit."

Wilson looked off. "There's a dirt road over there," he volunteered. "The Major could have seen it as he came down. Perhaps he walked down there."

Ward nodded. "Perhaps. We'll have a look." He was increasingly worried. A downed pilot is supposed to stay with his chute. For easy spotting. Tom Darby knew that.

The road was about a quarter of a mile away—and it was not easy going. They'd only made a couple of hundred feet when Wilson bent down to pick up something from behind a clump of weeds.

"Major Ward!" he called. He sounded shaken. "Look at this!" He stared at a bright red object held gingerly in his hand.

Ward and Hays hurried over to him. "It's the Major's, all right," Hays said.

The face plate on the helmet was shattered, the glossy red surface scratched, the EMG sight broken off. On the left side a ragged, broken dent marred the smooth surface where the helmet had been crushed in.

Ward took the helmet from Wilson. Carefully he ran his fingers across the inside jagged edges of the break. They came away discolored and sticky with partly clotted blood.

Wilson stared at it, wide-eyed. "Man," he said in awe. He looked sober. "Must've been some whack to do that."

The three men looked at one another, their faces mirroring their concern. "We have to find him," Ward said, his voice grim. "He can't be far away."

"It was lying over there." Wilson pointed. "The helmet. Near that crevice."

Quickly they walked to the spot. The crevice was an extremely narrow passage between two huge, bulbous boulders. It was about twenty feet long. They could see daylight at the other end.

Hays looked at the sandy ground. "Someone's been here," he said. "Or—some thing."

Ward examined the ground. There were scuff tracks leading into the fissure. It was impossible to tell what—or who—had made them. Ward started to squeeze through the crevice. "Let's take a look at the other side," he said.

Hays and Wilson followed him.

On the other side the big boulders gave way to a more rocky, mountainous terrain. The ground was hard. It was impossible to make out any tracks.

"Look around," Ward said. "See what you can find."

Sergeant Hays was searching among the rocks and the scraggly weeds and brush growing in thick clumps all over the area. He was concerned. Puzzled. What the hell did the Major think he was doing? If he'd have only stayed with his chute, they'd have had him halfway back to the Base by now, instead of running all over the devil's half-acre searching for him. He knew Tom Darby. He liked him. An OK dude. A guy who seemed to enjoy hanging his hide out over the edge on a regular basis. One of the best damned test pilots at Edwards, though you'd never know he knew his own importance from talking with him. But he sure knew his stuff. So what the hell was he pulling now?

He brushed through a clump of shrubs. Nothing. He turned toward another stand of brush growing up against the steep side of a rocky hill. He bent the brittle branches out of the way. Behind them he could make out what appeared to be a small cave opening. He stooped down to peer into the dark interior.

Sudden, explosive motion shocked him into split-second immobility. And in that flash moment an indelible sight seared itself on his mind.

Leaping from the gloom of the cave, a—a "creature" catapulted itself at him. Eyes forced wide, lips drawn back in a vicious snarl and hands clawing in front of him—it was Tom Darby! High on the crown on the left side of his head, dry, caked blood had matted his hair. His flying suit was torn and stained and his face streaked with blood. He looked wholly wild, dangerous—and terror-stricken.

With a lightning, panic-born swipe of his clawed hands, Tom violently shoved Hays out of his way, raking long gashes across his cheek in a dash to get past him. The sudden, savage impact sent the Sergeant crashing to the ground. And Tom raced away into the tumble of weirdly shaped boulders and rock formations.

Ward and Wilson came running up to the Sergeant, who was sitting stunned on the ground.

"Hays! What happened?" Ward knelt beside him.

Hays touched his bleeding cheek in bewilderment. "It was— it was the Major, sir." He sounded dazed. "It was Major Darby. He jumped me."

He looked at Ward uncomprehendingly—almost pleadingly. "I've known the Major for three years—and—and he tried to kill me!"

Suddenly Wilson shouted, "Hey! Look!" He pointed into the rocks.

On a large smooth boulder in the distance a lone figure stood silhouetted against the blue sky. It was Tom. Stiffly he stood gazing back toward the three men at the cave.

Ward ran a few steps toward him. "Tom!" he called. "Wait! Stay where you are! We're coming to help you!" The three men began running toward him.

For a moment Tom stood immobile. Then he abruptly whirled about, jumped off the boulder and disappeared among the craggy rock formations.

The three rescuers quickly reached the big boulder where Tom had been spotted. He was nowhere to be seen. Bewildered, they looked around.

Hays shook his head. "Why?" He looked at Ward. "Why is the Major running away?"

Ward stared out over the rocky wilderness. "I don't know, Sergeant," he said quietly. "I don't know. . . ."

They all saw him at the same time, briefly visible as he jumped from one rock to another a short distance away.

"There he goes!" Wilson shouted.

At once the three men took off in pursuit.

Tom was obviously winded—trembling with near-exhaustion. He breathed in short, shallow gulps as he scrambled up the steep, rocky hillside. For a moment he paused and looked down toward the faintly heard sounds and distant calls from his pursuers. His taut and grimy face was filled with fear. He touched the wound on his head; it was bothering him. He turned and clambered up the slope.

He reached a mesa. The flat, boulder-strewn area stretched before him. At once he began a loping gait out across the level ground.

Sergeant Hays was the first to crest the mesa. "There he is!" he called. Ward and Wilson climbed up to join him. In the distance out on the plateau Tom could be seen—running away. The men set out after him.

Tom was fleeing across the treacherous, rocky ground. He did not look back. His pursuers were far behind. Suddenly he stopped.

In front of him the ground gave way. A ravine. Fully twelve to fifteen feet across. Tom looked down into the abyss. It was deep and dark, its rocky sides virtually perpendicular.

Trapped, he ran a little way along the gorge, first one way, then the other. There was nowhere to cross. The ravine cut across the mesa in both directions.

He stopped and turned toward the oncoming men. There was a wild fire in his eyes—and terrified, uncomprehending despair in his face. His stance was wary and taut.

Ward saw Tom stop. He slowed his run. Deliberately he began to walk toward the petrified figure.

"Tom!" he called soothingly. "Don't run away. We want to help you."

Slowly the three men moved in.

Close enough to see Tom's face, Ward was deeply shocked. He could see Tom was badly hurt—but he could find no glimmer of recognition or reason in his distraught face.

Tom's eyes moved rapidly from one to another of the slowly approaching men. Like a cornered dog, he backed away from them, never taking his eyes from them—nearer and nearer the ravine behind him.

He stopped, his eyes wild with desperation. He was at the edge of the steep chasm. Trapped . . .

He threw a quick glance down into the abyss. His eyes flitted toward the opposite rim—so far away. . . .

The three men steadily, cautiously advanced toward him, Ward keeping up a continuous soothing monologue. "Easy, Tom, easy . . . Don't be afraid. . . . We're your friends. . . . We want to help. . . . Tom—listen to me. . . . Easy . . . Easy . . ."

He watched the terror-stricken figure crouched tensely before him. Almost. Another few feet. They'd get him back to the Base hospital at once for medical treatment. . . . Another few feet . . .

Suddenly Tom burst into action. He whirled around, took a short run and, with the reckless effort born of panic, leaped out over the gaping void, arms stretched out for the far edge. He thudded into the hard, rocky brink—hanging over the rim. He began to slip. He dug his fingers into the rough ground, his legs desperately searching for a foothold.

Slowly he pulled himself up. Never having uttered a sound, he looked back across the ravine at the three men standing shocked and bewildered on the other side, staring at him in stunned silence.

Wilson looked wide-eyed at the figure of Tom huddled on the ground across the crevasse.

"Man," he breathed, deeply awed. "Did you see that?" He asked the question of no one. "He jumped that ravine like a—like a big cat."

"He could have killed himself," Hays said, shaken. "He sure could. Easy . . ."

On the far side Tom got up. Without a glance back, he trotted off—disappearing among the rocks.

Wilson stared after him, his face thoughtful.

"I wouldn't have believed it," he whispered. "If I hadn't seen it. No, sir . . . It—it couldn't be done. . . ."

4

A1C Carole Goodman was bored. She had hoped for a more glamorous job when she had been assigned to the Flight Test Center, and she was not too charmed with her present duties at the Message Center at Edwards, routine—and mostly dull at that. She glanced at the teletype machine as it began to clatter, expecting another routine message—but the words being typed out on the machine brought her instantly to attention.

> URGENT   URGENT   URGENT
> PERSONAL FROM CHIEF OF STAFF
> TO COMMANDER AIR FORCE FLIGHT TEST CENTER
> EDWARDS AFB

She turned toward a non-com sitting at a desk. "Sergeant," she called. "Take a look at this!"

The non-com joined her at the teletype. The message continued.

> MAJOR DARBY F-15 CRASH EXTREMELY REPEAT
> EXTREMELY SENSITIVE DUE MARCUS XM-9 TEST.
> IMPERATIVE

The Sergeant quickly strode to his desk. He picked up the phone. "Get me General Ryan's office," he said. "Urgent!"

The teletype machine fell silent. The message was finished. A1C Goodman tore it off and immediately prepared it for delivery.

Three sober-faced men were facing General Ryan as he stood in his office, the teletype message in his hand: Dr. Theodor

Marcus; the Test Flight Director, a light colonel; and Colonel Howell. Ryan was reading the message to them.

" '—imperative ascertain cause of accident at once. Use procedures appropriate to situation as determined by officer in the field. Project vital, repeat vital to national security. Keep advising.' " He looked up at the men standing before him. "It is signed: 'Warfield, General USAF, Chief of Staff.' "

He looked from one to the other. "Have you any idea of what went wrong up there?" he asked. "Colonel Harnum?" He addressed the Flight Test Director, the man Marcus knew as Control One. Marcus glanced at the man. So that was his name. He'd have to try and remember.

Colonel Harnum shook his head. "It happened at the instant the XM-9 was fired, sir." He frowned. "We don't know what happened. . . . It may have been the laser activator. Or one of the pressure tanks. It could be one of a thousand factors. We just don't know yet. We had trouble with the telemetry. I haven't had a full report on that as yet. I don't know the full extent of the malfunction."

"Can we rule out sabotage?" Ryan asked.

Harnum looked soberly at the General. "Sir," he said. He sounded subdued. "At the moment we can rule out nothing."

Ryan nodded. He turned to Marcus. "Dr. Marcus?"

Theodor Marcus had been crushed with disappointment when the accident occurred. But the recuperative powers of his inquisitive spirit had not diminished with the years. He spoke firmly.

"I should be able to come up with some answers once I get the XM-9 mechanism from the wreckage. I understand it lies in a pretty inaccessible spot. I should like to get it as soon as it *is* retrieved." He shrugged. "Until then—anything I can say would be pure guesswork. I just hope we get there before some curiosity-seekers bent on collecting souvenirs." He thought for a moment. "And, of course, it is absolutely imperative that I debrief Major Darby as quickly as possible."

Ryan looked at Howell. "Jon? Where do we stand now?"

Howell looked uncomfortable—and he was. It was not a state of affairs he was used to, and he didn't like it.

"The plane pretty much disintegrated in the air," he said. He looked grim. "The wreckage is scattered all through the damned mountains. The Combat Mobility Forces haven't as yet located any main impact area. Or—areas, for that matter. As soon as they do, we'll cordon them off with Security Police."

He glanced at Marcus.

"I echo Dr. Marcus' concern," he said gravely. "There are hikers and climbers all through the crash area. We can only hope nobody runs across any—vital piece of equipment before we do. . . . It's happened that way before."

Ryan nodded.

Howell went on, "As for the status of the search-and-rescue operation," he said, "we've only had preliminary reports. "As you know, General, they have had some—eh, trouble getting to Major Darby."

Ryan nodded. He turned to Marcus and Harnum. "Thank you," he said. "That will be all."

The two men left.

Ryan studied Howell. "What the hell *is* going on out there, Jon?"

"I don't know the details yet. It seems Darby is—evading, actively evading the rescue team. And he is injured. It is not known how seriously. I'm waiting for Major Ward's detailed report."

Ryan frowned in thought. He looked at the teletype message in his hand. He walked to his desk and placed the paper in a folder. He looked at Howell.

"We're obviously not confronted with a routine rescue operation." He pursed his lips pensively. "I want you to sit on this one, Jon. Give it top priority. I want results."

Howell nodded.

"The F-15 is your baby," the General continued. "Has been all along. And you've also been briefed on the XM-9 project." He glanced at the folder on his desk. "Do whatever you have to do, *but—*" he looked soberly at the junior officer—"stir up the least amount of turbulence possible."

"Yes, sir." Howell nodded.

"Keep me informed."

"Yes, sir."

Howell turned to leave. General Ryan stopped him.

"Jon," he said earnestly, "we're dealing with a high-security matter. You're juggling a basket of eggs. Easy does it. . . ."

5

Only a single, feeble light bulb provided illumination on the narrow stair landing of the old apartment building—barely enough to identify the green uniforms so familiar to the people of East Berlin. The two men standing before a glass-paned door belonged to the *Volkspolizei*—Vopos. The People's Police. With black-gloved hand one of them rapped imperiously on the door. He let only a few seconds go by before he banged on one of the glass panes with his fist. In the hallway beyond, a light went on, casting a pale yellow glow out onto the landing. The fist grew more insistent.

A shadow showed indistinctly in the frosted-glass door panes. With obvious apprehension the voice of a man called out:

"*Wer ist da?*"

"Police. Open up!" the Vopo ordered brusquely.

There was the rattle of a chain being removed, the sounds of a bolt being drawn back and a latch unlocked. The door was opened and an elderly man stood silently in the doorway. His hair tousled, his eyes sleep-puffed, he looked frightened.

"You are Dr. Wilhelm Krebbs?" the Vopo asked gruffly.

The old man nodded. Nothing has changed, he thought bleakly. Nothing . . .

"I am," he answered. "What—"

The Vopo cut him off. "You are to come with us," he said. "Now."

For a brief moment Krebbs stood frozen.

"You will allow me to get dressed?" he inquired. "Or must I come like this?" He pulled at the frayed old robe he held around him.

"Be quick about it," the Vopo snapped.

Krebbs nodded. He turned and walked down the hallway. The two men followed.

The night streets of the city were all but deserted as the police car sped toward the *Stadtmitte* some five kilometers from the Weissensee residential district where Krebbs had his flat. The old man huddled silently in the back seat next to one of the Vopos. They took the most direct route, cutting through side streets where the grim evidence of the destruction suffered by Berlin during the war still remained. The headlights of the car swept across the old ruins. Momentarily the beams captured a sign erected in the rubble—a ghostly warning from the past:

EINSTURZGEFAHR
Betreten verboten!

DANGER OF COLLAPSE
Entrance forbidden!

Forbidden. Krebbs sighed. Nothing has changed, he thought once more.

He had already guessed where he was being taken. To one of the new government buildings on Unter den Linden. He was not able to keep from feeling increasingly uneasy as they drew nearer to their goal.

He glanced at a long red banner strung across the front of a huge building under construction:

WIRKSAM PRODUZIEREN—FÜR DICH, FÜR DEINEN BETRIEB,
FÜR UNSEREN SOZIALISTISCHEN FRIEDENSSTAAT—D.D.R.

PRODUCE EFFICIENTLY—FOR YOURSELF, FOR YOUR FIRM,
FOR OUR PEACEFUL SOCIALIST STATE—D.D.R.

Posters.   Banners.   Slogans.   Nothing changed . . .

He swallowed his bitterness. D.D.R.—the German Democratic Republic. Without mirth he recalled the cruel joke bantered about by the West Berliners: D.D.R. does not stand for

Deutsche Demokratische Republik, they laughed, but for *Der Doofe Rest,* The Stupid Leftovers. . . .

Leftovers, yes. But is it stupidity to have no choice?

The big new building on Unter den Linden near the Spree River looked forbidding—and somehow foreboding. It was dark except for the entrance hall and a row of windows on the third floor. The police car came to a halt before the main entrance and Krebbs was marched inside.

With a minimum of words, muttered out of earshot of their subject, the two Vopos received a receipt for him from a sullen officer, and Krebbs was turned over to two flat-eyed guards. Without a word they marched him up a sweeping staircase to the offices above.

When the man sitting in the office finally looked up from the clutter of paperwork on his desk, his face broke into a wide smile—as if someone had pulled the switchcord on a light. It was not a pretty sight. The grimace never reached the eyes. Only the bloodless lips seemed to move as if totally separate from the rest of his face. "Ah, Dr. Krebbs!" he exclaimed.

He stood up and came around the massive desk. He walked up to the waiting Krebbs, who stood just inside the door, flanked by the two guards.

Obviously a man of importance, Krebbs thought uneasily. His office was richly furnished albeit with a heavy touch. Large, expensively framed portraits of East German leaders adorned the walls, and at one end of the room a comfortable sofa and several leather easy chairs were grouped around a solid oak coffee table. Krebbs judged the man to be his own age—perhaps a year or two older. Sixty-five? Corpulent, balding, he wore a three-piece suit which somehow seemed out of keeping. A heavy gold watch chain ran from a pocket on one side of his vest through a buttonhole to a pocket on the other side. It gave him a peculiarly old-fashioned look. There was something disturbing about the man. Krebbs thought he knew what it was. The man was an ex-Nazi. Everyone knew that the most avid Nazis made the best Communists. He seemed cordial—but there was an oddly chilling effect to his cordiality.

"So good of you to come, *Herr Doktor.*" His voice was deep, beautifully modulated. "A pleasure to meet you." He extended his hand.

Krebbs took it. "Of course," he muttered uncomfortably. "Of course . . ." He glanced at the two guards.

The official nodded to them. "Leave us," he said, obvious authority in his voice. The guards came to attention and left. Krebbs was led to the coffee table. On it had been placed a cut-crystal carafe and two brandy glasses.

"Sit down, my dear *Herr Doktor,* sit down," the official urged. "I am quite sure you will not mind a little brandy." He chuckled and smiled his switchcord smile. "It is such an ungodly hour."

He poured two generous portions of brandy and held up his snifter, cradled in his hand.

"Zum wohl, Herr Doktor!"

Krebbs accepted his glass. He was nonplussed. "Thank you, *Herr. . . ?"*

The man's eyes widened in consternation.

"Ah, forgive me, my dear *Herr Doktor* Krebbs," he exclaimed expansively. "How very thoughtless of me. I am Colonel Gerhardt Scharff. Ministry of State Security." He paused, looked closely at Krebbs. "Foreign Intelligence."

The startled look that flitted across his visitor's face was not lost upon the Colonel. He was satisfied. He leaned toward Krebbs and spoke in a confidential, almost conspiratorial voice.

"I shall be brief, *Herr Doktor,* in view of the hour. Come straight to the point." Again he peered closely at his visitor. "You were an associate of Dr. Wernher von Braun, were you not?" It was obvious he already knew the answer. "In the development of the—eh, V-2 rocket?"

Krebbs was genuinely surprised. It had been long years since he had thought of his days at Peenemünde.

"I was," he acknowledged. "I—"

"And today you are still active in rocket research," Scharff interrupted. "Electronics, primarily. Am I correct?" He knew he was.

Krebbs nodded. "Quite correct, *Herr Oberst."* He sipped his brandy. He needed time to collect himself. Von Braun?

Peenemünde? "Really on a consultant basis these days," he continued. "It—"

"Of course." Scharff flashed his switch-on smile at him. He plowed on. "In the forties, when you were developing the V-2, you had a colleague named Marcus, yes?"

For the second time, surprise startled Krebbs. Theo? So many years ago . . .

"Yes," he said. "Dr. Theodor Marcus. A most—"

"Exactly." Unsmilingly Scharff broke in. "I presume you know that Dr. Marcus went with von Braun when he—eh, transferred his loyalties to the Americans in 1945?"

Krebbs was suddenly flooded with apprehension. He felt the nervous sweat collect in his armpits. He knew Theo had—"defected"—to the Americans. He also knew he himself would have done the same, had he been offered the chance. Had in fact solicited it. Did Scharff know that? What had Theo to do with his sudden forced night visit to this Colonel in the State Security? What did they want of *him?* After all these years? Was it, once again, guilt by association? No matter how long ago? He squirmed in his chair.

"I—I was aware of it," he said, trying to keep his voice calm, and not entirely succeeding. "I—I have not been in contact with Dr. Marcus since—since—"

Scharff flashed him one of his switchcord smiles. "Oberammergau. Quite, *Herr Doktor.* I am aware of that." He did not feel it necessary to tell Krebbs of his own involvement with Marcus so long ago. When Richter had come up with Dr. Wilhelm Krebbs as one of the erstwhile colleagues of Marcus, he'd recognized the name, of course. He'd been curious to meet "the one that got away." Although, he thought—with the familiar and bitter chagrin that had plagued him ever since he'd learned of the splash Marcus had made in the American scientific community—*he* was the real "big one" that got away. And he, Scharff, had had the man in his net. It continued to gall him and he was eager for another chance to gaff his prey.

This time not the man himself—but his life's work.

It would be fully as satisfying. . . .

Again he leaned toward his visitor. "But—to the point, as I promised you. Working with the Americans, Dr. Marcus has developed a—a certain device for them. A device that could be immeasurably important in the—eh, scheme of things. We have known of its existence for some time."

He let the intelligence sink in.

"I see," Krebbs said. He was deeply worried. Why tell *him* this?

"It is vital for our security, Dr. Krebbs—I am certain you understand—and that of our allies, of course, that we learn everything we can about this—eh, device." Scharff sounded deadly earnest. He contemplated the scientist sitting in awkward discomfort across from him. "Now, *Herr Doktor*—and this is in the strictest confidence, of course—we have just been informed that this, eh, Marcus device was being tested, mounted on one of the newest and most sophisticated American fighter planes. The test flight took place only hours ago. The plane crashed." He gave a short laugh. "Nothing we can take credit for," he said. "An accident."

He spread his hands. "We have been informed—reliably, of course—that the pilot survived. But—curiously—he is lost somewhere in the mountains of Southern California."

Krebbs looked genuinely puzzled. *"Herr Oberst,"* he ventured, "I am afraid I don't—"

With a quick gesture Scharff silenced him. "You will, *Herr Doktor.* You will." Again the quick, disconcerting smile—which almost at once turned into a look of solemnity. "You see, we are interested in enlisting your expert help, Dr. Krebbs. Let me explain. There is a possibility, a bare possibility, mind you, that I—that *we* may come into possession of the—eh, Marcus device. The physical device, that is. At the moment it seems to be—'up for grabs,' as the Americans so picturesquely express it. In what state is unfortunately impossible to tell." He flashed a smile. "So of course we at once thought of you, my dear *Herr Doktor* Krebbs. A former close colleague and friend of Dr. Marcus who undoubtedly is quite familiar with his way of thinking—and working."

Krebbs was taken aback. "But—I—"

Scharff firmly cut him off. "Now, *Herr Doktor*, straight to the point. If we should find ourselves in a position to furnish you with—eh, certain material, what would you need to be able to—to reconstruct the work of Dr. Marcus? Outside of his blueprints, of course." He gave an unpleasant little laugh.

"Need?" Krebbs was dumfounded. He thought quickly. There did not seem to be any direct threat to him, after all. Some of his apprehension left him. Need? "Well," he said pensively, "the device itself would certainly be a great help . . . or as much of it as possible, as you indicated. We might—"

Scharff interrupted impatiently. "I understand. If that proves unfeasible—what else? Any other possibilities? What else might be of help to you?"

Krebbs frowned in thought. He was beginning to get caught up in the challenge. "Notes," he said. "Theo's—Dr. Marcus' notes. They—" Scharff made a negative gesture. "Or perhaps an operations manual," Krebbs went on. "A repair manual, that sort of thing. Procurement orders?" Scharff was listening. He said nothing. Krebbs continued. "Someone who had worked on the project might be of value. Or—the pilot. He would have had to be thoroughly familiar with the device in order to test it effectively."

Scharff sat up, suddenly wholly interested.

Krebbs went on. "That would certainly have been the case with the top technicians conducting the tests at Peenemünde. If we could get a chance to question the pilot, we might learn enough from him to accomplish a reconstruction of the device." He was suddenly aware that he was allowing himself to be carried away with the problem. Easy . . . "Only a possibility, of course," he added lamely.

Scharff looked thoughtful. "Of course," he echoed. "A possibility." Sudden menace crept into his voice. "Though it may have to be a little more than that, my dear *Herr Doktor.*"

It was perfect, he thought. If they were not able to find the device itself in the wreckage before the Americans got it, they might be able to get the pilot. The Americans did seem to be having trouble finding him. If he "disappeared," no one would wonder why—or how. He would simply have perished in the desert. Somewhere. Never to be found. It was perfect. . . .

He stood up. "Until we know exactly how matters develop, I must ask you to hold yourself immediately available." He flashed his disturbing smile. "In fact, I have taken the liberty of having some of your things brought here so you can be close. I am certain you will be—comfortable."

Krebbs paled. All his apprehensions crowded back upon him. He, too, stood up. He looked at the Colonel. He had to play it out.

"Colonel," he said. "This—device. I shall have to know what its purpose is—if I am to attempt a reconstruction."

Scharff gave him a quick glance. He walked over to his desk and stood for a moment in thought. Then he looked up at Krebbs, his quick smile more chilling than ever.

"Yes," he said. "You will, won't you? Eventually." He seemed to be making a decision. "Perhaps—now. It may give you a head start. In your thinking." He looked steadily at the scientist. "Your friend Dr. Marcus has developed a Laser Activated Energy Beam. A particle beam. Extremely powerful. The Americans call it the XM-9. It is a far cry from the high-energy laser with which they first shot down a drone target over the New Mexico desert in 1973—as far a cry as their moon-lander from their Model-T Ford." He glanced at Krebbs. "You are familiar with the case, Dr. Krebbs? And with the—eh, tank-like mobile laser developed by the American Army some years later?"

Krebbs nodded. "Not in detail, of course."

"Of course," Scharff said dryly. He went on. "Coupled with their new eye-movement sight that is mounted on the pilot's helmet, this device has the capability to destroy any attacking missile, rocket or aircraft. Unerringly, *Herr Doktor* Krebbs, and instantly. In flight. Regardless of any evasive maneuvering attempted."

He let his words sink in.

"Instantaneous intercept, *Herr Doktor*. And total destruction. It makes it *impossible* for our defense forces to bring down any enemy bomber or ballistic missile equipped with this Marcus device. It is impervious to any intercept. It makes it possible for our enemies to deliver anything anywhere. And unfailingly. The implications should be clear to you."

He walked up to the intently listening Krebbs. "As you can see, it is imperative that we learn all the specifications of this device. Possessed unilaterally by the Americans, it could completely upset the balance of power between them and us—in their favor. We cannot allow that to happen. That is obvious."

He turned away and sat down at his desk. "As you can see, you are now privy to a top state secret," he said dispassionately. "I am confident that you are fully aware of the implications of that, too. Good night, *Herr Doktor*. The guard outside will show you to your quarters."

He watched the dazed scientist leave the room. He smiled to himself. He felt quite certain of the man's unreserved cooperation. He had no doubt that he would be able to ensure it. His early training as a young SS officer in the Gestapo during that organization's most powerful years had been very useful to him in his present position. He anticipated no problem. Not with the good *Herr Doktor* Wilhelm Krebbs . . .

But there *were* other matters. He picked up the phone. He spoke crisply:

"Richter, get me OV III—Major Blücher." Impatiently he waited. "Blücher? Scharff here. This is a top-priority request. . . . Yes . . . Have we any sleeper agents with technological knowledge in Southern California? . . . I need it at once. . . . I'll wait."

He drummed his fingers on his desk as he waited. Was it an old Nazi marching song?

He let his thoughts wander. . . . He had a twinge of doubt. Was he doing the right thing? Was the action he was about to take in *his* best interest? He brooded over it. He needed a big case. He needed *something* to solidify his position at the highest level. He needed it badly. He still grew coldly furious when he thought of the memo he'd intercepted. "Not decisive enough," it had said. He! Gerhardt Scharff! His service in the Gestapo from the first had been exemplary. He had the commendations to prove that. From Himmler himself. Still hidden away among his possessions. And his service to his new masters had been equally valuable. Always. So what if he *did* look out for his own welfare first? . . . "Replacement with a younger man should be considered." He knew those "younger men" clawing their way up. *Zum Teufel damit!* No young postwar brat could begin to do his job as efficiently as he, Gerhardt Scharff.

And now this Marcus thing. He knew it had been a big question for a long time. He knew the Russians wanted information about it. Badly. He also knew they did not yet want to risk creating an international incident by an overt act, such as— eh, abducting Marcus himself or one of the few others who were familiar with his—eh, device. But this pilot, lost in the wilderness as he was—that was another matter. His—eh, disappearance could easily be explained without any suspicion falling on outside forces. And he would be able to give valuable information about the device he had been testing, to him and to the Russians. If *he*, Gerhardt Scharff, could get the information— preferably by obtaining the device itself, but that seemed problematic—or through the pilot . . . If *his*, Gerhardt Scharff's, actions should succeed where nothing else had—his post would be secure. He would be important.

If.

He'd had to make a decision fast. As soon as he'd learned of the opportunity. And he *had* decided. Decided to go ahead— on his own. Without consulting anyone and thereby running the risk of losing the full credit.

What if it *did* go wrong? The whole damned situation admittedly *was* a long shot. But careers were built on long shots. The chance seemed worth taking. It would be unfortunate if the attempt failed—but not dangerous. The risks were minimal. And if anyone at a later date objected to his unilateral action, he could plead the urgency necessary to launch the undertaking. He'd *had* to make a fast decision. That, after all, was what he was paid to do.

Anyway, some risk had to be taken. And taken now . . .

Or he might be terminated.

In his business that meant only one thing.

Was he over-reacting? Was he letting his judgment be influenced by his preoccupation with Marcus, and his need to rectify past mistakes? With the threat of—termination. . . ?

He was brought out of his reverie as the voice on the telephone came back. He listened briefly.

"I see. . . . Two." His face grew dark. "One of them broke his cover to transmit the XM-9 crash information? . . . No, I did *not* know!" He sounded annoyed. "Is he still safe? In place? . . . Good. Here are your orders—effective at once."

His voice became hard.

"Activate them both."

6

Colonel Jonathan Howell was angry—and when he was, he didn't mind showing it. It made no sense to him to let a good, honest emotion go to waste. Paul Jarman and Quentin Ward stood before him in his office, both looking tired and grim. He glared at them.

"Damn his hide," he growled. "I'll throw the damned book at him. Walking away from his chute."

"He is not responsible, sir." Ward spoke firmly.

Howell fixed him with an icy stare. "Explain."

"The head injury, sir. Of course, without an examination, I—"

"I don't want a medical diagnosis, Major," Howell cut him off. "Just an explanation."

"His brain may be affected," Ward said. "Damaged. He is not himself."

"Are you telling me that Major Darby has lost his mind?" Howell asked acidly.

Ward was not to be put off. "I am saying that I believe him to have suffered brain damage, Colonel. He may be mentally deranged. It's the only explanation for his aberrant behavior," he said reasonably.

Howell stood up. He turned his back on the two junior officers and stood for a moment, pensively looking out the window into the night.

Ward made sense. He and the other search parties had re-

turned when darkness fell. They had not been able to spot
Tom again.

"You're right," he said, without turning around. "That would
account for him leaving his chute. Attacking Sergeant Hays.
Running away."

"It would," Ward agreed.

Howell turned back to the two men. "We'll have to get to
him. Fast." He looked directly at Paul. "As fast as possible.
Captain Jarman, are you settled in enough to take command?"

"Yes, sir."

"Good." Howell nodded. "I know of your ties to Major
Darby." He looked straight at Paul. "It'll be your baby. You
will be in charge of the search-and-rescue operations in the
field."

"Yes, sir."

"Major Ward, the medical responsibilities will be yours."

"Of course, sir."

"We'll start for the area at 0400 tomorrow," Paul said.
"That'll put us there as soon as it's light."

Howell looked at him seriously. "Captain Jarman," he said,
"Tom obviously needs help. But apart from all humanitarian
reasons, we *must* find him—and bring him back here."

He picked up a paper from his desk.

"The report from the crash-investigation team states that
the plane exploded and burned on impact. It is a total loss.
Total. Everything." He looked closely at the two men, troubled.
"The telemetering transmissions were cut off completely during the critical period. There are *no* reports—no information
at all. Tom is the only man alive who knows what went wrong
up there. He has the only answers." He paused. He scowled.
"We've got to know. Or we can start from scratch."

Paul nodded. He understood what Howell was saying, but
it was difficult to think of anything except getting Tom safely
back. "I'll organize a maximum search-and-rescue effort. I'll
get out the Emergency Service Teams, and—"

"Captain," Howell interrupted sharply, "you will mount a
minimum operation. I do *not* want to advertise what's happened. I don't want the press to blow this thing up to a major
media event. Understood?"

Paul looked at his superior, uncertain. "Sir?"

"I don't want to alert every Tom, Dick and Ivan to the fact that we have a mentally deranged test pilot with his head crammed full of top-secret information running loose in the area." Howell looked soberly at Paul. "And, more importantly, I don't want the damned place filled with curiosity-seekers," he said quietly. "If they got to him before we did—in his condition—they could harm him greatly." He looked at Ward.

Ward nodded. "That is certainly possible," he said.

Howell turned to Paul. "I want this handled as—routine, Captain," he said. "You should have no trouble finding him."

Paul nodded. "I understand."

The telephone on Howell's desk rang. He picked it up. "Colonel Howell . . . Yes." He looked startled. "Where? . . . I see." He glanced at the two men watching him intently. "Yes. Get a complete report. . . . Right." He hung up. "Well," he said crisply, "your job's been made easier for you."

He strode to a big wall map of the Southern California area taking in the Mojave Desert with its large military installations, the Naval Weapons Center at China Lake, Fort Irwin Military Reservation and, of course, Edwards Air Force Base; the Sequoia National Park; Death Valley National Monument and the Sierra Nevada mountain range. "That was a report from an Inyo National Forest Ranger station," he said. "Tom has been seen—halfway up the highest mountain in the continental states."

Shaken, Ward exclaimed. "Mount Whitney!"

"They didn't get a good look at him in the dark, but he was spotted at Whitney Portal—"he jabbed a finger on the map—"here—about an hour ago."

The three men stared at the map.

Paul nodded thoughtfully.

"Taking to the high ground," he said. "Like a wounded animal."

DAY TWO

1

He had spent the night curled up in the hollow he'd scooped out in a thick layer of pine needles under a stand of evergreens. He had slept the sleep of deep exhaustion. . . .

When he had fled from the frightening things that pursued him, screaming unintelligible sounds at him, he had taken refuge, making his way ever higher up the rocky mountainside. When everything had grown darker and darker, he had been terrified. It had been but one of the countless terrors that had assailed him in this world made up entirely of unknown terrors and threats.

Finally he had curled up under the trees. He gave no thought to who—or what—he was. He just—was. . . . He had no recollection or inkling of any existence before. He had no comprehension of the new experiences that crowded in on him. He only knew that most of them frightened him. There was only one existence. His. Now.

His first memory was that of finding himself entangled in a web of cruel restraints and enveloped in billows of suffocating softness. With the strength of panic he had struggled and had managed to free himself from the grip of the straps and from the cloying flimsiness. . . .

When he awoke, he was instantly alert. He lay still in his little burrow, listening, breathing the musty scent of the pine needles. The forest around him was awakening. A soft breeze coming down from the majestic mountain peak towering above the forest whispered in the trees; there were small, intimate rustling noises all around him, and he could hear the peaceful gurgling of a creek cascading down the steep mountainside a little distance away, its white water calming and winding its way through the big trees.

He was aware that the brilliant disk of warmth and light,

so strong that it hurt to look at it, was back high above him, and once more he could see clearly. He stirred cautiously. He felt stiff and it bothered him to move. The spot on his head that felt thickened and hurt when he touched it, ached. His mouth was dry. Instinct attracted him to the water nearby. Slowly, warily, he left his lair.

The crystal-clear water rushing along looked cool and inviting as the creek wound its way between boulders and rocks through a small green clearing. Tom stopped at the edge of the thicket. He watched uncertainly.

Suddenly he started. Instantly he crouched down, hiding among the shrubs. A small sound from the thicket not far away had alerted him. From the trees a deer came slowly to the edge of the bushes. Tom watched it, wary, immobile. The deer stopped at the edge of the clearing and looked around, ears alert, turning toward every little sound. It was a doe. Reassured, she walked daintily down to the creek and began to drink.

Tom watched. Instinctively he dismissed the deer as a menace. He stood up. Slowly he began to walk down to the stream. At once the doe looked up, alert to danger. Tom stopped. For a moment the two of them stood watching each other in silent appraisal, then the deer returned to drinking. Tom continued to the stream, crouched down and, plunging his face into the cool water, greedily began to drink.

The sudden roar of a motor being gunned in the distance, beyond the woods on the far brink of the creek, made the doe look up in alarm. Both she and Tom stared intently in the direction from which the sound came. Again the motor noises shattered the silence. The doe turned, bounded off and disappeared into the thicket.

Immediately Tom followed.

He was moving through the forest at a half-run. He was acutely aware of a deep, growling rumble somewhere behind him. He did not know it for what it was—the sound of several vehicles laboring up an incline—but it made him uneasy. He kept running.

Ahead of him the forest thinned. He could see several large rocks and a big, smooth, shiny area. As he came closer, he realized it was water; not alive and splashing over the rocks like the water of the creek, but quiet and calm. It was a little lake. On the level dirt area nearby stood rows of flat wooden boards on legs of different heights. The place was deserted. It was too early in the day for picnickers.

He slowed down, cautiously looking over the area. He stopped at the water's edge and looked across the lake. It did not seem far to the other side, but the water stretched out through the forest both to his right and to his left. For a moment he hesitated. The rumbling noises were coming closer. They frightened him. He made up his mind. The water was friendly. He knew that. He walked into it. Soon it became too deep for him to reach bottom and he began to swim, using his arms and legs in a dog-paddle stroke.

He waded ashore on the far bank, shook the water from him and, with a brief glance back toward the oncoming motor noises, trotted into the underbrush.

The vegetation was getting sparse, the trees smaller, and the rocky ground began to slope down steeply. He could see out over the land far into the distance. The world lay below him, quiet and motionless. Perhaps also without unknown terrors. He started down.

He was making his way around a large rock outcropping when he stopped abruptly. Instantly he fell into a guarded crouch. A short distance before him he saw movement among the vegetation. A small creature was burrowing rapidly with its legs into the loose dirt, enlarging a hole in the ground. Quickly it disappeared into the earth, out of sight. He watched in wonder. He started to move again, but suddenly he froze.

Off to one side a short distance away he saw it. Another creature. Larger. Looking dangerous.

Moving slowly, stealthily, across the ground, it was totally intent on a clump of vegetation. Pointed head stretched forward, ears laid back, bushy tail held straight back, the creature delicately placed paw before paw as it moved ahead. The stalking coyote was utterly unaware of Tom.

Suddenly it pounced. Sharp teeth snapped shut, catching the small, furry-gray thing that suddenly leaped from hiding.

A piercing screech was cut off in mid-agony as the thing was given a savage shake, held firmly in bared fangs.

Tom stayed motionless as the coyote trotted off with its prey, the dead baby rabbit dangling from its maw. He felt no emotion. Some deep-seated knowledge told him what he had witnessed: a creature feeding upon another. He was vaguely aware of an unfilled feeling within himself—but it was unimportant. Hunger had not yet made its pangs felt. He continued down the mountainside. . . .

On a road across the wide gorge high above him an Air Force scout was parked. Three men were sitting in it: A1C Wilson behind the wheel, Paul in the seat beside him and Sergeant Hays in the back. Paul and Hays were searching the mountain area with field glasses.

They had driven up to Whitney Portal early that morning. There had been no sign of Tom. Paul had left the two other search parties with Major Ward in charge to comb the area where Tom had been spotted by the Ranger observation station. On a hunch he'd driven a short distance down the road toward the valley below.

He let his field glasses slowly travel across the mountainslope on the far side of the wide canyon. From left to right—up a notch and back—from right to left . . . He had a clear, unobstructed view.

Suddenly Hays half rose up out of his seat. "There he is!" he shouted excitedly. "There, sir!" He pointed. "Way down . . . over to the left."

Paul shifted his binoculars. He searched the spot Hays had pointed out. There! A movement among the rocks and scrub trees. A tiny, lone figure.

Tom!

For a moment Paul watched him. Tom was making his way down the slope, scrambling over the rocky ground. He was almost at the bottom of the foothills. Ahead of him, like a gigantic contour map, lay the expanse of Owen's Valley. He seemed to move effortlessly. Paul felt instant relief. Tom could not be badly hurt. But the relief was short-lived. It also meant that he was capable of giving them a hell of a run for their money.

He plunked himself down in his seat. "He's headed for the valley," he said. "Come on, Wilson. Let's go!"

At once Wilson started up the scout. He slammed it into gear, and the little vehicle leaped forward. Paul clung to the windshield as Wilson raced down the narrow, winding road recklessly, skillfully, lurched around hairpin curves inches away from thousand-foot drops and careened headlong toward the valley below.

Twenty minutes later he came to a gravel-spurting stop where the canyon met the flatlands. Paul jumped from the scout. He climbed up onto a large rock and searched the area with his field glasses. Before him lay a vast expanse of jumbled rocks and boulders.

Hays joined him. "Anything?"

Paul shook his head. "He could be anywhere in that damned mess," he said bitterly. He turned toward the scout. "Wilson!" he called. "Get Major Ward on the radio. Have the other parties join us here. On the double!"

"Yes, sir."

Paul turned to Hays, his face set. "We'll scour this whole godforsaken area," he said grimly, "if it takes us all day."

Hays nodded. He touched the fresh bandage on his cheek. "We'd better find the Major soon," he observed soberly, "or he's gonna kill himself. . . ."

2

Randi knew she appeared tense and distraught as she sat on the edge of her chair in Colonel Howell's office, listening to him. The other officer in the room was a man she did not know. A Major Trafford. Arthur Trafford. He seemed nice enough, but Randi had been too unsettled to do much more than acknowledge him when Howell introduced them.

Howell had told her about the crash—and about Tom's strange behavior. She was frightened and confused.

"I think that'll give you an idea of what we're up against, Randi," Howell said, not unkindly. "You know we'll do everything possible to reach Tom."

She nodded miserably. "I know, Jon." She was deeply troubled. "Only—"

"The search-and-rescue effort is already under way. Captain Jarman is in charge. He's up there right now. We have a top medical officer on the job, too." He tried to reassure her. "We'll find Tom—even if his actions are . . . unpredictable."

Randi looked at him anxiously. "How—how bad is he, Jon?"

Howell evaded a direct answer. "I'll personally supervise the entire operation. We'll do the best we can under the circumstances. We—"

Randi stared at him. "Circumstances?" she inquired tautly. "What circumstances?"

"Randi," Howell said firmly, "this *is* a military operation. We *know* what we are doing. But we *are* faced with an unusual situation."

Randi watched him with growing anxiety.

"Tom is not just another pilot down," Howell went on. "We have to consider his—his state of mind." He looked at the distraught woman sitting across from him. He wished he could tell her of the other considerations that were dictating his actions. And he knew he could not.

With a conscious effort Randi controlled herself, but she was at the edge—and she knew it. "What's wrong with his mind, Jon?" she asked, her voice catching in her throat. "What's wrong?"

Howell looked grim. "Randi," he began, "you *must*—"

Major Trafford suddenly stood up. He came over to the desk.

"Colonel Howell," he said, his voice calm and unruffled, "I wonder if I might talk to Mrs. Darby for a moment." He looked steadily at Howell. For a brief instant Howell glared at him. He glanced at Randi. She looked stricken—on the verge of breaking down. He nodded.

Trafford turned to Randi. He sat down on the edge of Howell's desk, unobtrusively interposing himself between them.

"Mrs. Darby," he said quietly. "Randi, is it?"

Randi nodded.

"Randi. I am a neurosurgeon. I have already looked over all the available information about your husband very closely. Let me try to explain."

Randi looked up at him, her eyes moist. Somehow she trusted him.

"Please," she whispered. "Just—tell me the truth."

Trafford nodded reassuringly. "I will."

Howell watched. He knew what Trafford was doing. He kept silent.

"We know that Tom received a head injury when he landed in the rocks," Trafford continued. "We know where on his head the injury occurred. He probably has a fractured skull and a severe cerebral concussion."

Randi looked at him in alarm. He smiled—an almost fatherly smile. "Medical terms, Randi," he said calmly, "sound much worse than they are."

"But—why should that make Tom act so strangely?"

Trafford nodded slowly. He leaned down toward Randi. "That'll take a little more explaining," he said. "We can't know for certain, of course." He looked at her gravely. "And I want you to know that with our present limited knowledge about the *physiological* dynamics of the various stages of head injuries and the lack of precise ways to relate them to *psychological* functions, it is a difficult task at best to assess the exact nature of the post-traumatic processes in an individual patient. The range can be very great—and unpredictable. And in this case Tom has, of course, not had the benefit of any examination at all." He looked at her compassionately. "But I must be confusing you. I didn't mean to do that."

"Please—tell me what you think is wrong with Tom," Randi pleaded.

"Well—it seems that the pressure of the broken bone on Tom's brain and the probable subdural hemorrhage—"his eyes held hers—"internal bleeding have—eh, impaired the most vulnerable higher brain centers. Where memory, judgment and learned skills are seated. All the—eh, social functions of man."

"Is he—is he in pain?" Randi asked.

Trafford pursed his lips. "I want to be completely honest with you, Randi," he said solemnly. "But I can't give you a precise answer to that either. There's bound to be some pain. How severe, we can't know. Certainly Tom must have a dull, crushing feeling in his head. A continuous—eh, pressure. He may have occasional dizzy spells."

He paused. Randi watched him raptly. She stayed silent. Trafford went on.

"From the indentation on his helmet we know the injury occurred on the right side of Tom's head." He gave Randi an inquiring look. "Your husband is right-handed, isn't he?"

Randi looked puzzled. "Yes."

Trafford nodded. "The right side of the brain is where the higher centers, such as the speech centers, are located in a right-handed person," he explained. "The motor centers are on the left side. They should be unimpaired—the ones that govern his physical activities. Tom is still able to function on a—eh, biological level." He looked closely at her. "But the integration capacity of the higher brain centers is lost . . . in fact, producing what we know as total amnesia."

Randi was shaken, but she kept herself under control. "Tom has—lost his memory?" she breathed.

Trafford watched her closely. He nodded solemnly. "Suppressed is more the word," he said. "But, from all indications at the moment, it would seem so. The memory centers are the first to go. All sophisticated knowledge. Tom may be subject to fear reactions. Rage reactions." He looked her directly in the eyes. "We can only make a guess, Randi, an educated guess. But Tom may suffer *amnestic aphasia*. That means the loss of power of speech. Certainly complete *retrograde amnesia*— absolutely no memory of his past life. It is a rare occurrence, but it has happened. It *can* happen. . . ."

Randi stared at him, aghast. "Then—what's left?"

"Only his senses, Randi. And his basic instincts. Everything he experiences now must be new—and frightening—to him."

Randi swallowed the lump that was rising in her throat.

Trafford went on, "Of course, a lot of knowledge is still in his mind—but without his conscious knowledge of it *being* there." He contemplated her. "If that sounds complicated, it's only because it is. But I think you understand what I mean."

Randi wiped her eyes. Dammit, She would not cry! "But—how—if he remembers nothing at all . . . how can he cope?" she asked wretchedly. "With anything? How does he know how to feed himself? Take care of himself? How—"

"Nature, Randi. Instinct." Trafford put his hand on her arm. "It is not so difficult to understand. Remember, every newborn animal, every newly hatched chick instinctively knows what to do. Where to seek nourishment with the mother. How to hide from enemies. A baby kangaroo, only an inch long at birth, instinctively knows the way to crawl through his mother's fur to the protection of her pouch and attach himself to a nipple. The natural instinct is a wonderful thing, Randi. Tom will have that—and much more. He still has the native intelligence of a human being, even though he may suffer total amnesia."

"Is it—permanent?" Randi asked fearfully.

Trafford shook his head. "No. Tom's memory is still intact. He has lost the ability to tap into it. Right now he is building new memories—which will be suppressed when the old ones are restored. This kind of amnesia can be cured by surgery. As soon as the pressure of the fractured skull on his brain is relieved and the trauma has worn off, he'll be all right . . . if we can get to him in time, and if there is no further damage or complication." He looked at her gravely. "Any additional injury to the head could possibly result in death. That is why the search for him must be conducted—just right."

Randi buried her face in her hands. For a brief moment she sat in silence. When she looked up, her eyes were bright with unshed tears. "He's afraid," she whispered, almost to herself. "Like—like a wild, hurt animal. Running away from the very people who would help him." She turned to Howell. "Jon," she said firmly, "you've *got* to find him!"

"Of course," Howell said. "That's why Captain Jarman—Paul—is up there. That's why I put him in charge of the rescue operations in the field. And as Security Officer he'll have the manpower he needs in his own command. Including—as a last resort—the EST. They're a crack outfit."

"EST?" Randi looked questioningly at him.

Howell gave her a crooked smile. "That's the latest designation for the TNT—the Tactical Neutralization Teams. EST sounds a little less—explosive. It stands for Emergency Service Teams. Trouble-shooters."

Randi looked puzzled.

"They're a little like the police SWAT teams," Howell explained. "They're specially trained and outfitted. They handle especially—eh, difficult situations. Barricaded suspects. Hostage situations. Terrorism cases. Downed Aircraft Security. That sort of thing."

"Why use them as a last resort?" Randi asked.

"Because I think the mission mounted at this time will more than do the job. I have great confidence in Captain Jarman."

Randi felt a mixture of reassurance and resentment. Paul was so—overbearing. So—chauvinistic. To most of Tom's pilot friends the concept of manhood, manliness and manly courage was terribly important. To Paul it seemed almost a religion. It wasn't that she was all fired up about Women's Lib. She didn't think non-discrimination meant the right of women to be in attendance in men's locker rooms and showers. But she *did* believe in the equality of men and women—where such equality was warranted. And she felt her opinion was less than enthusiastically shared by Tom's friend. But Tom had said he was good at his job. And he *had* saved Tom's life once before. Maybe he would again.

"I know Jarman is a close friend," Howell continued. "And I also happen to know he's done a good deal of big-game hunting. Should come in handy."

Randi stared at him in alarm. "Hunting?" she exclaimed. "Are you going to *hunt* Tom? Like—like some wild beast?"

"Of course not." Despite himself, Howell sounded irritated. "But Paul's experience in tracking down and trapping wild animals may be of value. Don't you see?"

Trafford broke in, his voice reassuring. "You mustn't forget, Randi, that your husband at this moment acts more like an animal than a man."

"He is not only dangerous to himself," Howell added, "but to others. Like a wild animal, he may even kill, if he believes himself in danger."

Randi sat up, her face determined. She brushed a tear from her cheek. "What can *I* do?" she asked. "I won't be left here. Waiting. Not knowing."

"As a matter of fact," Howell said, "Major Trafford already suggested that you accompany us."

"We don't know the exact state of your husband's mind, you see," Trafford explained. "It is quite possible that the sight of you—the sound of your voice, perhaps—might break through to him. It's a chance that seems worth taking."

Randi nodded. "Of course. I'll go."

Howell looked at her, his face serious. "I've just had a report from Paul," he said. "Tom is headed for the desert. In the direction of Death Valley."

Randi looked at him, her eyes shocked.

"But—they lost his trail," Howell finished.

"The desert . . ." Randi was deeply troubled. "This time of year. Death Valley . . . Oh, Jon, the most desolate, the most hostile place he could have chosen."

"I'm sure he'll never get that far, Randi. We'll find him long before. Death Valley is over eighty miles from where he was last seen." Howell stood up. "You'd better get your things together," he said. "We'll take off for the area first thing tomorrow morning. We're using the Ranger Headquarters in Death Valley as our base of operation." Randi shot him a questioning glance. "There's an airfield there," he explained. "We can cover the entire terrain between the mountains and the valley."

Randi stood up. She looked straight at Howell, her eyes haunted. "The desert . . . Oh, Jon, why the desert? The worst place of all . . ." She gave a small sob. "He won't have a chance!"

Howell looked away, busying himself with the papers on his desk. He could not bring himself to contradict her. He knew she was right.

Survival in the desert in the heat of summer could be measured in hours for the hardiest of men.

And Tom had sustained a severe injury.

3

Like a tarnished, titanic devil's mirror shattered into an intricate network of cracks by some giant's blow, the vast expanse of one of the many dry lakes at the edge of Death Valley lay stretched out all around him, its surface of scorched silt and mud baked by a blazing sun into a myriad weirdly shaped fragments.

Tom was trudging across the desolation, his long shadow moving ahead of him, licking the crazy-quilt pattern of parched dirt. He was headed for a range of low mountains in the distance, purple and indistinct in the last rays of daylight. He was nearing the edge of the dry lake, making his way toward a stretch of desert dotted with withered weeds and misshapen Joshua trees. Obviously uneasy at being out in the open, he kept glancing back. But there was nothing to be seen except emptiness.

By the time he had crossed the dry lake and reached the sparsely vegetated desert beyond, at the foot of the mountain range, darkness had fallen. The bright, round disk high above had once again gone away. This time he had watched it disappear into the ground. And once again he had been filled with apprehension. He was exhausted, but his fear drove him on. He came to a small rise in the desert floor and sank down to rest against it. His mind swam with fatigue and pain; he dozed fitfully. . . .

Suddenly he jerked upright with a start—fear instantly awakened in his eyes once again. He strained to listen. From the distance a low, rumbling thunder reached his ears, growing louder with each passing instant. Quickly he scrambled up onto the embankment. He stared into the darkness toward the growing rumble that filled the night. In the distance a bright point of brilliance was rushing toward him. As he watched, it rapidly grew into a round spot of blinding light. In horror, he began to back away from the onrushing blaze. He was terror-stricken. The searing round light from above had come down to chase him! He whirled away from it and began to run from the blinding monster.

The rumble became a clattering roar that drowned out all else. He raced along the embankment as the demon from the sky hurtled down on him, holding him imprisoned in its blazing beam of light. His breath was like sharp stabs in his lungs, his head was racked with pain. He ran. . . .

Ahead of him, the monstrous light pursuing him was reflected in the shiny smoothness of two straight, narrow rails that reached into the darkness as far as he could see, mesmerizing him to race between them.

Suddenly, howling above the thundering rumble, an eerie, piercing blast of a horn shrieked through the night. Tom screamed. The blazing monster was upon him. In stark terror, he tumbled from the rise, eyes wild with fear, mouth split open in a harrowing scream—drowned out as the train thundered past in a crescendo of noise.

Raw panic seized him. He rushed headlong, aimlessly, through the night desert as the roar of the train slowly died in the distance. In the grip of terror, he imagined that the distorted limbs of misshapen Joshua trees that reached and groped for him were the huge, deformed arms of misbegotten demons. He pounded through the darkness, finally to fall in terrified exhaustion; to lie prostrate among the shadowy, warped shapes that loomed over him like ghoulish guards, their grotesquely twisted limbs faintly silhouetted against the dark sky.

He was gulping air, each breath a searing pain in his chest. He was trembling. With a deep-throated sob of ultimate despair he buried his face in the sand.

For a while he lay motionless, the pain slowly leaving him. With a great effort he lifted his tortured head and peered into the gloom around him, his eyes still haunted with abysmal dread. Ahead of him he could make out a jagged, dark shape among the shrubs. He crawled toward it, seeking its protection.

The black, quiet interior of the broken, rusty car wreck promised to be a snug and safe hiding place. Cautiously he peered into the empty iron cave. Carefully he crawled inside. He shrank back to the far corner and, drawing his knees up toward his chin, he settled down, his back against the protective wall.

He had quieted down. Lulled to a sense of security by the steel womb of refuge, he fell into a coma-like sleep.

Only a shadow of pain—or fear?—flitted across his face.

He was two days old.

His ordeal of terror had just begun.

DAY THREE

1

When he awoke, gray dawn was seeping into his refuge. He was instantly alert. He crept to the opening and cautiously peered out. The blinding light was nowhere to be seen. He stretched. His body was cramped and his muscles ached. He crawled from the wreck and stood up. He looked around. The low mountain range was close, and he started to walk toward it. He was utterly alone. . . .

After a while he came upon a stretch of desert that was different from the rest and from the dry lake bed. Smooth and hard, it seemed to run in a narrow ribbon forever in both directions. For a short time he followed it—the going was easier than in the sandy ground, but it made him feel uneasy. Exposed. To what, he did not know.

He searched the low mountains before him. All was peaceful. He looked back—and froze. Far away, up from the ground, the blazing round light was rising. Blood red, it seemed larger and more menacing than ever before. He began to run—slowly at first, then faster and faster—away from the frightening, luminous disk, terrified that it had come to pursue him again. He ran heavily in the soft sand. Frantically he looked around for refuge. He found none. Except—there! Straight ahead, among the clumps of desert shrubs, close to the ribbon of hard desert. The two hulking shapes, huddled close together, reminded him of the cave in which he had hidden from the monsters of the darkness and safely spent a time of rest. Perhaps here, too, was safety.

He ran toward the squat lumps half concealed in the desert brush. He raced up to the nearest one. There was an opening in it—hidden by a sheet made of a rough, pliable substance, the kind that covered his own body, hanging in tatters from his arms and legs, but heavier and stiffer. He squeezed through a slit in it into the cave beyond. It was warm—and had a pungent, comforting odor, and the floor was covered with withered vegetation. He peered out through the slit in the sheet hanging across the cave opening. The dazzling light still hung in the sky. It stabbed at his eyes, brighter and more ablaze than before. He withdrew. It would not see him if he stayed hidden. He crawled to the far end of the cave and crouched down in a corner.

He became aware of a dull ache in his stomach. And his mouth was dry. It made him think of the creek—and food. He was hungry. Over the pungent odor permeating the cave he became aware of another smell. It was sweet and pleasant. He was surprised to find that his mouth grew moist. In the half-light he looked around. The smell came from a lumpy object leaning against the wall in the other corner. He crept over to it. Cautiously he touched it. The smell was strong. The bulky thing was also made of some kind of material, rough and yet soft. It was bunched together at the top with something wrapped tightly around it. He could not get it loose. He tore at the material itself; it gave way and ripped apart. Through the hole several brightly colored round objects spilled out onto the straw on the floor. The sweet scent came from them. He picked one up. He sniffed it. He bit into it. The taste was bitter—but he ate it. The inside was sweet and dripping with moisture. It was not like the water he knew from the creek, but it quenched his thirst. Contentedly he ate the oranges spilled from the torn sack, quickly learning to discard the rind and eat only the inside pulp.

Suddenly a grating sound rent the silence. He stiffened in fear. The sound almost at once turned into a deep, steady rumble—the cave lurched and began to swing and sway.

For a moment he sat petrified in the pitching cave. Then, mustering all his courage, he crept to the opening and looked through the rift.

Terror-stricken, he stared. The world was racing away from the lurching cave. The desert, the clumps of vegetation, the long, hard ribbon—everything was rushing away from him at terrifying speed. He scrambled back to the safety of the far corner of the cave and pressed himself into it. He closed his eyes and waited, trembling, for the world to stop running. . . .

Lupe was whistling to himself—off key. He felt better. He shouldn't have had those last two Dos Equis at Mama Rosita's in Lone Pine, they'd made him feel *muy mareado*. But he was pleased with himself. He'd done the right thing, pulling over and taking a snooze in the cab. It would have been foolish to try to negotiate the winding road through the Panamint Range into the valley—especially since his little pick-up had only one good headlight. *A la chingada.* They would wait a few more hours for him to pick up the nag.

Faded lettering on the beat-up horse trailer hitched to the pick-up read:

McSWEENY STABLES
Renting—Boarding
BISHOP, CALIFORNIA

Lupe had borrowed it. He was on his way to Furnace Creek in Death Valley to pick up a horse. The poor *caballo*, he had gone lame trotting fat *turistas* all over the godforsaken place. His tourist-trotting days were over now, and he, Lupe, was buying him—cheap—from Juan, the stable wrangler. He grinned to himself at the thought of how pleased his *chamaquito* would be. *Dios mio*, he deserved it. He had six sisters—but he'd always wanted a horse. *Muy bien*, he would be easy to keep—out back.

He'd gotten a late start. He stepped on the gas pedal. He suddenly felt thirsty. *Aiii*, the heat of the day was beginning already. Should he stop and get a couple of oranges from the sack he was bringing to Juan? The hell with it. He'd wasted enough time. In another couple of hours he'd be wrapping himself around another Dos Equis. . . .

He'd left Stove Pipe Wells Village in the valley behind and had turned south on the road to Furnace Creek. He'd been driving for about an hour and a half. He shifted in his seat. Someday he'd have that tear fixed; the damned springs were coming through. He was uncomfortably aware of his full bladder. Half of it Dos Equis, no doubt. Beer always filled him up. The road was deserted for miles—he'd stop and take a leak. . . .

Huddled in his corner, Tom became aware of a change in the swaying, tossing motion of his cave. Nothing had happened to him, and he was beginning to lose some of his terror. He crept to the opening and peeked out.

The world outside was slowing down—and it had changed. It stopped. Now was his chance to escape from this disturbing place. He jumped to the ground and raced for the nearby foothills.

Lupe was opening the cab door. In the rearview mirror mounted on it he saw a quick motion. His mouth dropped open. He jumped from the pick-up in time to see the figure of a man racing into the desert. What the hell?

He had a sudden thought. He ran to the back of the horse trailer. He threw the canvas flap aside and looked in.

"Caramba! Pinchi pendejo!" he swore. Juan's sack was ripped open; the floor was littered with half-eaten oranges.

He shook his fist at the rapidly disappearing figure.

"Wait!" he shouted at the top of his lungs. "Wait! . . . I'll report you! *Ladrón!* . . . Thief! . . . The Rangers will crush your *cojones!"*

He kicked the worn tire on the trailer wheel in frustrated anger and stalked back to the pick-up. He almost forgot the reason he'd stopped. He strode to the edge of the road and unceremoniously relieved himself, watching the steam rise from the thirsty sand.

He glared after the fleeing orange-thief—no more than a dot disappearing into the foothills.

"Me meo sobre de ti!" he grumbled in disgust. "I piss on you!"

2

The sign over the modern, one-story stone building read:

DEATH VALLEY NATIONAL MONUMENT
RANGER HEADQUARTERS

ELEVATION:
150 FEET BELOW SEA LEVEL

A USAF scout came racing into the parking area in front and came to a stop alongside several other military and Ranger vehicles.

There were anger and impatience in the way Colonel Jonathan Howell dismounted and strode toward the building. He was followed by a man wearing a Ranger uniform, Chief Ranger Charles Stark.

In Stark's office, a large, sunny room adorned with several framed color photographs showing the undeniable splendors of the Death Valley wilderness. Paul, Ward, Major Trafford and a young Ranger were poring over a large map spread out on the table. When Howell and Stark entered, the officers started to get up.

"Sit down," Howell said, his manner and voice even more brusque than usual. He strode over to the table and studied the map for a moment. Sharply he turned to Paul.

"Two days," he snapped. "Two days—and no results."

Paul looked grim. "This is no ordinary rescue operation, Colonel, or we'd have picked up Tom long ago."

"He's actively evading us, sir," Ward added. "Running away. Hiding. There's no telling how long it'll be before we find him."

"I want him found," Howell barked. "And I want him found fast!"

"We've turned over every stone in the Alabama Hills—sir." Paul sounded testy. "And we've scoured Owen's Valley from one end to the other after that Southern Pacific Railroad engineer saw his 'weird creature' caught in the headlight. We have *not* been able to find him." He looked at Howell. "We are doing the best we can."

"Not good enough," Howell said coldly. "Have you any idea where he is?"

"No, sir," Paul admitted bleakly. "No, we don't. We—"

"Well, *I* do!" Howell snapped. He slammed his open fist down on the map on the table. "Here! Right smack in the middle of Death Valley."

The men looked startled. "Here?" Paul exclaimed. "How could he possibly have traveled that far? In a few hours? It's impossible."

Howell looked at him icily. "Chief Ranger Stark just had a report," he said. "A complaint. From an irate citizen of Mexican descent. Claims a hitchhiker—a weird *hombre*, as he put it— stole him blind."

Paul shook his head incredulously. "Tom? A hitchhiker?"

"Stowaway is more the word. Seems he holed up in this fellow's empty horse trailer. Made off with the Mexican state treasury—and ate his way through a ton of oranges."

"At least he's getting nourishment," Ward observed.

"And this—this Mexican gentleman unwittingly brought him here," Paul finished.

"Exactly," Howell stated. "Tom *is* somewhere out there. In Death Valley."

"Two million acres of desolation," Paul said soberly. He turned to Howell. "Colonel Howell, we need a lot more men to cover this area. We owe it to Tom."

"Time *is* of the essence, Colonel," Ward broke in.

Howell gave him an arctic look, then he turned to Paul. "You've got your search teams," he said flatly. "And Chief Ranger Stark has pledged his full cooperation. His Rangers will be at your disposal also. That will have to do."

Paul glared at his superior officer. "Why?" he bristled, his tone of voice bordering on rebellion.

Angrily Howell returned his glare. "All right, *Captain*

Jarman, I will tell you why," he said tightly. "Besides the reasons I've already given you—I don't want Tom to kill himself!"

Paul listened, tight-lipped. He was about to make a sharp retort when Trafford intervened.

"Maybe I can clarify that statement a little," he said, his voice calm. "As a hunter, Paul, you know that some wild animals, when they are hopelessly cornered, will try to destroy themselves rather than be captured. Or attempt to do impossible things that result in their destruction." He turned to Ward. "I understand that Tom already was in such a situation—and took a chance against near-impossible odds in order to get away. An act of desperation that might well have killed him."

Ward nodded soberly. "That's correct," he agreed. "When he jumped that ravine."

"Precisely," Trafford said, with the air of a man who has brought home an important point.

"Next time he might not make it," Howell added. "Now that he *knows* he's hunted, we'll have to be extra careful. That is the reason for no large-scale man-hunt, no media-wide publicity. We cannot afford to make him desperate."

Trafford nodded. "I concur in this, Captain." He looked solemnly at Paul. "And I must add to your problem, I'm afraid. You will have to reach Tom at a spot where he cannot try to do something dangerously impossible—or find a way to destroy himself before you can get to him."

Paul nodded thoughtfully. He looked deeply concerned. "I understand," he said quietly. He turned to Howell. "Colonel," he said, "what about Randi? Why was she brought up here?"

"Major Trafford and I feel she can be of help," Howell answered. "Communicate with her husband when he's located."

"Okay," Paul said reluctantly. "As long as she stays out of the way."

"I'm afraid you don't understand, Captain," Howell corrected him, his voice suddenly tight. "Mrs. Darby is to be available to communicate with her husband in the field. She will accompany you."

Incredulously Paul stared at his superior officer. "Me!" he

exploded. "What the hell am I going to do with a female tagging along? I've got nothing against Mrs. Darby. But who needs that?"

He was aghast. Dragging a woman along, for crissake! No way. He'd had intimate knowledge of only two types of women in his life. The Saigon Sallys—whatever their home towns might be. And the cute little hero-worshippers that tumbled in and out of his bed. He'd never run into a female who had evoked feelings of respect, of trust and confidence. Sure, he liked women. But not as a part of a man's world. In their proper place.

And that did not include a rough search-and-rescue operation with a life at stake.

"I need to be saddled with a broad on this mission like I need having a broomstick up my ass," he fumed.

"We can do without your vulgarities," Howell said sharply.

"What the hell do you expect me to do?" Paul asked, outraged.

"I expect you to follow the best course of action to reach Major Darby," Howell said icily. "And that includes taking his wife along on the search." He looked coldly at the junior officer. "In fact, Captain, I'm making you personally responsible for her safety."

Paul glared at him. "Is that an order, sir?"

"That is an order!"

"Yes, sir."

"Where is she now?" Trafford asked, his voice conciliatory.

"Over at the ranch," Howell answered.

Trafford nodded slowly. "It will be rough on her," he said. "But she *can* be of use. When Tom is sighted. Let us hope it will be soon. . . ."

Howell brusquely cut the discussion short. "You had better plan your next moves," he said. "In this damned heat Tom won't last long without water. And water is hard to come by in this godforsaken place." He fixed Paul with cold, hard eyes. "You know what's at stake," he said. "I repeat: I want Tom found. And I want him found fast! I suggest you start looking. Now!"

He turned on his heel and, followed by Chief Ranger Stark, he left the room.

Paul glowered after him. "I wonder," he said bitterly. "I wonder what he's most worried about. Tom—or the test results on his precious F-15!"

With an angry gesture he snatched a tourist brochure from Stark's desk. Needing something to do to calm down, he cracked it open. He glanced at the page.

D E A T H   V A L L E Y

TEN COMMANDMENTS

1. Consult with park rangers before traveling into backcountry.
2. Avoid overexposure to the sun.
3. Stay out of old mines.
4. Carry drinking water.
5. Make frequent checks of gas, oil and radiator water.
6. Keep tires at normal pressure.
7. Shift to low gear on all grades.
8. Watch car temperature gauge.
9. Carry cloth to wet and wrap around fuel pump in case of vapor lock.
10. Stay with your car in case of breakdown.

He stared at the printed page. Ten commandments. For Tom, he thought bitterly, they could all be lumped into one. Survive!

Any way you can . . .

The telephone on Stark's desk rang. Ward answered it. He looked at Paul. "It's for Howell," he said. "General Ryan's office."

Paul turned to the young Ranger. "Adams," he said, "see if you can catch him."

Ranger Adams hurried from the office. In less than a minute he returned with Howell. The Colonel picked up the phone.

"Colonel Howell," he said. He listened.

Paul watched him expectantly. Perhaps they'd seen the light, he thought. Perhaps the General was giving the green light to go all out.

"Yes, sir," Howell was saying. "I'll take off at once." He hung up.

"I'm flying down to Edwards," he said. "Carry on."

Quickly he left the office.

An hour later he stood in the office of General Clifford Ryan, staring in grim disbelief at the Test Flight Commander and Dr. Marcus. He had not thought it possible that the situation could deteriorate any further.

It had.

Ryan had shown him a top-secret directive from the Pentagon. Unless the test malfunction and crash problems were solved within three days and the Marcus device as a result definitely was proved totally without danger to the population—the XM-9 project would be discontinued!

A small group of Senators and Congressmen, known for their opposition to any armament projects, had gotten wind of the XM-9 test and the crash of the F-15. They had presented their ultimatum to the Secretary of Defense before going public and informing a press and public—still skittish from the nuclear near-catastrophe at Three Mile Island—of this new "possible danger." Dr. Marcus' assurances that there could be no possible danger to any U.S. citizen resulting from the XM-9 tests had fallen on unresponsive ears. The same assurances had been given by the nuclear proponents. The Secretary had been hard pressed to persuade the legislators to give him the three-day grace period. They would sit on it that long—and no longer!

Marcus looked stricken. "Forgive me, Colonel Howell, for repeating myself," he said disconsolately, "but Tom Darby is the *only* one who can help us now. There is *no* other possible way."

Howell nodded, his face troubled.

"I know you understand, Jon," Ryan said, the gravity of the developments showing in his voice. "If we're forced to scrap the XM-9 as we've been forced to scrap other projects in the past—instead of having an edge, we'll be back in the hole. Instead of an advantage in this damned power-balance game, we'll be handed a setback. A setback we can ill afford." He looked at Howell. "Find him, Jon. Alive."

"Any change in procedure?" Howell asked hopefully.

Ryan shook his head. "I wish to God I could give you the whole Base," he said. "But I can't. The matter is still highly sensitive. The word is still—caution . . . or we'd be doing the publicizing ourselves."

Howell nodded. In other words, he thought cynically, *Run faster, but tie your legs together.*

3

Paul had deployed his search teams, integrating their sectors with those covered by Stark's Rangers. On the map it had looked as if they would be able to cover in their first sweep a pitifully small area of the vast Death Valley.

He was driving the USAF scout himself, with Randi in the seat next to him. Sergeant Hays sat in the back with the compact radio equipment. The heat of the day was building rapidly—it promised to be another scorcher.

He sat in silence. He felt resentful and uncomfortable. It was not his way. A problem had to be out in the open, not kept in. He pulled over. He turned back to Hays.

"Sergeant," he said gruffly, "get lost for a moment."

Hays looked at him. If he was surprised, it didn't show. "Yes, sir," he said evenly. He climbed out of the scout and walked off a short distance.

Paul turned to Randi. "Listen, Randi," he said, his voice harsher than he had intended, "I might as well be blunt with you. I want you to know you're here over my objections."

Randi listened in grim silence.

"It wasn't my brainchild for you to tag along," Paul went

on. "I think it's a piss-poor idea. It's not going to be a picnic up here."

"I am well aware of that," Randi said firmly. "I'm not here to *have* a picnic."

"It's going to damned rough, for crissake! No place for a woman."

"I want to help."

"This is *my* job, Randi. And I know my job. There's nothing you can do here that I can't do."

For a moment Randi looked at him, her eyes steady. "Let me be blunt, too, Paul. I think there *is*. And I'm here to do whatever I can. I'm here to stay. Regardless of what *you* can or cannot do. I expect no preferential treatment. I want you to treat me exactly as you would anyone else on your search teams. But that includes using me when I *can* be useful. Is that understood? I'll keep up with you or you can send me back."

For a moment he stared at her. Then he snapped: "You got it!"

He motioned for Hays, and the Sergeant came back and climbed into the scout.

With an angry jerk the little vehicle started up and took off.

They were driving slowly through the mountains on a narrow dirt road. Ahead of them rose a ridge of weirdly shaped, beautifully colored rock formations. Paul stopped. With his field glasses he searched the hill. Baked mud, sand and rocks in a profusion of different pastel hues burned into them by eons of blazing sun—huge splashes of green, red, purple, golden yellow, brown and black—the hillside was a riot of color in the broiling, forbidding wasteland. He felt discouraged. They would need a hell of a lot more than their share of luck to spot Tom in this labyrinth of buttes and bluffs, gulches and gullies that made up the freaky scenery. He hated it for that— no matter how spectacular it was.

He drove on. Perhaps a higher vantage point would offer better possibilities. Zabriskie Point. It overlooked a large part of the valley.

He turned to Hays. "Radio the Ranger truck in our sector," he said. "Have them meet us at Zabriskie Point. We should be there in fifteen minutes."

"Roger." Hays at once began to make contact. . . .

Tom was making his way through a shallow gully up into the eroded foothills. He was looking for a place of shade where he could rest, away from the noisy, frightening monsters he had observed tearing along the hard desert ribbons below, spewing raucous, rumbling sounds into the hushed silence of the yellow sands. The climb and the heat had fatigued him. His injured head pounded and his legs had grown leaden. He stopped and looked around. There was no shelter to be seen. The hillsides arched around him were bare.

He raised his sweaty face and squinted apprehensively up at the blazing sun suspended in the naked sky high above. Its scorching rays beat mercilessly down on him—and on the sun-baked land.

Drops of moisture ran from his forehead into his eyes. He wiped it away. He looked at it with curiosity. He licked it off his hand. The taste was unpleasant. He worked his mouth to get rid of it. It did not lessen his growing thirst. He trudged on. . . .

Randi was subdued as she sat beside Paul. The scout was laboring in low gear up the steep slope toward the high vantage point, the motor noises reverberating through the naked hills. She shivered in the heat—a whisper of growing despondency. She had been overwhelmed by the wild vastness of Death Valley. It terrified her to think that her husband was out there somewhere in that hostile wilderness. Alone. Injured. Terrified. And in total incomprehension of what was happening to him. How would they ever find him? It seemed hopeless . . . even though she knew that Paul had selected as his sector the one where that Mexican man had last seen Tom. But that was hours ago. Tom could be anywhere by now. . . . She ached with worry.

They reached the final switchback that led to the observation level at Zabriskie Point. They drove onto the small flat area. Paul lifted his binoculars and scanned the surrounding hills.

The view was breathtaking. The age-old, eroded bluffs stretched all around them, looking like the wrinkled skin of a gigantic, sleeping prehistoric reptile. Far below, through a pass cradled between golden rock peaks and huge brown rounded mud humps, the expanse of the valley could be seen spread out before them, hazy blue in the heat. Randi felt the awe of it clutching her throat.

A Ranger pick-up drove up to the observation point and stopped behind the scout. Ranger Adams dismounted and joined them.

Paul turned to him. "Adams," he said, "take the right." He pointed."I'll take the left."

"Okay, Captain." Adams began to search the area with his binoculars. He could not help feeling keyed up. It was the first time in his five months with the Park Rangers that something exciting had happened. He enjoyed it. He had a pang of guilt. Enjoy? A man was lost out there. Dying. He glanced at the young woman tensely staring out over the barren landscape. He felt genuinely sorry for her. He wished very much to find her husband for her. Soberly he returned to his sweep of the ridges and cliff before him.

Paul let his field glasses roam. He searched the crest of a bluff, swept down the weather-wrinkled slope—down into a dry wash far below. Its dark-gray flow snaked through the scalloped hillocks toward the valley.

Suddenly he started. Rounding a bend, a tiny figure came plodding along the wash.

Tom.

"There he is!" Paul shouted. "My God! *There he is!*" Excitedly he turned to Randi. "Randi! Call to him! Shout! As loud as you can."

Randi tumbled from the scout. She ran to the low parapet surrounding the observation ledge. "Tom!" she shouted. "Tom! It's me!" She cupped her hands around her mouth. "Tom! It's *me! Tom!*"

Far below, Tom stopped dead in his tracks. Alarmed, he

looked up toward the new, alien sound that came down to him from above. He was afraid—but an angry defiance was building up in him. He felt a burning hatred for his pursuers. They would give him no rest. He lifted his face toward the distant sound. The heat from the blazing sun beat down on him and drained him of strength. And the frightening monsters chasing him would give him no respite—always closing in on him.

For a brief moment he listened to the faint calls from above. The shell of injury clamped around his head was penetrated by the sound—but not by its meaning.

Abruptly he turned and ran down the wash the way he'd come.

High above, Paul saw him disappear around the bend.

Randi was shattered. "Tom! Wait!" she called, knowing it was in vain. She sobbed. "Please—please wait," she whispered.

She seemed to collapse a little within herself. With unnaturally bright eyes she turned to Paul.

"He didn't listen, Paul," she said, holding back the tears. "He didn't know me at all. . . . You were right. I'm no good."

He looked at her. Of course he was right. But he suddenly realized the crushing strain on the girl, the anxiety and desperation she must be going through. The "I told you so" died on his lips.

"Perhaps he couldn't hear you," he said, himself unconvinced. "It's a long way down there."

"Yes." Randi clung to the tiny shred of hope. "Yes—that could be it. We'll have to get closer to him."

Paul turned to the young Ranger. "Adams," he said briskly, "how do we get down there? Fast? Cut him off?"

Ranger Adams already had a map spread out on the hood of his truck. He shook his head. "We can't get through to him from here that fast," he said. "But I think we have a chance to corner him." He pointed to the map. "There."

Paul at once turned to the Sergeant. "Hays," he ordered, "get Major Ward."

"Roger!"

He spoke urgently into his mike. "Armadillo Two. This is

Armadillo One," he called. "Come in. Come in."

He switched to receiving. Static crackled from the set. With concern Hays glanced at the surrounding mountains.

"Armadillo Two. This is Armadillo One. Come in. Come in!" Unconsciously his voice grew more insistent. *"Come in!"*

He listened. . . .

Wilson was guiding the scout around a large boulder fallen onto the trail as the vehicle emerged from a steep-walled canyon. The radio sputtered: ". . . Armadillo Two. This Armadillo One. *Come in!"*

Ward, sitting next to Wilson, picked up the mike. "Armadillo One. This is Armadillo Two. Go ahead."

Paul's voice came over the radio. "Ward! We've spotted him. He's headed for Desolation Canyon. Take the west entrance. We'll go in from the east. And step on it! Over."

Ward was at once alert. "Roger, Armadillo One," he said. "Leaving Hell's Gate immediately for west entrance to Desolation Canyon. Over and out." He replaced the mike.

"Let's make tracks, Wilson," he said.

The scout took off in a cloud of dust. . . .

Tom had a strong premonition of danger. His heart beat faster. Adrenalin shot through his system. His pursuers were narrowing the gap. He suddenly thought of the little gray-furry creature that had been stalked by the larger beast on the mountainside. Now *he* was the one being hunted.

At a half-trot he loped along the bottom of the gorge. It was narrowing markedly. The sides were getting steeper. He came to a dirt trail entering the gully from the left and disappearing into the narrowing canyon ahead. The high, steep walls cast a darker strip of shade along one side. Tom ran into the ravine, welcoming the relief from the direct sun beating down.

He ran on, his footsteps echoing in hollow cadence between the sheer rock walls rising abruptly on both sides of the narrow gorge—adding to his growing panic. Uneasily he glanced up the precipitous walls of the deep chasm, searching for the thin ribbon of blue sky high above his head. He kept on running. . . .

At the west entrance to Desolation Canyon, Ward's scout

came careening down the desert trail toward the canyon mouth. Slowing only a little, Wilson drove into the ravine. . . .

At the east end, where the trail swung into the steep-walled gorge, Paul's scout negotiated the turn and began to threadneedle a course between the perpendicular rock walls of the narrow canyon. . . .

Tom was running at a half-trot through the close-walled crevice. In growing alarm he glanced up the virtually unscalable sides that shaded the canyon floor. He sensed he was trapped. The shade had given him relief from the burning sun, but he knew that what had lured him into the ravine had been the bait for his plight. He sped on, every step a painful effort. He would soon come out the other end of the chasm. Soon . . .

Suddenly he stopped. Gulping air, he stood rooted to the spot, listening. From behind him the now familiar and feared deep rumbling noise of the creatures chasing him came rolling down the gorge. He redoubled his efforts, racing along the sandy ravine floor.

He drew up short. Wild-eyed, he stared ahead, listening intently. The distant sound of a motor laboring at a different pitch reached him. Slowly it was drawing nearer.

He stood stock still. Both from behind him and from in front of him the dreaded noises of the pursuing terrors were closing in on him. Frantically he looked around, fear and despair contorting his sweat-streaked face. The canyon walls imprisoning him seemed higher and more forbidding than ever.

He ran a short distance—first in one direction, then the other. But he was trapped. He stretched his arms up the steep rock wall as far as he could reach, searching for a hold. He found none. He ran to the other side. The rim above was just as unreachable. He tried to claw his way up the insurmountable stone wall—but he fell back.

Like a rat trapped in a pit, he turned around and around, desperately searching for a way out.

There was none.

Again he attacked the precipitous wall, his nails already torn and bleeding. In a crack grew a small, withered clump of spiny weed—yellow and dry—like the ones that grew sparsely along the bottom of the canyon walls. He grabbed hold of it, oblivious to the thorns, in a frenzied attempt to pull himself up—out of the trap. The dead weed tore loose in his hands and he dropped back to the ground.

For a moment he stared at the shriveled plant in his bleeding hands. Then he looked up, nostrils flaring in fear.

The demon noises were coming closer. . . .

Paul stared ahead into the shadows of the narrow canyon—its walls towering over the scout on both sides as the little vehicle crept along. Any moment he expected to catch sight of Tom. Randi sat beside him, hands clutched together in her lap, knuckles showing white. Faintly they could hear Ward's scout rumbling toward them. . . .

Ward was standing up in the scout, his eyes searching the canyon in front of him. Wilson was driving slowly, carefully. Tom could not be far ahead.

They drove around a bend—and Ward stared in astonishment. Less than a hundred feet in front of him, Paul's scout was drawing up—coming to a halt.

Tom was nowhere to be seen.

Wilson drove up to the other vehicle and came to a stop almost hood to hood. In utter perplexity the men dismounted and gathered around Paul's scout.

"Did you see him?" Ward asked. He knew it was an inane question, but he had to say something.

Paul shook his head. "I'm positive he went in here," he said, sounding far from positive. He frowned up at the steep canyon walls.

"He must have climbed out," Hays said. It was obvious that he didn't believe it himself.

Randi fought to check her bitter disappointment. Disheartened, she looked at the precipitous rock walls. "He—couldn't have," she said quietly, voicing what they were all thinking.

Paul nodded grimly. "It would be impossible," he agreed.

"Well," Wilson said, "I guess nobody told him that, so he went and did it."

Unsmiling, they looked at him. He shrugged.

"We must have missed him," Paul said. "Somewhere." He turned to Wilson. "You got enough room to turn around here?" he asked.

Wilson nodded, glad to be off the hook. "Sure." He jumped into the scout and began to maneuver it expertly, turning it around on the narrow trail.

"We're meeting Stark at the Ranger Headquarters in about half an hour," Paul said to Ward. "We'll follow you down there."

Ward nodded. He got into the scout, and the two vehicles drove off down the ravine toward the valley. The laboring motor sounds faded and died in the distance. Once again the deep gorge was silent and deserted.

Suddenly, on the shaded side of the canyon, there was a small movement in the loose sand and gravel at the edge of the hard-packed trail. Near one of the yellow, withered weed clumps growing there a small ripple stirred the sandy ground— and slowly, probingly, Tom's arms emerged from the soft sand where he had burrowed into it like a desert fox. He brushed the cover of dirt and rocks from him and pushed aside the dead weed that had covered his sweat-and-grime-streaked face.

He struggled up to a crouch and for a moment sat looking in the direction of the departed vehicles. He shook the sand from him and peeled off some bits of dry straw stuck to his parched lips.

He stood up. He began to trot up the ravine, casting a final glance after the enemies he had eluded.

Was there a glint of triumph in his eyes?

4

Chief Ranger Stark squinted up at the sun almost directly overhead as he emerged from the HQ building. The oppressive heat was like a physical blow when you came from an air-conditioned office. The three Rangers following him already looked uncomfortable.

He watched as two scouts covered with dust drove up and came to a halt. Paul helped Randi from one of the vehicles. Stark walked up to him.

"I don't have to ask," he said.

Paul shook his head.

Stark indicated the three Rangers. "I'm bringing my complement up to emergency strength," he said. "I figure we can use all the help we can get."

"Right. Thanks."

"I'll have them in the field in no time." He glanced at Paul. "You know," he said thoughtfully. "Tom may be moving at night. When it's cooler."

Paul nodded. "Howell's putting one of the new rescue choppers equipped with the *Pave Low* night rescue system on the project."

Stark looked questioningly at him.

"It's an infrared tracking system. Makes observation possible in the dark. It's still in the development stage. Howell had a hell of a time prying a bird loose for us. They'll be flying night search missions starting tonight."

Stark nodded. He looked up as a Ranger truck drove in. Ranger Adams was behind the wheel. Stark turned to one of the new Rangers. "Gordon," he said, "do you know where the motor pool is?"

The man nodded. "Yes."

"Take Merriman and Sanchez. Wait for me there. I'll only be a few minutes."

"Right."

Gordon and the two other Rangers started off. Stark walked toward Adams.

Paul turned to Sergeant Hays. "You and Wilson get something to eat," he said. "And gas up. Meet me here in one hour."

"Yes, sir." The big Sergeant climbed in behind the wheel of Paul's scout.

Paul looked at Randi. There was a budding respect in his eyes—even though it was a grudging one. The girl had endured the scorching sun with the best of them, and not a word of complaint. And, dammit, she had stood her ground against him.

He took her arm. "Come on, Randi. Let's get out of the heat."

Randi shook her head. "In a minute, Paul. I—I want to be by myself for a little while."

Paul nodded. He understood. He and Ward walked briskly to the HQ Building entrance.

Randi slowly walked toward a small stand of gnarled and twisted, half-dead trees nearby. Her thoughts were in turmoil, her emotions battered and beset. She fought against the black despair that seemed to envelop her mind and hold it in a tightening grip. She was determined not to be weak. As long as Tom was out there, there could be nothing else. . . . But self-doubt and incertitude nagged and picked at her.

She reached the stand of stunted trees. Their scraggy trunks and limbs hugged the ground as if fearful of reaching up into the scorching heat. She sat down on a sun-bleached branch paralleling the ground and wearily rubbed the back of her neck, moist with perspiration.

Major Trafford watched her from the Ranger HQ entrance. He frowned with concern. He walked over to her. She looked up as he joined her.

"Randi," he said kindly, "you look beat. Why don't you go lie down for a while? Out of the heat . . . Rest . . ."

"I'm all right," she said huskily. "I—I'll just sit here for a minute. I'm—fine." Her appearance and her lackluster tone of voice belied her words.

Trafford sat down on a squat stump beside her. He watched her searchingly. "Are you?" he asked softly.

The strain, the fatigue, the heat had all taken their toll, and Randi was desperately vulnerable. Suddenly she broke down. She put her face in her hands and cried softly, her slender shoulders trembling.

Trafford watched her, his face solemn with compassion. But he made no move to interfere. Presently Randi stopped crying.

She wiped her eyes with the back of her hand. She had long since forgotten about the niceties of cosmetics. Contritely she glanced at Trafford.

"I'm sorry," she said, her voice catching slightly. "I hate women who cry at the least little thing."

Trafford gave her a little smile. "A good cry never hurt anybody," he said. "Sometimes I wish I could write a prescription for one." He looked into her tear-stained face. "But you mustn't give up. They'll find him."

"It isn't that. It's—"

She stopped. She looked away.

Trafford gave her a quick look. "*What* is it, Randi?" he asked gently.

Suddenly the last of Randi's barriers came tumbling down. She fixed her troubled eyes on the older man. "It's *my* fault," she said miserably. "It's *my* fault Tom crashed. It's all my fault—if he dies!"

Recognizing the importance of the turn the conversation was taking, Trafford was careful not to press too hard. He said quietly: "That's quite a responsibility you're taking on, isn't it?" He paused. He looked into her eyes. "Why do you feel that way?" His voice was calm, reassuring. Despite it, he felt Randi's rising anguish.

"Because he was worried. Because perhaps he didn't—*couldn't*—concentrate enough. He may have done something wrong—and crashed—because of me . . ." A little sob escaped her. Her guilt crowded in on her.

"Why, Randi?" Trafford probed gently. "Why do you say that?"

Randi was on the verge of losing control. "Because I—I—" With a conscious effort she got hold of herself. She took a deep breath, and in a flat, monotone voice she went on. "Because for months our marriage hasn't been—a marriage. Because *I* haven't been a wife."

Trafford watched her with growing comprehension. Deliberately he remained silent, letting her talk.

"I—I don't know what to do," she said hopelessly. "We—we do love each other. We—we used to be so very close. . . ."

She dug her knuckles into her eyes, but she did not cry. "I'm so—confused. I don't know what happened to me. I . . . ."

She stopped abruptly. She looked almost defiantly into Trafford's face. Now that the dam had been broken, she let her innermost thoughts, her feelings and fears, pour out.

"Yes—I *do* know," she said. "I lost the baby. We wanted a child so very, very much—and I lost it. After carrying it for more than eight months, I lost it." She squeezed her eyes shut. "And Tom . . . Tom . . . ."

Her voice broke. She lowered her head and sobbed in stark anguish.

Trafford did not want to lose her. Softly, gently he prompted: "Tom . . . ?"

Randi shivered almost imperceptibly. She looked up, staring at the man—past him—not seeing him, staring into a nightmare remembered by a tormented mind.

"I was lying there," she said tonelessly. "Alone. For hours. Waiting. But he wasn't there. . . . I knew I would lose the baby. I knew. I knew . . . And we had made such wonderful plans . . . such wonderful plans. . . ."

And once again the inexorable nightmare that had been born as cruel reality flooded her mind in all its horror and anguish. A memory—harrowing, tortured—unreal . . .

Once again she stood in the sunlit nursery, seeing all the wonderful things placed there in anticipated celebration of their love. Hers and Tom's. The gaily painted dresser for baby's things; the colorful cut-outs on the walls; the white lace curtains; the funny-looking bassinette; the cuddly stuffed toys. And the crib. Once again she smiled down at her stomach, big with love, and once again she touched it, feeling the lusty little kicks within. . . .

And she reached for the little child's wind-up phonograph Tom had bought. And she turned it on, listening to the cheerful, tinny voices of children singing the familiar nursery rhyme:

> "Run, run as fast as you can,
> You can't catch me,
> I'm the gingerbread man . . ."

and she watched the little running figure mounted on the spindle slowly turning with the music. . . .

And once again she picked up the multicolored mobile from the dresser—the one to be hung above the crib from the ceiling hook which had once held a lighting fixture. . . .

The nightmare quality of her remembrance slowly heightened, as she knew it would. As it always did. As she dreaded it . . .

And she relived its horrors in somnambulistic detail. . . . The stool next to the crib . . . Stretching to reach to hook high above—and the heart-stopping moment when she knew she was going to fall . . .

The mobile flying from her hands, and everything—the dresser, the bassinette, the pictures, the toys—spinning wildly, crazily and forever as she fell . . .

The searing pain when the sharp corner of the wooden crib gouged into her swollen stomach and the life inside . . .

The agony of struggling to her feet, holding on to the dresser, drawing herself up and coming face to face with the running figure on the spindle top, suddenly menacing and foreboding . . .

Her trembling hands clasped over her pain-racked womb—and her silent scream of deep, deep anguish when the red spot appeared between her feet on the bright yellow carpet . . . growing larger and larger until it engulfed the world . . .

Once again she knew the despair of lying helpless, pain-ridden and alone on the floor in the nursery so suddenly turned into a nightmare. . . . Watching the door. Forbidding. Unreachable. Silent. And closed. Closed . . . Offering no help—as the new life within her, the life she had wanted so very much, dissipated itself on a yellow rug, its moisture anointing her loins . . .

Swimming, struggling in and out of consciousness, sinking into an abyss of oblivion—and clawing herself back up . . . Waiting. Waiting for Tom to come and make everything right . . .

And watching. Watching the door. Closed.

Closed . .

And then—after an eternity of waiting and suffering . . .
Tom.

Silhouetted in the open door, the setting sunlight glinting
from the silver wings on his uniform jacket . . . Tom—hurrying
to her side, staring down at her, his face a mask of horror . . .

And the scream. She had not known it was hers. . . . Arching
back; straining in desperation; seeing the staves in the crib—
her eyes racing along them to oblivion . . .

And once again fighting her way back and watching the
formless, immobile shape become Tom. Tom, standing before
her, his bloody, bundled-up uniform jacket cradled in his
arms . . .

She stared at Trafford, not seeing him—still reliving her
nightmare. She knew she was telling him. Everything. But she
was not aware of words. Only remembered horror and pain—
and grief . . .

"She was dead," she whispered bleakly. "The baby was
dead. . . ."

She took a deep breath, returning to *now* once again. "And
after that," she said tonelessly, "everything fell apart. . . . I—
I couldn't stand Tom touching me. I'd see him standing there—
holding . . ."

She sobbed. She looked at Trafford, anguish in her haunted
eyes. "I—I just freeze up every time he comes near me. Nothing seems to matter anymore. We used to be so close. Now
we can't seem to—to communicate at all. . . . Sometimes I
even blame *him* for the baby's death. For weeks he'd promised
to hang that mobile, and he never got around to it. Why
couldn't he have been there? We needed him so desperately.
He—he didn't even *have* to be away. It was just something
he wanted to do with his friends." She looked down at her
lap. "I—I don't even know if I do want him back. I—"

She stopped, horrified at her own words. She looked up
quickly. She sobbed. "Oh, God! I don't mean that. I *do* love
him. I do. . . . But now—I don't even think I can be of any
help. Up here . . . I saw him. I called to him. And he didn't
answer. Didn't react at all. . . . And the night before his crash,
he—"

She stopped.

"He what, Randi?"

"He wanted me . . . and I—"

"How long has it been?"

"Seven months," she whispered.

He nodded.

"But—he's been . . . very gentle. All the time. He never tried to—to force anything." She bit her lip. "And look what I've done to him."

"All right, Randi, *let's* take a look," Trafford said. He spoke calmly, reasonably. "Tom had an accident. What went wrong up there wasn't your fault. It was beyond your control. And what happened between you is in no way to blame for Tom's condition. His injury is. Exactly how, we still don't know. There's a lot we don't know, Randi. A man's mind is still a wilderness. A seven-inch wilderness." He looked closely at her. "But I can tell you this: what happened between you and Tom certainly won't lessen your importance in being able to reach him. You *can* help."

"I want very much to believe that," Randi said earnestly. She was finding new strength. She knew she would never be able to forget her loss. She knew she would have to learn not to assign blame. Either to Tom or to herself. She would have to learn to cope. Could she? Not without a scar. *What deep wound ever closed without a scar?* she thought. A remembered stanza. Byron, it was. From her high-school days. Funny she should think of that now. . . . There'd always be a scar. But a scar *is* a sign of healing.

She looked at Trafford, new determination on her face. "We must find him," she said.

"We will." Trafford patted her arm. "He needs you, Randi. And when he's back home—you and I will have a talk. Agreed?"

Randi nodded. "Agreed."

She gave him a sidelong glance.

"I guess—Tom and I—we're both a little lost."

He pulled off the road and came to a stop on the gravelly shoulder near a sign that identified the mountain highway as California State 190.

For a moment he sat staring out over the vast, pale and desolate expanse shimmering with heat below him. It was his first view of Death Valley.

Shit!

He had the feeling his assignment would not exactly include all the comforts of home.

He'd anticipated a good, long, quiet time as a sleeper in place, after receiving his engineering degree back East and being transferred to the Coast and given a new identity. Then, dammit, out of the blue, he'd been activated and given a mission. Highly technical. In the Sierra Mountains.

And then, without explanation, someone'd done some button-pushing, and he'd been pulled off what had promised to be an exciting cat-and-mouse search with minimal risks involved—to hightail it to this crappy place. Mission: Locate and abduct a downed USAF pilot. He could make no sense of it. But he'd do the job. If he could find the bastard. Of course, he would have help on that score.

Political kidnapping was nothing new. He'd been involved in a case once before. But—in a godforsaken place like Death Valley, for crissake!

He was not impressed with the piece of useless information he'd picked up—that the valley was seventy million years old. It had just had that much more time to become real uncomfortable.

He hawked. Better get himself in the right frame of mind for his new job.

He finished the can of forty-weight he'd been drinking on the road. Coors. His favorite. He threw it out of the car.

He started off again and went rubberbanding it down the highway. The road quickly began to wind and he slowed down. Might as well keep the shiny side up and the greasy side down—and get there in one piece.

Even if the stinking place was the pits.

And he did have a job to do. . . .

5

Colonel Gerhardt Scharff did not feel at ease. Things were not progressing the way he'd wanted them to—in fact, had anticipated they would. The situation made no sense. For the tenth time he went over the last transcribed report from L.A. He found it difficult to make head or tail of it. But it was certainly not optimistic. It made him acutely uneasy.

Suddenly the door to his office opened. He'd heard no knock, certainly had not acknowledged any, and he felt instantly annoyed. With a sharp remark on his lips he looked up—and at once sprang to his feet.

"Comrade Minister!" he exclaimed. "I—I didn't—"

The man who strode into the office was small of stature and wore old-fashioned, steel-rimmed *pince-nez* spectacles. Scharff knew he had a habit of adjusting them at crucial moments, a gesture that was chillingly ominous.

"Sit down, Scharff," the man interrupted sharply. He himself took a chair opposite Scharff without waiting to be asked. Coldly he contemplated the apprehensive intelligence officer.

"I want some facts, Scharff," he said, his voice deceptively calm. "Not conjectures. Not possibilities. *Facts!*"

"Of course, Comrade Minister."

The man waved his hand impatiently. "First. That device of Dr. Marcus'. It is destroyed?"

Scharff nodded soberly. "Yes," he said. "Totally destroyed. It is of no possible use to anyone. Even the Americans. We—"

"Do they know what went wrong?" the Minister interrupted.

"No. My information is that they do *not* know the cause of the malfunction. They have no idea why the crash occurred."

"Your information is reliable?"

Scharff nodded. "We have two agents," he said, "both in place. And active. At this moment the pilot is their target. They are both top men. They—"

Again the Minister interrupted. "What is your communications set-up?"

"Reports every four hours—and on an urgency basis," Scharff explained. "The agents in the field have a contact schedule to be maintained with the L.A. control through the telephone system, using only public telephones that cannot be tapped. Orders and information are relayed to them and to us."

"Adequate." The Minister nodded curtly.

"Information and instructions can be exchanged within half an hour, Comrade Minister."

The man gave him a cold look. "The pilot?"

Scharff's face grew cloudy. "Developments are—confusing. You are already aware of the—eh, extraordinary situation reported to us. I—we—eh—" He stopped his stammering. He could feel the sweat of acute discomfort itchy on his skin. He knew that his face would soon begin to glisten with it. He resisted the urge to wipe it. He did not want the supercilious bastard sitting across from him to have the satisfaction.

"It would now seem," he continued, "that it is most doubtful if the pilot will fall into our hands. Alive. Developing circumstances are very much against us. There is—"

"I do not know at what level this operation has been mismanaged," the Minister broke in. He glared icily at Scharff. "But I intend to find out."

Scharff felt anger rising in him. He hid it. Well. He was used to that. Instead he automatically flashed one of his switchcord smiles. He wished to hell that he'd never heard of that *verfluchte* Marcus device. And most of all the damned crash, which had seemed like an orange falling into his Aladdin turban; a chance to penetrate the secrecy of the Marcus project— a feat that so far had proved impossible—and with risks that should have been minimal. Now the damned risks were growing—and they had become risks to *him.* He cursed. He knew a scapegoat had to be found. So far *he* was the logical one. A part of his mind set out to find another, as he went on.

"I admit, Comrade Minister, that—based on the information given me—my first evaluation of the situation and the windfall it might have afforded us was, eh, perhaps optimistic—"

"*Overly* optimistic," the Minister interjected acidly.

"—overly optimistic. I shall, of course, instigate a thorough investigation of how the mission was handled—eh—in the field. I felt—"

Again the Minister interrupted, a small sneer of contempt on his face. He adjusted his *pince-nez* eyeglasses—a gesture not lost upon Scharff.

"So, *Herr Oberst,*" he said. "Am I correct in assuming that without the device, or part of it, and without the pilot, it will be impossible for Dr. Krebbs to accomplish anything?"

Scharff nodded heavily. "You are correct. But—"

"But Marcus *can* duplicate his work." It was a statement, not a question.

"Of course. But even *he* will not know *why* his equipment malfunctioned, *why* the plane carrying it crashed, until he can talk to the pilot. That is essential. We—"

"Then we must see to it that he does not do so, mustn't we, my dear Scharff?" Again the man's voice was deceptively gentle.

Scharff looked sharply at his superior. "I—understand," he said.

"Excellent." The Minister adjusted his *pince-nez.* "I shall leave it in your hands, then. Entirely."

He stood up.

Scharff at once rose to his feet. He almost clicked his heels. Some habits linger for a long, long time.

"Of course, Comrade Minister," he said.

Without another word or a glance the Minister left the office.

Standing behind his desk, Scharff contemplated the closed door. He was troubled. The Minister had come to *him.* Not a good sign. But—there *was* a way, a way to come out of this shitty situation without his own skin being befouled. . . .

His mind flitted back to another state minister he'd known. Long ago. He, too, had worn *pince-nez* spectacles. When *he* had been at his most considerate, his most calm and friendly, another meat hook in the Gestapo building was about to be occupied. He shivered. He suddenly realized he was still standing stiffly behind his desk. He sat down. Heavily.

He picked up the phone and jiggled the cradle.

"Get me Blücher," he snapped. "OV III. At once."

He waited. He fished a handkerchief from his pocket and wiped his face. As he had expected, it came away soggy with sweat. *Zum Teufel damit!*

"Blücher?" he said. "How fast can you get new orders to our agents in California? . . . Next contact at 1600 hours, their time. Good . . . Here are the orders to be transmitted to the agents in the field at once: Effective immediately, your target is to be eliminated."

He took a deep breath.

"I repeat. *Kill your target!*"

6

Tom's eyes smarted. He squinted out over the open valley exposed before him as he emerged from the mouth of a narrow canyon. The broiling sunlight shimmered on the sands, the heat creating hazy false horizons. He eyed the stretch of desert immediately in front of him, a flat, rough area dotted with large, humpbacked islands of hard-packed sand, overgrown with spiny vegetation. He studied them. They promised shade and concealment. Hesitantly he started down the gentle slope of the alluvial fan extending from the gorge, headed for the nearest dune. He was bone tired, and his whole body ached with exhaustion. Half running, half stumbling, he made for the island of safety. . . .

The two seventeen-year-old boys lying in the shade of one of the brush islands near the road giggled at one another. The joint they had been smoking was taking effect, and the world was their oyster—although admittedly a damned hot one and totally misplaced.

They'd been visiting Scotty's Castle in the north end of the valley and were on their way back to the campground at Texas Springs, in no hurry to get to the place—and parental supervision. They'd enjoyed the far-out Moorish mansion, lavishly built by the equally far-out Death Valley Scotty two lifetimes ago, and they'd joked over the old pictures of Scotty from his days as a prospector and as a trick rider with Buffalo Bill's Wild West Show. But they had been pissed off when the two super-skirts they'd tried to pick up turned out to have their folks in tow and the hoped-for little bit didn't come off. They hadn't even been able to cop a feel.

It had been a long, hot and tiring trip, and when they'd begun to check their eyelids for pinholes on the way back, they'd decided to get horizontal for a while—and the brush-covered sand dune had seemed as good a rest-'em-up place as any. Now the joint was gone, their fancy mopeds were pushed in under the brush, out of the sun, and all was well with the world.

Suddenly one of them sat up and peered toward the nearby foothills. He pointed.

"Hey!" he giggled. "Look! What's *that?*"

"What?"

"Over there. By that gorge. See it?"

They both looked.

In the distance a figure could be seen making its way down the slope from the ravine, moving in a curious, staggering half-run. It was impossible to make out what it was, but it seemed human, with tattered clothing hanging from it, moving in a half-crouch.

"Looks like a spaced-out OM."

"That's no old man. *You're* spaced out," the boy giggled.

"Well, he sure's no superjock," his companion countered. "He looks wrecked!" He looked eagerly at his friend. "Hey! Let's go mess around with him."

Quickly they hauled their mopeds from under the brush. They started up and careened toward the foothills, cutting across the desert.

"Come on!" one of them shouted exuberantly. "Drop the hammer down! You don't have to double-nickel it. There're no Evel Knievel smokeys out here, man!" He managed to perform a half-assed wheelie as both roared across the desert.

Tom looked up in wild alarm as the high-pitched whine from the mopeds shattered the silence around him. Across the desert two terrifying creatures were hurtling down on him, spewing sand and dust, their racket angrier and more frightening than any of the others that had pursued him.

In quick panic he looked around. There were no places to seek refuge. He began to back away from the strident menace racing toward him. He glanced back toward the canyon from where he'd come—and scrambled back up the slope toward the break in the humpbacked hills.

On the desert below, the two boys had come upon a dirt trail that led up toward the canyon mouth. They gunned their mopeds—mufflers rolling thunder over the sand—and raced to cut Tom off.

Terror-stricken, Tom clambered up the rock-strewn slope. The roaring monsters were gaining on him. He did not know why he was being hunted. But instinctively he fled.

Suddenly he lost his footing on the loose gravel and crashed to the ground. He got up at once and sat crouched on his haunches, his hands on the ground before him, regaining his strength. He turned his wild, sweat-streaked face toward his pursuers and watched them with fear and hatred.

The boys drew up. Startled, they stared at the strange apparition squatting some distance before them.

"Man!" one of them exclaimed. "What kind of weirdo is that?"

"Looks like a fugitive from a funny farm," his companion giggled. "Let's go put a net over him!"

He gunned his moped, and both boys raced toward their prey.

Tom leaped to his feet. He streaked toward the canyon, the noisy, terrifying creatures in close pursuit.

He reached the break and ran into the ravine. Still fairly wide, the canyon had a near-perpendicular wall on one side and a steep slope strewn with boulders and rocks on the other.

Tom was no match for the speed and mobility of the mopeds. They easily overtook him. Whooping his triumph, one of the boys raced past him and skidded around to a stop, gunning his idling motor.

Tom stopped short. Terror tore at his mind.

He was boxed.

The boy in front of him gunned his motor. The rumbling sound reverberated between the canyon walls—the roar of a demon. With a shrill Wild West war whoop the boy raced his moped a short distance toward the terrified Tom, slewing to a gravel-spurting halt a few feet from him. At once, from behind, the other boy, yelling with excitement, roared at his ambushed prey, raising a cloud of dirt and dust as he laid his bike on its side in a sliding stop.

Tom was frantic, gripped by a terror that robbed him of his breath. The noise hammered at his ears. Desperately he sought a way to escape the ravening monsters that herded him between them, closer and closer.

To the boys his frenzied attempts to flee were great sport. They gunned their noisy bikes and bellowed at their quarry, taunting and tormenting him until finally he was trapped between them, his back to the precipitous canyon wall. There was nowhere he could go.

Wild-eyed, lips drawn back in a snarl, he stood facing them. Raw panic ripped his mind apart. A savage fury took possession of him. A terrifying scream tore from his throat—and with the feral desperation of a cornered rat he hurled himself at the nearest enemy.

Shocked by surprise, the boy tried to avoid the maddened charge. He gunned his moped. It leaped ahead with a sudden lurch. The loose gravel shot from the spinning wheels; the boy lost control and the bike crashed into a huge boulder, pitching the rider headlong into the rock. Limply he slipped to the ground.

In the grip of uncontrollable rage, Tom did not stop his onslaught. His tormentor was still there, lying before him. He rushed upon the motionless boy and the still racing machine, its wheels spinning as it lay on the ground. With unbridled fury he attacked. He seized the noisy, frightening demon that had been tormenting him. With strength born of blinding rage he lifted it over his head and slammed it violently into the rock. The gas tank split open and immediately flames and black smoke shot up from the mangled bike.

Tom drew back. His fury unabated, he whirled on the other rider. Shaken with horror, the boy gunned his moped, turning it away. He found himself headed for the steep incline that formed one wall of the canyon, his crazed assailant in close pursuit. Hammer down, he covered ground, trying to scale the slope. Gravel, sand and rocks spewed from the racing wheels as he urged the moped up the steep canyon side. Suddenly the vehicle bucked. It pitched over backward and tumbled down the hill, the boy—thrown from it—plummeting after. Gathering speed, the moped hurtled down to crash into the burning bike at the boulder below. A thunderclap explosion rocked the ravine and rolled through the hills.

Tom was thrown to the ground by the blast. With heart-stopping fear he stared at the flames that licked the remnants of his enemies. A momentary inner vision of another fireball burned through his mind—never reaching the conscious level. It filled him with primeval terror. Quickly he got up and ran for the mouth of the ravine—the way now open to him.

He felt utterly spent, but the rage had left him. His terror of the monsters pursuing him had been vastly reinforced, but there was also a self-satisfied realization.

The fearful monsters *could* be fought.

And vanquished.

Without a glance back he ran from the ravine, leaving behind two still figures sprawled on the ground and a blazing fire sending billows of black smoke up into the burning sky. . . .

On the road a little more than a mile to the south Wilson brought his scout to an abrupt stop. He pointed.

"Look!" he called to Ward. "What the hell is that?"

In the distance a column of black smoke rose over the foothills, climbing higher and higher into the stagnant air. . . .

To Paul, the map of Death Valley lying spread out on Stark's desk was becoming a symbol of something sinister and evil. The Chief Ranger pointed to a spot on the map.

"Here," he said. "Here's where he attacked the two moped drivers from the trailer camp."

Paul frowned. "Attacked?" he queried. Grim-faced, he turned to Ward.

"I know," the medical officer said. "It sounds—unbelievable. But—fact is we've got one kid with a fractured skull and another with a broken collarbone and a hide covered with contusions and lacerations."

Scowling, Paul returned his attention to the map. He was beginning to hate it. He put his finger on it.

"Here's where *we* lost him," he said. "Desolation Canyon."

"I still don't see how it was humanly possible to get out of that ravine," Ward said.

Paul glanced at him. "*Humanly* possible? Maybe it wasn't." He returned to the map. "And here's where you found the mopeds and the two boys. He can't have gotten too far. We'll place observers in a ring around the area." He traced a line on the map. "Here." He turned to Stark. "Tell your men to keep their eyes open. He's got the cunning of a desert fox."

Stark nodded. "If he's there, they'll spot him."

"Our search teams will patrol the area inside the circle," Paul continued. "We'll be in position to move in as soon as they do. Get on it."

"Right." Stark left.

Ward looked solemnly at Paul. "He's getting dangerous, Paul."

"Meaning?"

"Meaning that we'd better get him before he really attacks someone. Or kills them."

Paul stared at him, his face dark. He was about to make a remark when Randi entered the office. He turned to her.

"Randi," he said, concerned, "why don't you get some rest? This heat is enough to bake all your energy right out of you."

Randi nodded. She looked out the window at the sun-scorched desert. "One of the rangers told me that the Panamint Indians called this place Tomesha. It means Ground on Fire." She turned to Paul. "Tom is out there, Paul. How will *he* rest?"

"Randi—"

"Are you going out?" Randi asked quietly.

"Yes."

"I'm going with you," she said.

He started to protest.

"Remember our bargain," she cut him off firmly.

He grinned. "Dammit, doll! You drive a hard one."

7

The fight with the two tormenting foes in the ravine had robbed Tom of his remaining strength, and still he was fighting enemies. Enemies infinitely more deadly than the ones he had defeated. Enemies he could not hope to conquer: exhaustion, heat—and thirst . . .

He peered in agony up at the relentless sun, sweat rolling down and caking the acrid dust in the stubble on his cheeks. His lips were cracked, and he could conjure up no moisture for his tongue to soothe them.

He staggered as he made his way along a trail toward a group of craggy rock formations that cradled pools of shade among them.

He passed a round, smooth boulder raised above the burning ground on stubby legs. For a moment he leaned against it. It felt different from other rocks. He worked his parched mouth and squinted toward the shade of the rugged peaks a little farther on. The earth before him seemed to smoke from the fury of the incandescent disk that watched him malevolently high above. Near collapse, he hesitated. There *was* a little shade where he stood—but the round boulder was out in the open, exposed. He struggled on, brushing past the meaningless markings on the boulder—W A T E R—and ignoring the spigot with the admonition to use the water in the tank for radiators only, and to close the tap firmly after use.

He reached the rocks. Scraggly, withered clumps of desert brush grew sparsely among them—and also a few spiny, bulbous objects.

He fell to one knee. The world grew fuzzy and seemed to pulsate with indistinctness. He collapsed completely, lying prostrate on the sand. He wiped his face with a grimy hand and peered ahead with sun-blinded eyes, straining to see. Through the shimmering heat rising from the ground he could make out a craggy nook of shade. He struggled to his feet and dragged himself toward the spot. Again he stumbled. He fell, raking his knee across the tough, sharp needles of a small hedgehog cactus. Sudden rage surged through him. Enemies were everywhere. Enemies that frightened, tormented—and hurt. He whirled on the pain-inflicting foe, and with a booted foot he stamped on it—again and again—crushing it.

Spent, he sank down beside it. Dully he looked at the trampled enemy. In the pulp, beads of moisture sparkled. He touched it. With his hands he scooped up the moist cactus pulp and buried his burning face in it, sucking the wetness into his parched mouth. . . .

There were four vehicles drawn up on the little spur road that led to the mountain observation point overlooking the valley—two scouts and two Ranger pick-ups. The blazing sun stood high in the cloudless sky and the only shade was a narrow strip along each vehicle.

Paul glanced at his watch, more out of impatience than a need to know the time. It would not be long now. He had always hated waiting. They had reached the time where each second seemed twice as long as the one just past. As soon as he got word that the ring of Ranger spotters was complete, they'd start to patrol the area—hopefully flushing their quarry into the open where he could be spotted. If . . .

If he *was* in the area at all.

He looked toward Sergeant Hays standing by the radio in his scout. Good man. And the only one whose face wasn't dripping sweat. He let his mind wander. He was glad to have the big black on his team. The man was experienced, reliable. Paul knew he'd seen service on bases all over the world. There was a strength about him that was infectious.

Ward and Ranger Gordon were conferring over a map, their faces glistening with perspiration, their shirts spotted with dampness. And Wilson was sitting on the ground in the strip of shade cast by the scout, leaning against it, slowly spooning the contents of a canned ration into his mouth. Paul marveled. It was too damned hot to eat.

He wiped the sweat from his forehead. He glanced at Randi sitting next to him on the rocks, her head lowered, staring down into her lap. The enervating heat was obviously draining her. Later he'd start her on salt pills.

He was suddenly astounded. He found himself thinking about the girl, evaluating her as he would the men under him. Okay, she *was* living up to her word. She *was* keeping up. He approved. She was all right. For a woman. Actually, he admitted to himself, he sometimes even forgot she *was* a woman.

Randi looked up to meet his eyes.

"You okay?" he asked.

She gave him a wan smile. "Yes, Paul. Fine."

He offered her his canteen. "How about a drink?"

She took it and drank. For a moment she sat staring at the canteen, lost in thought.

"What is it?" Paul asked.

She looked at him. "Oh, nothing. I—I was just thinking. It's so terribly hot and I was so thirsty." She looked at the canteen. "I have water. What about Tom? What must it be like for him?"

He had no answer. Clumsily he tried to change the subject, get her thoughts away from her fears.

"Quite a view," he said, nodding at the desert panorama below them.

Randi sighed. "Yes. Magnificent," she said, not really aware of her answer. She knew what he was trying to do—and she liked him for it. She looked closely at him. She found herself buoyed by his strength and stamina, his decisiveness. She understood why Tom called him friend. Not once, since their talk, had he shown resentment of her—or been overly solicitous. He *had* treated her with complete equality. She respected him for it. It would have been so easy for him to show his displeasure and to make her ill at ease by treating her as a fragile female. He had not.

"Must have been quite a sight seeing those twenty-mule-team wagons plowing along down there," he said.

Randi gazed out over the vast expanse of the valley below. She spoke, a sudden catch in her voice.

"I—I wish the place could be filled with people," she said. "Looking for Tom." She turned to Paul, sudden anger on her face. "Tom's giving his life for the Air Force," she flared. "Where are they now?"

Paul put his hand on her arm. "You know why we can't," he said quietly. "It's for Tom's own safety."

Randi looked away. "I know," she said miserably. "Oh, Paul . . . It's so terribly big. Tom could be anywhere."

She shivered. Shivering is not reserved for being cold, she thought. She glanced up at the incandescent sun high above. She pulled at the sweat-soaked shirt that stuck to her skin. Cold . . . She suddenly thought of the coldest she'd ever been. 165 degrees below zero. In Florida . . .

It had been at Eglin Air Force Base. Tom had been stationed there when he came back from Vietnam. It was there they'd met. She had been working in her first job out of college, where she'd majored in business management. It had been with the First National Bank in Fort Walton Beach. In the loan department. She'd met Tom when he applied for a loan to buy a car. They had their first date that same night. She still wasn't quite sure why she'd accepted. She'd never done anything like it before.

She'd visited the Base, and Tom had shown her the landing strip where Jim Doolittle and his volunteer crews had practiced short take-offs in their B-25s before carrying out their historic bombing attack on Japan in early 1942. She had quickly realized that Doolittle was one of Tom's handful of heroes—which included such wildly diverse personalities as Margaret Rutherford and Jules Verne.

They'd grown close. She'd always been curious about the huge Environmental Test Laboratories at Eglin, where the Air Force could create any kind of weather or temperature extreme—from a Sahara sandstorm to an arctic blizzard—in order to test their hardware under the most severe conditions. One of the labs held engines that had to withstand the cold of space itself. She'd been dying to know what it would be like, and Tom had wangled permission to take her in.

They'd put her in a jump suit several sizes too large. They'd told her to stay inside no more than five seconds. They'd instructed her not to breathe or she'd freeze her lungs—and they'd told her not to touch anything or she'd stick to it and would have to be cut loose.

She'd followed Tom through the air locks into the test chamber. She'd hardly been aware of the huge engine suspended in the starkly lit room. She had felt the freezing cold penetrate her skin, her flesh, down to her very bones in the few seconds she'd stayed inside. It had been incredible—frightening. . . .

When they'd walked outside into the Florida day, they were still so cold that in an instant the moisture in the air condensed all over them, turning them completely white. They'd eyed one another. They looked like animated snowmen. Tom had laughed. He had seemed to her like a boy showing off his newest toy. It was the first time she knew that she loved him. . . .

Again she looked up at the burning sun. She turned to Paul. "Do you really think he has a chance?" she asked quietly.

"Of course. We'll find him." He thought he sounded confident. "I promise."

"In time?"

He nodded. He said nothing. He was afraid he could not be convincing. It was quite possible Tom had already perished out there. Somewhere.

He stood up. "I'll check with Hays," he said. He walked over to the Sergeant. "Any contact?" he asked. He knew it was a totally unnecessary question.

"Only cross-traffic, sir. Some of the units are just moving into position."

"Let me know as soon as all units are ready." Another superfluous remark. He felt disgusted with himself. The tension was getting to him.

"Yes, sir," Hays said, unruffled.

Paul walked over to Ward and Gordon. Hays looked at the radio. Nothing. He contemplated Wilson sitting on the ground next to the scout.

"How the hell can you feed your face in heat like this?" he asked. "You're gobbling up that stuff like a vacuum cleaner with teeth."

Wilson looked up. "Me? Weather don't bother me none."

"Yeah?"

"Sure. Hey, man, I was once at a base where it got fifty below in the winter and a hundred and thirty in the summer."

"Shit, man!"

"You don't have to believe me, Sarge. But—like it's the only base I've been at where the *chaplain* went AWOL."

"Go choke the chicken, you bull jockey!" Hays exclaimed with mild exasperation.

Wilson grinned, and looked with interest at a spoonful of food from the can. "Say—what *is* this here stuff?" he asked.

Hays raised a surprised eyebrow. "You never had C-ration before?"

"No-o-o-o . . . Can't say I have."

"Where the hell did you get it?"

"It was in the Ranger emergency stores."

"Shoe leather and glue," Hays said dryly.

"Oh." Wilson sounded relieved. "I thought it might be something I couldn't eat."

The radio sputtered. Hays at once gave it his full attention.

"Armadillo One . . . Armadillo One . . . This is Ranger One. . . Come in. . . . Come in. . . ."

Paul came hurrying over. He listened intently. Hays spoke on the mike. "Ranger One . . . Ranger One . . . Go ahead."

"All units in position. . . . Repeat. All units in position."

Hays glanced at Paul. He nodded quickly.

"Roger, Ranger One. Out." Hays replaced the mike.

"Mount up!" Paul called. "You've got your sectors. Let's go!"

It was just past 1600 hours when Ranger Adams came barreling down the road toward the gas station in the little desert village of Stove Pipe Wells. The place was an oasis, lush with metal signs and wooden billboards rather than date palms and well poles. In profusion they sprouted everywhere: GAS—

SNACKS—TELEPHONE—CABINS—POINTS OF INTEREST—and the ever present COCA-COLA. A squat, fat Coke dispenser stood next to a tall, slender telephone booth, looking like a square, utilitarian Abbott and Costello.

A man started across the roadway from the station. Adams leaned on the horn—and, startled, the man jumped back. He glared after the disappearing Ranger truck, and with a booted foot he angrily kicked an empty Coke can, sending it spinning across the road.

Adams stepped on the gas. His new position was at Mud Canyon, a few miles ahead. He'd make it OK. . . .

Tom was instantly awake. He had been dozing fitfully in the shade of the rocks, refreshed by the moisture squeezed from the pulp of the crushed cacti. He did not know what danger had alerted him, but instinctively he pressed into the little crevice that had sheltered him.

He listened. All was quiet.

He had begun to relax when a tiny new sound caught his attention. He searched for it. Only a few feet away he located the source. A small creature, no bigger than a mouthful, scurried across the sand—and stopped.

Tom was intent on it. It was alive—was it something that could be eaten? Slowly he reached out a hand toward it.

The little creature scurried away on many legs—just a few inches. Again it stopped. It arched a long, curved tail over its body, a needle-sharp stinger pointing forward, and waved two tiny pincer-clawed legs in front of it.

Tom was fascinated. Again he reached toward the scorpion. Slowly. Closer . . . Closer . . . Close enough to pounce . . .

Suddenly he stiffened. The deep growl of a motor intruded upon the silence. The small life was instantly forgotten, and it scuttled into the safety of the crevice. Tom listened. The hated sound of his enemies was getting louder as it drew closer. Anger rose in him. And fear. He did not know how to tell them apart.

He sprang to his feet. He glanced toward the desert, from

which this new threat was approaching, and, hugging the rocks, he ran for the steep, rugged mountains and at once began to climb the jagged cliffside. . . .

Ranger Gordon turned his jeep off the main road onto the dirt road leading toward the foothills. He was alone in the vehicle. He preferred it that way. He had tried to reason out where that pilot they were chasing might have holed up. The canyon leading to the Natural Bridge seemed a good bet. Water rushing down the canyon through the ages had gradually undercut the softer rock and formed a massive natural bridge some fifty feet above the wash, and the steep sides of the ravine had been scoured into grottoes, arches and spillways—perfect for hiding. He crossed the broad expanse of the alluvial fan and stopped at the entrance to the canyon. He looked around. He searched the hills with his binoculars and turned the jeep into the gorge. The narrow dirt road snaked between craggy rock walls—steep, but not unscalable.

He drove slowly, carefully. He came to a sharp bend in the road where a rock outcropping all but strangled the passage. He stopped before it. For a moment he sat listening; then he dismounted and walked a few steps toward the bend, his heavy boots crunching on the gravel.

Again he stopped. He listened. Nothing . . .

He was just about to turn back when he froze. From the other side of the rock outcropping came the rustle of small stones trickling down the precipitous slope. He listened, watchfully. A faint scraping sound reached him.

Quickly, silently, he ran back to his jeep. He leaned into the front seat and brought out a shotgun that had been slung under the dashboard. Gun at the ready, he returned to the rock outcropping.

Cautiously he began to walk around the bend. Suddenly the figure of a man came tumbling down the slope in a torrent of small rocks and crashed heavily onto the road directly in front of Gordon. He jumped back. Instinctively he brought up his gun—and froze. He stared at the young man sprawled in the dirt, gaping wide-eyed up at him.

The disheveled tumbler shook his long hair out of his eyes and held up his hands. "Hey, man, don't shoot!" he cried. "I just lost my footing."

Gordon lowered the gun.

The man got up. He examined his boots. "Shit!" he said in disgust. "Scuffed all to hell."

"What were you doing up there?" Gordon scowled at him.

"Working, man. Working." The young man looked around. He spied what he was looking for, a drawing tablet lost in his fall, lying among the stones. He picked it up. He handed it to Gordon. "I'm doing a series of, you know, desert sketches. For a book. Like fantastic!"

Gordon looked at the drawing. It was quite good, he thought grudgingly. He had taken an instant dislike to the artist. Perhaps because the man had so obviously startled him. In the lower right corner the sketch was signed with a flamboyant *Jerry Hayden.*

"You're Jerry Hayden?" Gordon asked.

"That's me." The artist brushed himself off. "Slightly the worse for wear and tear."

Tartly Gordon handed the sketchpad back. "I suggest you be more careful," he said. "Especially if you travel about the valley alone. An accident up here can be serious. If not fatal." He enjoyed the little threat.

"Sure, man. Sure . . ."

Gordon glanced around. "How'd you get here?"

"In Sarah."

"Sarah?"

"My buggy." The artist grinned. "She's parked around the bend."

"Just be sure you don't block the trail," Gordon admonished sourly.

"Really." Hayden grinned amiably at him.

Gordon turned on his heel and stalked to his jeep. The artist looked after him, the grin on his face fading slowly as the Ranger got into the vehicle, skillfully turned it around and drove from the canyon.

Indelicately he waved a finger at the departing jeep.

There were at least a dozen of them, crushed and ravaged, scattered on the ground. Ward bent down. He fingered the stringy pulp. It had not yet dried brittle hard.

"He's been here," he said. "And not too long ago."

Wilson kicked one of the crushed cacti. "Cactuses can't keep you alive," he said. "They only help you die a little slower."

"Cacti," Ward said automatically.

"Yeah. Cacti." Wilson glanced at him. "You sure it was the Major?" he asked.

"Yes," Ward answered. "Reasonably so." Was anything ever more than reasonably certain? he thought. He looked at the trampled cacti. Inwardly he felt pleased. Tom was learning to survive. With some surprise he realized he'd actually expected it. Tom had come through the grueling Air Force survival course in better shape than anyone else in his group. Ward knew that for a fact. He'd been the examining doctor. . . . It was amazing the great amount of stamina and inner resources man possessed, he thought. He remembered his father's harrowing stories about the notorious Bataan Death March. In 1942. He'd been there. Sixty miles of forced marching under the most grueling, inhuman conditions imaginable. Twelve thousand American boys had begun that ordeal, most of them sick or injured; all of them starved. One in five had died. Miraculously the others had found the strength and stamina to survive. . . . Perhaps it was no miracle, Ward thought. Perhaps man *does* have a reservoir of unsuspected resources within him.

He gazed up into the rugged mountains. "He may still be up there," he said. He glanced at the sun, dipping down toward the horizon. "We'll still have about an hour of light," he estimated. "Let's take a look."

The two men got into their scout and slowly drove into a narrow wash between the steep and jagged rocks. There was no road and the going was rough.

Presently they stopped. They dismounted and scanned the weather-furrowed mountain peaks towering over them, edged in golden pink by the setting sun. Already the shadows below were deep and dark.

Suddenly Wilson started. Excitedly he pointed. "Up there, sir!" he called. "On that ridge . . . See it?"

Ward ran a few paces into the draw to get a better vantage point. His eyes searched the ridge high above. There . . . Movement . . .

It was Tom.

Wilson joined him. "It's the Major, all right," he said. He cupped his hands. "Hey! Major!" he called. "Major Darby!"

High above they could see the figure of Tom abruptly turn and look down upon them. For a brief moment he stood frozen—then he scrambled to reach the crest. In his efforts he dislodged several small rocks and they came trickling down the steep slope, gathering speed and loosening other stones, sweeping them along.

Ward and Wilson shielded themselves from the rain of pebbles that pelted the wash.

When they looked up at the crest again, Tom was gone.

"Dammit!" Ward said. "It'll be dark in less than an hour." He started to run back to the scout. "Wilson!" he called. "Get on the radio! Notify Captain Jarman we've spotted him!"

Wilson ran with him. He glanced up at the ridge as he ran. "How long will the Major keep running away?" he puffed. "When will he learn we're only *people?*"

They reached the scout. Wilson at once picked up the mike.

"Armadillo One," he called urgently. "Armadillo One. This is Armadillo—"

A growing rumble from above made him look up.

Down the jagged mountainside, bouncing from one protruding rock formation to another—like a grotesquely misshapen ball in a giant, crazily tilted pinball machine—a huge boulder tumbled toward them, rapidly building an avalanche of rocks and stones, rushing with increasing speed and noise directly down on them.

They leaped for the cover of the canyon wall—even as the huge boulder came crashing down into the draw, narrowly

missing them. With an ear-grating crack of torn metal it slammed into the scout as a hail of smaller rocks pelted the vehicle
and the cowering men.

The dust settled. The silence was suddenly oppressive. Ward
went over to the scout. The rear was dented and buckled;
one wheel hung askew on a broken axle.

And the radio was smashed. Totally destroyed.

Ward gazed up at the ridge high above. He stared down
the wash. He looked at the mangled scout. They were without
communication. It would be a long walk back. He looked at
Wilson.

"He's learning," he said quietly.

"Yeah," Wilson said. "Learning to fight back!"

8

He had him in his sight. There was no doubt—it was the
downed pilot. He could make out the green flying suit even
in the deceiving twilight. With his field glasses he followed
the man's laborious progress down the eroded ravine. He had
seen him come across the far crest, obviously wary and uneasy,
constantly looking back over his shoulder and stopping to sur-
vey the terrain before him.

Lying quietly among the rocks at the vantage point on the
ridge overlooking the gorge, he watched the man. The light
was getting poor. He could not take the chance of missing
his target. The pilot's course would bring him quite close within
a few minutes. Close enough to make missing him impossible—
even in the darkening twilight. And he did have a scope on
his gun.

He glanced toward his rifle, leaning against a rock nearby.
He'd put it there to keep sand from getting into the muzzle
and the sight—and to keep it out of the sun, which had still
been blazing down when he took up his position a couple of
hours before.

He'd made his 1600-hours contact with his L.A. control and

had been given his new priority orders. At once he'd gone up into the mountains above Furnace Creek and picked an observation post taking in the greatest possible area. It had paid off, dammit! He had the poor bastard spotted. He felt a grim satisfaction. On his next contact he'd report success.

The target was getting closer. He could still make him out quite clearly against the golden rock and sand of the eroded hill.

Suddenly he froze.

"Are you all right, sir?" a voice behind him inquired.

He whirled around.

A few feet away stood a Park Ranger, his pleasant young face contemplating the man lying prostrate on the ground.

"Is everything all right?" he repeated his question. "Can I be of help?"

He stood up. He brushed himself off—more for something to do than for the sake of cleanliness. With a pang of alarm he realized that the Ranger stood squarely between him and his rifle.

"No," he said. "No, thank you. I—I was just admiring the mountains in the sunset."

The Ranger nodded. "It can be quite spectacular," he agreed. He looked toward the rifle leaning against the rock. "I see you have a gun with you," he said. "Hunting is strictly forbidden within the confines of the National Park. Firearms are not allowed."

"I—I didn't intend to shoot anything—eh, Officer," he said. Perhaps pretending to be a bumbling tourist would buy him time, he thought. "I—well, I just get a kick out of sighting in on a wild burro—or something." He grinned sheepishly. "It—eh, it isn't even loaded." He made a move toward the rifle.

The Ranger stopped him. "That's all right, sir," he said. "I'll take it." He picked up the gun. He worked the bolt. A round jumped from the breach and plopped down on the sand.

Neither man uttered a word. The Ranger bent down and picked up the bullet. He glanced at it and put it in his pocket.

"Perhaps you'd better come with me, sir," he suggested calmly.

"Where to?"

"Ranger Headquarters. I think it would be better if the Chief had a word with you." He motioned him down the hill.

The situation was intolerable. His mind raced. Under the circumstances he could not possibly allow himself to be taken in. He glanced at the Ranger making his way down the slippery incline a few feet behind him.

The man would have to die.

His mind worked at peak capacity. On the narrow, one-way dirt road below he could see his own vehicle where he'd left it on the shoulder—and the Ranger pick-up pulled up behind it. He knew what he had to do.

Suddenly he lost his footing on the loose rocks and pebbles. He tumbled head over heels down the slope. Painfully he sat up. He tried to regain his feet—and fell back with an oath of agony. He put his hands on his left knee just above his heavy boot and rubbed it gently.

The Ranger was at his side. "Are you badly hurt?" he asked, concerned.

"It's my knee," he groaned. "I—I hope it's just twisted."

As the Ranger bent down to look at it, he exploded into action. With all his power he jabbed the sharply pointed knife, drawn from his boot, up into the Ranger's chest—twisting it viciously as it penetrated the rib cage.

With only a hoarse gasp of air expelled by the violent blow, the Ranger collapsed across his legs—his body twitching in the throes of death. He could feel the warm blood gush out over his loins in oily, sweet wetness.

He rolled out from under the dead man. He thought fast. He had been trained to do just that.

Quickly he emptied his pockets and took off his blood-soaked slacks. He pulled the pants from the dead Ranger and put them on himself, emptying out their contents on his own discarded clothing. He looked around. A short distance away there was a small fissure under an overhanging rock—just big enough to hold a man. He picked up the body and carried it over. He stuffed it into the crack. He returned for his bloody slacks, rolled them up with the Ranger's belongings and pushed them in after him.

He had a sudden thought. He pulled the slacks out again and fumbled for the man's wallet. He opened it. Twenty-two bucks. No big haul, but it would get him a new pair of slacks. He glanced at the man's ID card. *Adams.* He stuffed everything back under the rock and concealed the opening with stones. It would be some time before the man was found. Unless someone with a good nose happened by.

He ran toward the vehicles. He stopped and looked at the bright red spot on the ground. He began to kick sand over it, but stopped at once. The disturbed ground would be more of a giveaway than simply leaving the bloodstain. Tomorrow's sun would bake it to a blackish, unrecognizable blot. He picked up his rifle and put it in his vehicle. He ran to the Ranger pick-up and rummaged around in the back of it. He brought out a short length of sturdy rope and hitched the two vehicles together, bumper to bumper.

Carefully, slowly, he began to tow the Ranger vehicle away from the area. . . .

It was dark when he finally stopped in a steep-walled canyon several miles away.

He unhitched the Ranger truck. Once again he searched through it. He came up with a jack and a large, rusty nail. He threw the jack into his car and walked back to the pick-up. Carefully he placed the nail in front of the rear right tire, leaning against it, its tip resting against the rubber.

He climbed into the vehicle and eased it forward.

The nail was driven into the tire. It was already beginning to go flat as he dismounted.

He got into his own vehicle. For a moment he sat quietly, collecting his thoughts.

He had taken a chance killing the Ranger; the man would be missed. But he'd had no choice. He had made the right decision. He went over every move he'd made. He was satisfied he'd covered his tracks as completely as possible. Of course, the Ranger force might get even more officious than they already were; make things a little more difficult for him. And for his teammate.

He knew there had to be another agent on the case. It was standard. But he had no idea who it was. Only the L.A. control would know. Proper security procedure, of course. It could be anybody. Using any cover. Only *one* person in Death Valley it could *not* be, he thought wryly: Major Tom Darby.

He had a sudden thought. Wouldn't it be ironic if the man he'd killed had been his counterpart?

He wouldn't know. In the opinion of the big-shots, he had no need to know.

Was it carrying secrecy too far? He realized the reasoning behind it. It made sense. If the mission was important enough, the idea was not to entrust it to one agent only—and at the same time not put all your agents in one basket. If one was caught, he could not give the other one away. The mission was not totally aborted. And the chance of the two men "eliminating" each other was next to nil.

But it was a funny idea! If that crazy spy-spoof TV show *Get Smart!* was still in production, he might submit it.

His eyes fell upon the box of artist's materials on the seat beside him. He rather liked his cover. An artist could be anywhere, any time—no questions asked. He was actually quite good at it. He had been instructed to use his talent in creating his cover as a sleeper agent. He had been assured that he would be taken care of, and he did sell—enough to be comfortable. Sometimes he was astonished at some of the big-name customers who bought his work. He couldn't help wondering if they did so by choice or by instruction.

He started his buggy. He drove away. He cursed under his breath. He had missed his first chance.

There would be another. . . .

9

Darkness had come again. Tom was getting used to it. When he looked up, everything was black with many, many bright little pinpoint holes. It reminded him of the moving cave in which he had taken refuge from the fury of the blazing disk above. It had been covered by a thick, soft sheet of blackness, and through it he had been able to see the light outside as a wall of tiny, bright dots. Something black had now been pulled over the entire world once again, letting only light dots through; something that cast a cool black shade over everything.

Only one of the holes was larger; almost as large as the burning disk that blinded his eyes. But he could look at this hole in the darkness. It let in enough light so he could see, and it did not hurt his eyes. He felt no fear of it.

He continued down the rocky slope of the foothill toward the desert floor below . . .

Lt. Barlow was not in the best of moods. He'd planned on spending a cozy night in bed with his girl, Joan. Certainly not sitting in the *Jolly* staring at a video screen.

The huge HH-53 helicopter was equipped with the new *Pave Low* night rescue system. Barlow felt he'd already spent half his life flying around in the dead of night, staring at a red screen, testing and evaluating the infrared tracking system. And now this. . . .

The flight from Edwards to Death Valley had been routine. One-hundred-and-thirty-seven miles. Over Randsburg and Trona—right through the corridor between the Naval Weapons Center at China Lake to the west and the Naval Weapons Range and Fort Irwin Military Reservation to the east. Both he and his copilot had kept their video display screens on—overlayed with red plastic to preserve their night vision. The whole damned cockpit had a reddish glow. He'd watched the terrain slip by below, looking like a giant red negative.

It had been a suddenly mounted mission over and above his regular schedule. And an urgent one. "Get your bird up to Death Valley and search for a man on the loose in the area. He may try to evade—so keep your eyes on your screen. Report his location when you spot him, but do not try to apprehend." He wondered who the guy was—and what he'd done that it was so all-fired important to get him. He hoped it was worth losing a night with Joan. But he doubted it.

They were flying over the barren foothills just southeast of

Furnace Creek. On his eerily red screen the rocky ground below looked totally alien, utterly still. They'd been on the job a couple of hours. They'd seen nothing.

Barlow kept his eyes glued to the video display. Occasionally he'd work the slew switch on the console below the screen, changing the system's field of view.

Still nothing.

On either side of the big *Jolly* two Para-Rescue Jumpers, secured by their safety straps, were hanging out the doors watching the ground. With their thick, protuding night-vision goggles they looked like visitors from outer space ogling Mother Earth with great, luminous green eyes.

Barlow was aware of one of the flight engineers standing behind him, watching over his shoulder. He was newly assigned to the project and still fascinated with the *Pave Low*. Hell, it *was* a slightly incredible gizmo—able to turn the dead black night into crimson day.

Suddenly one of the PJs called on the intercom. "Sir! I think I saw something move. Three o'clock. 200 yards."

Barlow banked the *Jolly* and turned toward the indicated area. He watched his screen intently. He knew his copilot would also have his eyes glued to his own screen. The rocky terrain below looked eerily unearthly as it moved across the red video display.

Nothing.

Suddenly his copilot sang out. "There! Two o'clock."

Barlow at once made a slight course correction. He stared at the screen. And he saw it. A shadowy, indistinct form scurrying behind a large rock formation. He banked sharply and doubled back to hover low over the spot.

Suddenly a dark shape bolted from cover and raced away in panic, leaping across the rocky ground.

"Shit!" Barlow exclaimed. "Just a wild ass." Turning his view turret he watched the little burro streaking to safety. He changed course and headed down toward the flat valley floor. . . .

Tom looked up in alarm. The night silence was being disturbed by a deep, growling sound that seemed to beat the air. Far in the distance a misshapen, dark shadow with a huge, faintly glowing red eye was hurtling through the air headed straight for him. Following his first impulse he began to run from it.

The huge, red-eyed beast in the air was rapidly roaring closer. Terror-stricken, Tom searched for a place to hide as he scrambled down the rocky slope. In the dark he saw a craggy outcropping. At once he headed for it. . . .

From the doorway a PJ called. "Movement, sir." He sounded uncertain. "I—think. Eleven o'clock. 400 yards."

Barlow headed for the spot. Another damned donkey, he thought, disgruntled. He circled the spot.

Nothing.

Not a damned thing. . . .

Tom lay huddled, pressed against the rock outcropping, melting into the black shadow at the base. He didn't move, petrified with terror at this new, unknown menace. The huge, red-eyed monster was flailing the air directly over him—roaring its rage as it searched for him. Instinctively he knew that his only safety lay in complete immobility. He fought the urge to run in panic. He forced his body to lie motionless. Only his heart beat wildly. . . .

"Nothing down there," Barlow grumbled. "Let's try the next sector."

He banked—and gaining altitude the big *Jolly* flew off. . . .

For a while Tom lay still, trembling, listening to the whop-whop of the big chopper disappearing in the distance. The confusing, vague stirrings of familiarity meant nothing to him. They only disturbed him and he quickly forgot them. At last the night silence returned.

Cautiously he emerged from his hiding place—and continued down toward the valley floor. . . .

The ground was dotted with dry vegetation. Tom crouched among the brittle bushes. He looked up at the luminous disc high above that bathed the world in a soft bluish light.

And there was another light.

Warily he kept his eyes on it as he crept through the desert brush. It was different from the other lights. It was soft and yellow. It came through a square hole in a big square rock sitting by itself a short distance from the foothills. Nearby, the solid black of many tall, gently swaying shapes lay over the lighter desert floor and the horizon. He knew what they were; he had seen them before. They were tall, bushy plants on long, sturdy legs. They were no menace.

He crept farther down toward the lone, square rock. He worked his mouth. It felt dry and hot. His cracked lips hurt with a sharp pain when he moved them. Cautiously, silently, he moved on. Unerring instinct told him that water could be found nearby. . . .

Juan, head wrangler of the Furnace Creek Stables, was not in a particularly good mood. He had almost backed out of the deal with his friend Lupe. He had almost kept the lame old nag. But Lupe was still coming up with more *dinero* than the glue factory. Still, a deal was a deal, and the sack of oranges, dammit!, had been part of it. He did not for a moment believe Lupe's lizard-brained story of a weirdo *hombre* stowaway eating them all. *Estúpido!*

He was sitting at the wooden table in the adobe hut that served as both bunkhouse and harness room for the stables, working on a broken bridle. He glanced at the two other wranglers with him. *Gracias a Dios!,* there were not many *turistas* in the valley during the summer, so there was a chance to bring the equipment up to usable standards. He dipped his work-worn fingers in a can of saddle soap and began to work it into the leather. . . .

Tom was crouched behind a clump of withered sagebrush. He peered into the gloomy half-light. Ahead of him, behind an open barrier made of a few slender, long timbers running parallel to the sand, he could make out the dark shapes of several large beasts. The smell coming from them reminded him of the moving cave. It was familiar and he felt reassured. Quietly he crept closer.

Just inside the barrier stood a long, low trough. A couple of the big creatures had their heads bent down into it. One of them lifted up its head and shook it. Water dripped from its muzzle.

Tom was suddenly more conscious of his craving for water than ever; his nostrils dilated as the moist smell reached him. He crept toward the corral.

Uneasily the horses looked up, ears alert. Anxiously they turned their heads toward Tom and stirred with apprehension. Tom stopped. Fearfully he watched the wary horses. Instinctively he sensed they were afraid of him—and his thirst overcame his own fears. He slipped through the loose wooden fence.

One of the horses snorted in alarm; another took up the warning and neighed in fear; they all milled about in their haste to get away from the water trough—and the intruder.

Juan looked up at the sound of the agitated horses. He glanced meaningfully at his two companions. He grinned, revealing two front teeth missing. He wiped the saddle soap from his fingers with a dirty cloth, got up from the table and took down a double-barreled shotgun from a rack in a corner of the room. He checked it. Both barrels were loaded. He nodded to one of the wranglers, and the man put out the light. For a moment Juan stood motionless, acclimatizing himself. Then he walked toward the door. . . .

Tom submerged his face in the water. He drank deeply. The cool water soothed him.

He lifted his face. Water ran down his cheeks and dripped from the bristly stubble of his beard. A faint sound had risen over the scuffling noise made by the big animals in the enclosure. A different sound. He listened intently, feeling the acute tension of danger course through him. Uneasily he stared toward the lone, square rock.

The light was no longer there.

Instinctively he linked it with the sudden feeling of peril. Noiselessly he turned from the trough and crawled toward the timber barrier and the brush beyond. . . .

Outside the door of the adobe, Juan peered into the darkness, trying to see. . . . There! At the water trough. A half-hidden form slinking away through the fence. He raised his gun. . . .

Tom was through the barrier. He turned and glanced back toward the dark, square rock. Suddenly there was a quick, bright flash of light from it. In the same instant a thundering roar slammed against his ears and a violent blow struck him on the shoulder, spinning him around. Pain seared him. With a snarl, part rage, part fear, part pain, he snapped his head around to grimace furiously at his burning shoulder. He grabbed the wound with his hand. It felt wet and slimy. It hurt.

Again the explosive thunder blasted the silence and the ground spat little puffs of sand at him.

Terror gripped him. He sprang to his feet. He ran.

The darkness swallowed him. . . .

Randi gripped Paul's arm. "What was that?" she asked, startled. "Shots?"

"Came from that direction," Paul said. He stepped from the Ranger Headquarters entrance, where he'd been standing with Randi. He peered into the starry night.

Randi joined him. "Over by the stables?"

He nodded. "One of the boys must be taking pot shots at a bobcat."

"Bobcats? Down here?"

"They come down from the mountains during the night, now and again. Looking for water." He looked at her. "Raise havoc with the horses."

She nodded. "Good night, Paul," she said. "I'm going back to the cabin."

"You want me to drive you down?"

"No. Please. I—I feel restless. I'll walk. The air'll do me good."

"I guess it'll be all right," Paul agreed. "Any bobcats within miles would have been scared back into the hills."

"Oh, Paul," Randi said. "They'd be more afraid of me than I of them."

He smiled at her. "OK," he said. "We'll finish mapping out the search areas for tomorrow. Good night, Randi."

"Don't forget, I want to go with you."

"I won't." He looked closely at her. "Randi," he said solemnly, "it would be an empty gesture to say, 'Don't worry.' But—I promise you—we'll do everything we can."

She nodded, subdued. "I—know. . . ."

She walked off.

He looked after her. She was quite a girl, he thought. Tom was a lucky bastard. He, Paul, had never run into a chick like that. Uncomfortably, he suddenly realized he was a little envious.

He turned on his heel and went into the building. . . .

The quiet was cathedral. Black infinity arched above, its myriad eyes gazing down upon her as she walked in solitude toward the palm grove at the ranch. The silent calm of the night was in sharp contrast to the storm of emotions within her. Her mind was raked with doubts, with feelings of guilt, fear, frustration—and anger.

Was she to blame, after all? Despite what Major Trafford had said? Had she—had her frigidity and the frustration she had forced on Tom made him more prone to have an accident? *Was* she at fault? She did not want to do it. But she did not know how not to. Why should she be expected to carry all the guilt? It wasn't fair.

What would happen to them when Tom was found? And back with her again? Would it all be—like it had been? What if he was never found? Or died? Would she ever forgive herself? *Was* there anything to forgive?

She knew she would do anything to save her husband. But what *could* she do? . . . Did she love him? Really love him? She knew she did. His life was hers. Then why could she not—show it? *Was* it something in her—or was it in him? What was she doing wrong? Or he?

The questions, the doubts, the self-accusations and recriminations crowded in on her in greater numbers and with greater insistence than ever, now that she was confronting them. Questions—but no answers.

Only doubts and incertitude.

She found herself in the grove of tall palms—an oasis of quiet serenity. In anguish she turned her face up to gaze into the night sky. She watched the luminous disk of the moon glide in and out of the softly swaying palm fronds high above. So much like home.

She had a brief little pang of homesickness. She had them—

but only occasionally. She remembered how supportive Tom had been when her father died. Back in Florida. Suddenly. Only three years ago. He'd been showing a house to one of his real-estate clients when he suddenly collapsed with chest pains. He'd died that night. Tom had taken care of everything, quietly, efficiently, sparing her mother and her all the terrible details. She'd loved him for it.

Her mother was still in Tampa. Alone now. She suddenly shivered. How terrible it must be—to be alone. . . .

The palms above her rustled softly in a sudden, gentle gust of night wind. It brought her back. This was not Florida, however much it might seem so. It was Death Valley. It was California.

Tom was a native Californian. Opposites attract, he'd joked when he'd first courted her back in Florida. And you and I can hardly be more opposite—geographically speaking, that is. We ought to attract one hell of a lot.

Her eyes bright with unshed tears, her face pinched with torment, she stood for a moment in silence. Her voice was audible only to herself.

"Oh, dear God. Please let him be safe. . . ."

She lowered her head and walked on. She passed the gate to the Outdoor Museum near the ranch. For a moment she hesitated. Then she took the path leading into the grounds. Her cabin was directly across.

After a few moments she regretted having taken the short-cut.

The museum area adjoining the Furness Creek Ranch was crowded with relics from the bygone mining days in Death Valley. A giant twenty-mule-team borax wagon, heavy and high-wheeled, lorded it over weathered crushers, drillers, ore carts and pumps. A conglomeration of corroded tools and pieces of old machinery played court to a massive, rusty locomotive. The pale moonlight, stabbing through the twisted forms and shapes of the ancient equipment, peopled the night with weird and ominous shadow creatures as Randi walked through the deserted grounds.

She felt increasingly uneasy. She was acutely aware of her

footsteps crunching the gravel on the path, each step cutting at the silence that pressed in on her. It was the only sound she heard—except for the hollow pounding of her own heart. Unconsciously she speeded up her pace. The eerie indistinctness of the feeble light reaching down through the iron frameworks lent a disturbing aura of menace to the place.

She froze in mid-stride. Coming from the deepest shadows ahead of her, a faint, sharp clang of iron against iron had startled her. She stood stock still, staring into the darkness. Her heart raced. She listened, every muscle tense.

All was quiet.

She felt angry with herself. It was nothing but a little night creature scurrying among the old gear. She was being ridiculous. She could blame it only on the tension and exertion of the last two days. She walked on.

Ahead of her a towering, gibbet-like derrick loomed tall and foreboding in the night, casting a deep black shadow across the path.

She walked toward it.

Suddenly she screamed. A short, shrill scream, choked off by terror. From the blackness behind the gallows hoist a nightmare apparition jumped out, a fearsome specter that squarely blocked her path.

Tom!

He looked completely what he was—a dangerous, wounded creature, trapped, desperate—and ready to kill in defense of its life. The terrifying sight seared itself on her mind in one split instant.

The head injury, matted with dark, clotted blood; the wild, ferocious eyes filled with hatred and fear; the teeth bared in a maddened snarl that split his savage face, streaked with grime; the dirt and dust, caked in the stubble of his beard; his clothing tattered; the wound on his shoulder, wet and bloody, the cloth around it torn.

It was Tom.

It was her husband.

Instinctively she shrank back—and he leaped for her. His hands ripped at her blouse, tearing it.

She cried one anguished word—"Tom!"—and fell to the ground.

Tense. Taut. His face wild and savage, his hands held clawed before him, Tom stood poised over the prostrate form of his wife. He knew he could fight his enemies; he knew he could inflict injury and damage on them when they came at him. Destroy them. But this one lay quiet. Motionless. Presenting no menace. He waited. Lynx-eyed, he watched her. At the slightest sign of danger he would rip the life from her. He had meant to do it. Now. Traced to this place of hiding where he had crept to lick his wound. But this enemy on the ground did not stir. It was not like the others. Slowly, gradually, the terror-fury left him.

He stiffened when she opened her eyes and looked at him in horror. But she did not move. She only stared up at him. He saw fear in her eyes. And—something else. He did not know what. . . .

Randi felt the grip of terror tightening in her throat as she lay petrified, gazing up at the brutish creature that was her husband. As realization of his true state of mind grew in her, so did her horror. She saw no spark of reason; no hint of recognition. Only feral savagery. And—curiosity . . .

Slowly she sat up.

Tom watched her warily, ready to pounce. But a deep-seated instinct continued to tell him that this foe was different. This enemy meant him no harm. Absorbed, he looked down at the woman. He reached out a hand and pushed her on the shoulder. She shrank back. But she did not resist. He was deeply curious. He sensed—and scented—a presence that excited and aroused him. The presence of—a female. Again he reached for her.

"Good night, Frank."

Tom froze in alarm at the sudden sound of the man's voice coming from the distance. Instantly alert, defiant, he turned to face the new threat.

"See you tomorrow."

"Good night." Another voice.

There was the slam of a screen door swinging shut—and footsteps crunched on the ground.

Randi's heart beat wildly. Her thoughts raced. They would help. The men would help. If she could attract their attention, call out to them, they would help. . . . She glanced at Tom, her eyes filled with fear and desperation. She *had* to. She would call out.

With a sharp intake of breath she opened her mouth, her cry ready in her throat.

Instantly Tom whirled on her, his face dark with rage. He lunged toward her—and she cowered against the derrick in heart-stopped silence.

For a moment Tom stared at her. The footsteps were coming closer. He turned to flee. Almost immediately he whirled back and grabbed the woman, roughly hauling her to her feet. Dragging her along, he ran into the distorted shadows of the dead and silent mining relics.

Terror-stricken, Randi stumbled after her husband. Where was he taking her? Why? She found it impossible to think clearly. In the flood of thoughts let loose by her shock whirled the bits of knowledge and information about Tom she had gleaned from Major Trafford. In her terror she tried to gather them, to fathom what to do. She could not.

Through the palm grove they ran—and out onto the night desert.

Presently Tom let go of her. She stumbled after him, occasionally breaking into a half-run to keep up. She didn't know what else to do.

Ahead of them on the desert floor a large hillock loomed in the darkness. Overgrown with vegetation, blue-gray in the moonlight, the dune afforded protection and concealment. Tom headed for it.

The salt bushes, the desert holly, the creosote bushes grew densely on the little sand mound. Tom crawled in among them, pulling Randi along. In a small, sandy hollow they settled down. For a while they sat regarding one another.

Hesitantly Randi spoke.

"Tom?"

He watched her intently. But there was no recognition nor comprehension on his face.

"Tom . . . Please," Randi said. She tried to keep her voice from trembling. "It's me—Randi. . . . Please, Tom . . . Please know me."

He listened. This was not the grating, rumbling noise or the high-pitched whine of his pursuers and tormentors. This was not the roar of the light that struck him and hurt him. Unconsciously he touched the wound high on the crown of his head. He felt soothed by the soft sound. He watched. He listened.

But he did not know how to respond.

Slowly Randi lowered her head in despair. Her voice was a whisper in the wilderness.

"Oh, dear God . . ."

DAY FOUR

1

Paul could feel the hot anger born of frustration rise in him. He fought to keep it in check, but his grip on the telephone tightened until his knuckles showed white.

"Perhaps with more men, Colonel," he said, his voice taut and brittle. "With a *reasonable*—" He stopped, obviously cut off. He clamped his mouth shut, cording the muscles in his jaw as he listened. Ward, Trafford and Stark watched him steadily. The air-conditioning in the Chief Ranger's office was already going full blast, although the sun had just begun to tinge the Funeral Mountains to the east with pink.

"There *is* no doubt," Paul said firmly. "He was shot by one of the wranglers—near the corral. He was probably looking for water. The man thought he was shooting at a bobcat; but from the description he gave us of what he saw, it could only have been Tom." He listened. "No, I don't know how serious it is. But we—"

Again he broke off. Growing impatience darkened his face. "She *must* be with him," he said. "Why else would she be missing? And she's not been in her cabin all night. Tom's trail led from the corral to the Outdoor Museum. Randi's cabin is just across. She probably took a shortcut through there last night. And there *were* signs of a struggle."

Again he listened. He controlled his mounting anger only with difficulty. "All right, sir. I *will* take the responsibility. But I must also *insist* on getting the manpower and the equipment to conduct a full-scale search. There is *no*—"

He stopped. For a brief moment he listened. "Of course I realize nothing must happen," he snapped. "To either of them." He listened again. "In one hour? . . . Right." He slammed the receiver down. "Damn his hide," he swore. "He must have a conscience like a duck's ass!"

"What did he say?" Ward asked.

"He's sending half a dozen choppers. They'll be here within the hour."

"That's something, at least."

"Yeah. Something. But far from enough, dammit!" Paul couldn't shake his frustrated anger. "They'll quarter the valley. Try to spot them for us in a low altitude search. If. *If* they're out in the open." He walked over to the wall map. "He's also going to arrange for a photo mission. An SR-71 overflight. Ryan has to get Pentagon clearance."

Trafford looked interested. "The SR-71," he said. "That's that new high-altitude Strategic Reconnaissance plane?"

Paul nodded. "They'll make a run over the valley. Give us an overview of the entire area. From 80,000 feet."

Stark looked startled. "That's—that's twenty miles up," he said. "They're going to try to spot Tom from twenty miles?"

"Why not?" Paul shrugged. "We've got hardware in orbit that'll read the license plate on your car from a hundred miles up." He stood up. "The SR-71 flies out of Beale Air Force Base near Sacramento. It's a helluva plane. It has the capacity to relay overflight photos back to Base for real-time analysis. They *could* spot Tom."

"You know what beats me?" Ward said. "How does Tom keep evading all the top technology we can throw at him? One lone guy."

Paul looked at him. "He's got one hell of an ally," he said quietly.

"Ally?"

"Death Valley."

"Let's hope *someone* spots him," Ward said soberly. "We *are* running out of time. It's a miracle Tom has survived this long. Expending the energy he is—with an aggravated skull fracture."

"Perhaps the fracture itself isn't as traumatic as we thought," Trafford said. He sounded hopeful. "Perhaps it's not a depressed fracture that's causing the pressure on Tom's brain." He frowned in thought. "It could be a subdural hematoma—" he turned to Paul—"a blood clot, Paul, which has stabilized."

"That condition and the concussion might easily produce the same effect," Ward agreed.

Trafford nodded. "The *contrecoup* effect," he said. "The entire cerebrum would be traumatized, of course."

"If what you're saying gives Tom a better chance," Paul said fervently, "I hope to God you're right."

"It might tend to explain his stamina," Trafford said. "But there are still enormous dangers. The hematoma could progress—that is, enlarge from more bleeding. Tom could lapse into unconsciousness."

Paul looked at him, his face grim. "We've got to pick up their trail," he said. "Pretty damned soon." With a sudden thought he turned to Stark. "Any word about Adams?"

Stark shook his head. He looked deeply concerned. "No," he answered. "We found his truck. Flat tire. And he'd gone out without a jack."

"Any idea where he could be?"

"None. He must have gone for help and . . ." Stark shrugged helplessly. "I don't know what could have gotten into him. His truck was found way off his assigned sector." He frowned at Paul. "He should have known better. Dammit!—he *did* know better. We have our own ten commandments on how to survive out there. The last one is: 'If your car breaks down, stay with it. Do not attempt to walk for help.' . . . Adams himself posted warnings all through the valley."

Paul looked disturbed. "What the hell *is* going on out there?" he asked of no one in particular.

Ward looked at him. "Paul," he said uncertainly. "You don't think he—he could have run into Tom?"

Troubled, Paul shook his head. "I—don't know, Quent, I don't know. . . . Dammit!—this thing keeps getting more complicated all the time. First Tom. Then Adams. And now—Randi." He turned to Trafford. "What's she up against?" he asked. "What's likely to happen between her and Tom?"

Trafford slowly shook his head. "It's impossible to predict," he said. "Only one thing is certain: the situation will be dangerous for her."

They looked at him sharply.

"Remember, Tom Darby is not really her *husband* at this moment," Trafford explained. "He's more like a hunted, frightened animal." He sighed with regret. "No one can foretell what he might do."

"Could she have gone with him voluntarily?" Ward asked. "In an effort to—help?"

Paul shook his head. "No," he said emphatically. "I'm certain she didn't. Remember, I read the signs myself. There *was* a struggle." He turned to Trafford. "What if—if she did *not* go with him of her own free will?" he asked. "Why would Tom take her along?"

Trafford spoke deliberately as he gathered his thoughts. "He—eh, probably does not know *who* or *what* she is," he said slowly. "But he may be—eh, attracted to her—as a male to a female. Primarily by smell, I'd say."

"Smell?"

"I would say, almost certainly." Trafford nodded. "Most insects and animals are guided by pheromones—or scent signals. They mark territory, establish pecking order and send out sexual cues. That sort of thing." He looked at Paul. "Humans as well. We're just now learning how much in studies and research being done at various universities. Something of very basic importance does occur via the olfactory sense. It has, of course, already been determined that there's a connection between sexuality and odor. I would very much expect that to be a factor here. Smell. And touch. A pure male-female attraction. It—it may give Tom a certain—eh, feeling of security. Something he sorely needs in his present condition." He looked gravely at Paul. "He's not going to let her go," he finished.

Paul looked bleak. "Our damned problem has just doubled," he said, bitterness in his voice. "Hell! I wish we *had* tried to get close enough to Tom to use a tranquilizer gun. Long ago."

"Captain," Trafford said quietly, "you know why we decided against that approach. The risks were too great. Far too great. Risks that exist even for strong, healthy animals. Under controlled conditions. For Tom . . ." He let the sentence hang.

"I know," Paul said. "I know." He looked at the big wall map showing the vast expanse of the valley.

"If only I knew where the hell to look!"

2

Randi stirred fitfully. She opened her eyes. She felt cramped and stiff. For a moment she puzzled groggily over where she was—then the terrifying events of the night burst upon her. She looked up quickly.

Crouched across from her in the sand hollow among the desert brush sat Tom, watching her with intent curiosity.

She drew herself up and sat hugging her knees. She looked at her husband, knowing that he knew her not at all, at once both frightened of him and wanting to reach out to him. After a while she mustered up enough courage to speak to him.

"Tom," she said apprehensively. "I—I know you don't understand my words. But I . . . I want to help you." She kept her voice low and gentle, trying to let her tone of voice convey her compassion.

"I know you're confused," she continued. "Afraid. I understand. I do understand, Tom."

He listened, his eyes following the movement of her lips with fascination. Suddenly he winced. With a dirty hand he scratched at the wound on his shoulder.

Randi followed his motion. She became aware of the torn, blood-soaked cloth. Her eyes widened.

"You're hurt!" she exclaimed. And with sudden comprehension: "It was *you* they shot at!" She looked at him, shocked. "Oh, Tom. How frightened you must have been!"

Again he picked at the painful wound.

"Don't," she said, concerned, knowing he would not understand, but needing to express herself in words. "Don't touch it. You'll get it infected." She took out one of the handkerchiefs she had stuffed into the pockets of her pants. "Here," she said. "Let me . . ."

She reached for him.

At once he drew back, instantly alert, suspicious.

She froze. With sudden insight she understood. Tom was like an injured animal—suspicious of the hand that would help him, wary because of the weakness the injury presented. She would have to win his confidence before he would let her touch the wound. She would have to convince him, prove to him that she meant him no harm. She was frightened—but she persisted. "Tom. It's all right, Tom . . . it's all right." She spoke soothingly, reassuringly. "Be still now, Tom . . . it's all right."

He watched her uncomprehendingly—but his tension left him.

Again she reached out for him. He pulled back, never taking his wary eyes from her. But he let her touch the wound.

"There," Randi said. "You see? It's all right, isn't it?" Cautiously she began to peel the torn cloth from the clotted blood around the fresh wound. He trembled, but he did not interfere.

"Oh, my God!" Randi exclaimed. "The buckshot's still there!" She examined the little black pellets imbedded in Tom's skin. Now that the wound was exposed, she could see it was quite superficial. But the shot had to be removed. She looked earnestly at her husband.

"Tom," she said gently. "Be still, now . . . I know it's going to hurt . . . but—trust me. Please trust me."

Gingerly, using her nails, she picked a shot from the wound. Tom flinched. His lips drew back, but he did not move away. Instinctively he knew that she was helping him. Randi kept talking to him, steadily, soothingly.

"Easy, Tom . . . Easy. It won't really hurt. . . . Just—just a few more . . . There . . . I'll get help. As soon as I can. You won't have to run away anymore."

The last of the shot had been picked out. Randi cleaned the wound as best she could, folded the handkerchief and placed it inside the torn suit as makeshift protection.

She was encouraged. She felt she *had* reached him, communicated with him. There was hope in her eyes as she watched him.

Tom was looking at her with curiosity and growing interest. Suddenly he stiffened. Slowly he turned his head and stared intently into the surrounding brush. He had seen movement out of the corner of his eye.

Randi followed his gaze. A fat chuckwalla lizard, almost a foot long, sat in the sand, slowly moving its head from side to side.

Tom watched the lizard raptly. Slowly he reached out a hand toward it. Momentarily startled, the reptile moved out of the way. Tom froze, hand outstretched.

His eyes were riveted on the lizard. He had a flash memory of the coyote pouncing on its prey.

Imperceptibly he shifted his weight—and suddenly he threw himself, lightning fast, toward the big lizard. His hands grabbed the bloated body and he pulled it to him as it struggled frantically in his grip.

For a moment he gazed at the wriggling reptile in his hands—then he made a sudden, wrenching motion, breaking its back. He raised the still twitching body to his mouth and with his teeth he tore into the skin.

Randi stared at him, her eyes wide, her face frozen into a mask of unbelieving horror. She gagged. She clasped her hands to her mouth and swallowed hard, trying to keep down the burning bile that rose in her throat.

Tom ripped the skin from the dead lizard and tore strips of bloody meat from it. He pulled off the tail and threw it to Randi. Still jerking with a macabre life of its own, it lay before her.

White and nauseated, she fought to conquer her profound revulsion. She averted her eyes—from the hideously twitching tail, and from her husband, greedily gulping down the bloody lizard meat. Utterly horrified, shocked to her innermost depths, she realized her husband's true state.

And she despaired.

Tom threw the gnawed lizard carcass aside. He looked around. With a soiled hand he grabbed Randi and pushed her ahead of him as he started to crawl from the dune.

They were just about to emerge from the growth of desert shrubs when Tom stiffened. In the distance the dreaded, familiar and threatening rumble of an enemy could be heard, rapidly growing louder. At once he flattened himself among the weeds and pulled Randi down with him.

She peered out through the brush. Not too far away from the sandy hillock a road ran through the desert. In the distance a lone vehicle was fast approaching. . . .

Jerry Hayden's buggy was tooling down the road. He was

returning to the area where he believed his quarry to be, after having been to Stove Pipe Wells to make his 0800-hours contact with his L.A. control. He had reported last night's killing. He had not asked, but from the man's reaction he knew it was not his counterpart he'd eliminated. He was still not the only agent in Death Valley hunting the downed flier. He looked around. Pretty soon he'd pick a vantage point and take up his vigilance. Now? Here? Mentally he flipped a coin. He continued down the deserted road.

With mounting agitation Randi watched the buggy rapidly drawing closer. Her heart raced. She realized that Tom was mortally afraid of the vehicle and its disturbing noise. She also knew that their only chance was to be found—and helped. She glanced at her husband, lying stiff and tense next to her, watching the approaching vehicle with fear and hatred on his face.

The car was almost directly in front of them.

It would have to be now!

She rose to her knees. As loudly as she could she screamed: "He-e-e-re! Over *he-e-e-re!*"

Instantly Tom grabbed her. Roughly he pulled her down, snarling his rage at her. His hands pushed her into the sand; powerful fingers dug into her flesh as he held her down, sending waves of pain through her. Defeated, helpless, she did not—could not—resist. . . .

On the road Hayden pulled up. He stopped. Over the drone of his open buggy he'd thought he heard what sounded like someone calling out. A high-pitched sound. He picked up his binoculars lying on the box of artist's materials on the seat next to him and scanned the desert.

On his left it stretched up toward the foothills; on his right several hillocks and dunes overgrown with vegetation sparsely dotted the flat expanse, larger and farther apart than the little mounds of the area known as the Devil's Cornfield, through which he'd just passed. There the little dunes overgrown with arrowweed resembled rows of eerie corn shocks. He'd made sketches of them.

He searched the nearest dunes. Nothing. What he'd heard

was probably the hee-haw of a wild burro, he thought. They roamed the foothills all over the valley.

He started up again. He'd decided. He'd drive through Furnace Creek and into the mountains just south of there.

He hoped for good hunting. . . .

As the vehicle disappeared down the road, Tom relaxed his vise-like grip on Randi. She sat up. She rubbed her arm and shoulder where he had hurt her.

He scowled at her, puzzled and angry. Why would she want to attract the attention of the demons hunting him? He pushed her to get up. She did.

They emerged from the dune. Ahead of them stretched the barren, hostile desert. In the far distance a vast panorama of utterly naked, wind-sculptured sand hills could be seen, spilling its expanse of rolling, sun-baked Sahara-like dunes to the horizon.

He pushed her to go. She stared at the forbidding land.

"Oh, Tom," she whispered. "Not out there. We'll never make it." She turned her tear-bright eyes to him. "How can I make you understand?"

Roughly he prodded her.

Together they started out, trudging through the sand.

And the blazing sun rising overhead offered no respite. . . .

3

Someone was following them.

Once again he glanced in his rearview mirror. The little blue Volkswagen with the oversized wheels was still there. He turned to Hays.

"Sergeant," he said, "someone's tailing us."

"I know," the big black said calmly. "Blue VW. Been with us quite a piece." He nodded at the rearview mirror. "I've seen you checking him out."

Paul guided the scout along the dirt-road upgrade. It was tough going on the loose gravel and he was grateful for the four-wheel drive. They were headed for the site of a ghost town, Schwab, in the hills a short distance up Echo Canyon. If Tom had sought the high ground again, it would be a perfect spot to hole up. It was worth checking out.

And now they had picked up company.

Ahead, a flimsy iron gate hung across the road from two poles. A sign on it read:

C L O S E D

SITE NOT OPEN TO THE PUBLIC

Tacked up on one of the poles was a cardboard notice: *Due to extreme hot weather and lack of patrol this road is closed.*

Paul steered the scout around the gate. His was not the first vehicle to do so. He continued to labor up the washboard road.

Perched in the hills above the valley, Schwab was a mining town that had been born and died in a single year seventy-five years in the past. Several wooden structures and rundown board shacks, splintered and sagging with age, lined the sole street. Occasional boardwalks, edges curled by time, aproned boot-worn steps. A few rusty and broken pieces of mining equipment stood guard over the deeply weathered buildings, ghostly fragments from a brief boom period a quarter of a century after the little town's heyday, and the surrounding hillsides were dotted with mining adits and stopes. Schwab, dozing in the sun-baked hills, was a true ghost town—where time had died. Silent. Deserted. Not restored for the tourist trade.

They passed the age-worn markers of a venerable cemetery brooding on a windswept knoll, and turned toward the ghost-town street, which made a bend into the built-up area.

"Sergeant," Paul said, "as soon as we round the bend, I'm getting out. Slide over and take the wheel. Okay?"

"Yes, sir."

"Keep going. Slowly. Until you reach the end of town. Then stop. Get out and go into one of the houses. Leave the scout empty."

Hays nodded. He did not seem surprised at the instructions. They turned down the street. For a moment they were hidden from the VW tailing them. Quickly Paul jumped out and ran for concealment behind a tumbledown shack. Hays continued down the deserted street.

Paul crouched down, out of sight, near a pile of broken-down barrels, their staves split and unfettered by rust-crumbled rings and gradually drooping toward the horizontal. He listened. The stalking car was drawing near.

Slowly the VW crept around the corner. It stopped. Up ahead the scout could be seen, halted on the roadway. No one was in it. The VW driver leaned forward intently.

Paul stepped from the shack to stand behind the car.

"What are you doing here?" he asked brusquely.

The man behind the wheel stiffened. He did not turn at once.

A chill shot through Paul. He had an icy thought:

He was unarmed.

For a fraction of a second he regretted his decision not to carry any weapon on the mission. He suddenly felt naked. Angrily he dismissed the feeling. How could there possibly be a need for violence?

The driver got out of the car. He leaned against it, insolently peering at Paul.

The two men sized each other up. The VW driver was a young man; longish hair, a well-trimmed beard. He wore casual but good clothes. On the passenger seat in the front of the car Paul could make out a large thermos bucket, and a map was lying on the dashboard. The stranger was well prepared for his desert trek.

"What are you doing here?" Coldly he repeated his question.

The man stepped away from the car. He planted his booted feet in the dirt and faced Paul squarely.

"Why?" he asked brazenly. "What business is that of yours?" There was instant antagonism between the two men.

"You're trespassing on posted property."

"Are you the caretaker?" The stranger made a point of looking Paul up and down. "Is that what we're using Air Force officers for these days?" He smirked derisively. "Not a bad idea."

Paul chose to ignore the insult. "Didn't you see the sign?" he asked. "This place is closed to the public."

"What sign?" The young man sneered. "You mean the one you went around?"

"I have business here," Paul said icily. "You don't."

"Oh?" The man looked around in mock surprise. "What is this place? A secret Air Force base?"

Paul found it increasingly difficult to tolerate the young man's impudence. "I advise you to leave," he growled. "Now!"

"Or?" The young man raised a dubious eyebrow. "Or what? Neither you nor the Air Force have any jurisdiction here."

Paul glared at him. "Perhaps not," he snapped. "But I can sure as hell get someone up here in a hurry who damned well does!"

The young man contemplated him for a moment. Then he shrugged.

"I think you'll find I have a pretty good reason for being here, too," he said. He reached into his back pocket and brought out his wallet. He removed a card from it and handed it to Paul.

Paul took it. It was a press card. He looked at it. THE BERKE-LEY QUESTIONER. He looked up at the young man.

"You are David Rosenfeld, Jr.?" he asked.

The man nodded. He reached for his ID. Paul gave it to him. "I ask you again," he said grimly. "What are you doing here?"

"Oh, come off it, Captain." The reporter eyed him condescendingly. "You know that better than I. Why don't *you* tell *me?*"

Paul suddenly felt chilled. There had been a leak. The press was on to something. And of all possible media, a rag like the *Questioner.* It would have a field day with anything anti-military. "I don't know what you're talking about," he said acidly. He suddenly felt on the defensive. The roles had been reversed.

"Really?" Rosenfeld again raised a doubting eyebrow. "Well,

I suppose it's not the first time the Air Force has been in the dark." He grinned unpleasantly. "My information is that something *extremely* interesting is going on up here."

"Who gave you *that* information?"

"Really, Captain," Rosenfeld scoffed. "Haven't you heard? We don't have to divulge our sources. To anyone."

"Well, your *sources* are wrong!" Paul snapped.

"Really?" the young reporter demurred. He swept the area below with his eyes. "With Air Force brass huddling with Park Rangers? With you guys running all over the place in your cute little scouts? With Air Force helicopters churning up the sky? Wrong?"

He contemplated Paul scornfully. "I suggest to you, Captain, that something *is* going on. Something highly interesting. Something the public should *definitely* know about. Something *I* intend to find out about!"

Paul stared at the reporter. He suddenly knew what tack he had to take. He sighed. "Perhaps you're right," he said. "We hadn't sought publicity on this, you understand." He shrugged. "Actually, we didn't think anyone would be interested." He looked at Rosenfeld. "But since you're here, why not? The Air Force can always use some positive public-relations blurbs from you guys." He was gratified to see a shadow of uncertainty cross the cocky reporter's face. He gestured out over the vast expanse of the valley.

"That's a pretty hostile place, don't you agree?" He waited for Rosenfeld's reaction.

The reporter nodded. He was perplexed. Was the fly-boy about to come up with the real poop? Or was he going to hand out some cock-and-bull shit?

"In fact," Paul continued, "it's one of the most hostile and deadly desert environments on earth. Hot as hell. You know that. A lot of sand and rock and dead brush—and very little else." He glanced at Rosenfeld. "Don't you agree?"

"So?"

"So . . . With the international situation the way it is these days, the Air Force believes in being prepared. For anything." He lowered his voice, injecting just the right amount of confidentiality into it. "We're conducting a survival training exercise," he said. "Desert survival. What better place to do it than here? Let me give you a little background information, Rosenfeld. Why we chose this place. Did you know it's the hottest and driest spot on earth during the summer? Ten degrees hotter than the hottest African or Middle Eastern desert? It is, you know. Ground temperatures up here can get so hot that your feet blister, right through your shoes! So you'd better wear boots. Like you do . . ."

Paul was enjoying himself. He knew he was boring the young punk reporter to death. It was exactly what he had in mind. He went on.

"Why, some of the Rangers wear gloves. Gloves! Up here. You know why? Because they'd have no skin left on their hands if they didn't! It'd all be stuck to the handles, the steering wheels and ignitions of their vehicles! You saw that Charles Addams cartoon on the brochure they give you down at the Visitors Center? The one that shows a family driving into Death Valley and passing an open convertible full of skeletons on their way out? Well, it's only slightly exaggerated. You really have to know your way around the desert if you want to survive. *That's* why we chose this place." He looked closely at Rosenfeld. "We want our boys to be as fully prepared as possible. For *any* contingencies. Don't you agree?"

Sourly Rosenfeld looked at him, a speculative frown on his face.

Paul hoped he'd bought it. He knew exactly what he was doing. He'd given the bastard just enough of a story, hoping to satisfy his damned curiosity. He could see the headlines in his sheet: AIR FORCE TRAINS PILOTS FOR DESERT WARFARE . . . IS ARMED INTERVENTION IN THE MIDDLE EAST IMMINENT? Hell, it was no worse than the usual muck the yellow press dished up. And it would have no more credence. Most important, the XM-9—and Tom—would be safe.

If the bastard had bought it.

"As a matter of fact," he said conspiratorially, "if you really want the full story, I suggest you contact Colonel Howell. Colonel Jonathan Howell. At Edwards Air Force Base." He grinned to himself. Dammit! They deserved each other.

Rosenfeld was staring at him, a calculating but puzzled look in his eyes.

"I can probably arrange for an interview with the Colonel right now," Paul continued helpfully. "My sergeant has a radio in the scout." He raised his voice. "Sergeant Hays!" he shouted toward the distant scout. "Over here!"

"Yes, sir." The voice came from a few feet away. Both men started. Hays stepped from behind the shack. "I thought you might need me, sir," he said calmly.

"Yes. Fine." Paul caught himself. "Get the scout, Sergeant. Contact Base. Colonel Howell."

"Yes, sir." Hays started off toward the scout.

Rosenfeld glared after him. He turned away in disgust.

"Shit!" he spat. "Who the hell wants to interview a fucking colonel?"

He turned on his heel. He got into his car, slammed the door and took off in a cloud of ghost-town dust.

Paul gazed after the rapidly disappearing car. Perhaps he'd bought some time. For Tom. Enough?

The scout came barreling down the street toward him. Even before it came to a stop Hays called to him.

"Sir!" he shouted. "Get in!" His voice was urgent. "They've found a body!"

4

There were four vehicles pulled off the narrow dirt road that wound its way through the smoldering folds of the Black Mountains: Ward's scout, Stark's jeep, the Ranger "ambulance"—a converted station wagon carrying a stretcher—and a red 1969 Cougar.

Paul brought his scout to a stop behind them. He jumped out and joined the group of men standing at a prominent rock outcropping. Stark and Ward looked up as he approached. Both appeared grim and angry. On the ground, covered with a blanket, a still form lay stretched out. Paul bent down and lifted the blanket.

Someone had closed the young Ranger's eyes. Even so, his face had a disturbing expression of uncomprehending shock. Paul gazed at the young man. Nothing is as certain as death, he thought. Nothing as uncertain as when it will come. He turned to Ward.

"Knife wound in the upper abdomen," Ward said. "Upward thrust into the chest. He didn't have a chance."

Paul replaced the blanket. He felt bleak. A life had been lost in the search for Tom. He prayed it would be the only one.

He turned to Stark. "Any idea what happened here?"

Stark shook his head. He looked deeply troubled. "It's very puzzling," he said. "Someone exchanged pants with him. Emptied all his belongings from his pockets. His wallet is there, but his money is gone."

"You think the motive was robbery?" Paul frowned the question.

"I don't know," Stark said uncertainly. "I don't think so. Adams wore a rather expensive wrist watch. It's still on his arm." He looked off. "His pick-up was found quite a distance from here. Someone—the killer, I suppose—went to quite a bit of trouble to mislead us."

Paul was aware of strong relief—which at the same time made him uncomfortable. The killing of the young Ranger was a horrifying thing, but obviously it was not *Tom's* doing. "How was he found?" he asked.

Stark nodded toward the Cougar. "Couple found him. A Mr. and Mrs. Hastings. They're pretty shook up." He looked at Paul. "Captain," he said soberly, "I'll have to report this to the local law-enforcement agencies. You understand." Paul nodded. "I won't mention *your* purpose in being here," Stark went on, "unless it becomes absolutely necessary. No reason to. There's obviously no connection."

"Thank you," Paul said. Death Valley was entirely outside the jurisdiction of the Air Force. If the local sheriff or police or what-have-you became involved in the search for Tom, it would effectively negate their efforts to keep the XM-9 crash and Tom's plight from being played up big. He was grateful for Stark's understanding and support. He was lucky to have the man on his team. But of course the killing of Adams had to be investigated.

He walked over to the Cougar. An elderly couple sat in the front seats, both doors open. They looked hot, disheveled and distraught. On the back seat a brown mutt with a white ruff panted in the heat, his tongue dripping on the upholstery. Paul squatted down beside the car on the driver's side. The mutt's ears at once grew alert.

Paul addressed the man. "Mr. Hastings," he said, "I'm Captain Jarman, United States Air Force. Would you mind if I asked you a few questions?"

It was the woman who answered.

"It was Brendel that found him, poor soul," she said. "It was horrible. Absolutely horrible. We'd let him out to—well, to run a little." She reached back and scratched the dog's ears. He mustered up enough energy to wag his tail—just once.

"He ran over to that—that rock." She pointed to the outcropping. "And he started to bark and whine, carrying on something awful. And scratching at the stones. We called to him, but he wouldn't come. And he *always* minds. So Marvin got out and went over, and I went with him. And one of the rocks rolled away where Brendel was digging at it, and—and a hand fell out! Just plopped right out. It was—horrible. Just horrible. A dead hand. Just like that . . ."

Paul nodded. He knew that the grisly discovery had made the woman's trip. A story to be told and retold to anyone who'd listen back home. He resented it. He turned to the man.

"I wonder if I could have an address where you can be reached, Mr. Hastings," he said. "In case there should be any further questions."

"Of course," the woman said. "Marvin, give the officer your card." She looked at Paul, her face glowing with excitement. "Marvin's in hardware. We'll be glad to cooperate. Any way we can."

"Thank you," Paul said. "We appreciate it."

He walked back to his scout and Sergeant Hays. The matter of Adams was in Stark's hands. Finding Tom was his job.

He had a nagging feeling that the killing of the young Ranger had ramifications he was not aware of. But he was totally unable to put them together. It irritated him.

It bothered him that the killing was so elaborately done, so expertly concealed. It was too professional. No detail forgotten. And all for the money in Adams' wallet? The man couldn't have been carrying that much. Then—what? Why? Did it have something to do with Tom? The search for him was the only extraordinary happening taking place in Death Valley. If so— who could possibly be involved? And how?

Perhaps he felt the way he did because Adams had lost his life while he had been searching for Tom. That was probably it. But he did not feel satisfied. The answer was too glib.

Was he missing something? He dismissed it. He knew his priority consideration.

Find Tom.

5

The furnace-like heat lay over Death Valley like a suffocating blanket as Tom and Randi toiled across the burning sand.

Tired, spent, tortured by the scorching sun, Randi valiantly tried to keep up with her husband. Hot, grimy with dust and sweat, she ran a dry tongue over her cracked lips. She fixed her smarting eyes on Tom. Relentless, he plodded on. He seemed obsessed with the urge to keep moving—as if he felt himself in constant danger.

Hopelessly she let her sun-scalded eyes sweep the expanse of desert. She had the bleak feeling that she and Tom were the only beings left alive in the seething inferno.

She struggled to stay with him. Her mind clung to the thought that she was the only link to his survival. Somehow, somewhere she would be able to do something. If she stayed with him. She did not know what—but she had to believe she'd find a way. Perhaps she would be able to attract someone's attention, if the opportunity came again. Another thought pressed to enter her awareness: her fear of being left alone herself. To perish in the desert caldron. Alone . . . She refused to acknowledge it.

She slipped on the gravelly sand and steadied herself with one hand. She looked at her fingers. Her nails were broken and chipped from climbing among the rocks. She had always been proud of her nails. She'd always taken care of them. Her only fear when she played tennis had been breaking a nail. Not winning or losing. She'd won the Singles Cup in the last OWC Tennis Tournament, one of the big events in the Officers Wives Club at the Base. She belonged to the club, of course, although she'd never quite accepted the girls-together isolation of the other Air Force wives, nor the fact that as a Mrs. "Major" she "outranked" all the Mrs. "Lieutenants" and Mrs. "Captains" on the Base. No—not winning or losing, but breaking a nail . . .

And she'd joined the 500-mile Joggers Club at the Base— shooting for the 1,000-mile one—all in the last several months. Tom had called her an exercise nut, even while he did his own roadwork every morning togged out in a heavy sweatsuit. She'd felt he meant she substituted those strenuous activities for an active sex life. But he'd never said so. Practically the only sport she did not pursue was golf. Neither she nor Tom played. They simply didn't think it offered enough activity. . . .

She stared at her nails. Ruined. It did not seem important. It struck her that it wasn't—and she went on. . . .

Tom felt apprehensive and tense as he moved across the open desert. He had wanted to get away from the disturbing and noisy monsters that pursued him in the hills. But the open expanse of the desert floor made him uneasy. He eyed the distant mountains. They promised refuge. They were his goal. He never thought that the frightening sounds would be there as well. He was aware of his companion following him. He accepted it totally without question. It could not be otherwise.

His lips were parched and he worked his mouth and throat

in an impotent effort to swallow imaginary moisture as he squinted up at his blazing enemy in the sky. He had come to accept its presence—its disappearances and reappearances. He was still wary of it. His mind retained its memory of the terrifying attack in the night.

He stopped. For a moment he stood still, testing his surroundings. Randi caught up with him. He gave her a quick glance and began to run up a sandy incline. Dully Randi stared after him. Then she followed—drained with fatigue and thirst.

Tom crested the dune. Ahead of him lay a large pool of clear water looking inviting and refreshing. He ran for it.

He fell to his knees at the water's edge. He plunged his burning face into its coolness. Eagerly he gulped a deep draught. Immediately and violently he spat it out. His body shook as he gagged convulsively, racked with spasms of coughing.

He stopped, heaving air. He wiped his mouth. Stolidly he sat back on his haunches. Dully he stared at the water, his eyes uncomprehending.

Randi came hobbling up. She sank down beside her husband, cupped her hands together, dipped them greedily in the water and brought them to her face.

Tom looked up. Suddenly, savagely, he hit Randi's hands, making her spill the water before she could drink. Deeply shocked, she stared at him. He stood up. Roughly he grabbed her and hauled her to her feet, angrily pushing her away from the pool.

Wildly Randi tried to escape from his grip. She needed the water desperately. *Why? What was Tom doing to her?* Frantically she looked around. Her eyes fell upon a wooden sign erected near the pool.

And she froze.

Dismayed, she read the legend inscribed on it:

BADWATER

280 FEET BELOW SEA LEVEL
IN THIS AREA IS THE LOWEST LAND IN THE
WESTERN HEMISPHERE.

ON THE CLIFF IS A SIGN INDICATING SEA LEVEL.

THE WATER SEEN FROM THIS POINT CONTAINS
FIVE PER CENT SALTS.

THE SHRUBS NEAR THE WATER ARE PICKLEWEED.

She looked at Tom, wonder on her face. He had tried to
save her from the salty water.

She looked at her still-wet hands.

Little beads of moisture were forming at her fingertips.

She wiped them on her blouse. . . .

Paul replaced the water bag, hanging it on its hook on the
side of the scout. He had been drinking only sparingly. He
was always amazed at how cool the water stayed even in the
most scorching heat simply from the evaporation through the
porous canvas. His hands were wet from the droplets that
formed on the bag and slowly trickled down the outside. He
wiped them across his hot forehead.

He walked back to Hays, who stood frowning over a map
spread out on the hood of the scout. It was the master map
with every location already searched checked off and all team
sectors, both Ranger and Air Force, marked. He looked up
as Ward and Wilson drove up in another scout. He went over
to talk to Ward. Wilson joined Hays.

"Hot enough for you, Sarge?" the airman asked. He wiped
his brow and tried to loosen his sweat-clinging shirt from his
skin. Hays, studying the map, merely grunted.

Wilson looked with interest at the map with its markings
and notations. He glanced at Hays.

"Say, Sarge," he drawled, "we been all over this godforsaken
place. Where're we at now?"

Hays put his finger on the map. "Right—there!"

Wilson leaned over to look. "Death Valley," he read. "Funeral Mountains. Coffin Canyon . . . Jeez!" He shuddered melo-
dramatically as he eyed the map.

Hays glanced at him. "Superstitious?"

"Naw," Wilson dead-panned. "Just don't go putting me on
no graveyard shift."

Hays groaned. Wilson unhooked his canteen cup from his belt. He filled it with water from the canvas bag. He drank long and deep. He shook the last drops from the cup out on the ground. The dry sand sucked them up immediately.

It was late afternoon when Paul and Hays arrived at the last rendezvous spot of the day for the teams in their sector. The desert shrubs were letting their shadows out after having kept them tucked in beneath them during the midday hours.

They were the first to arrive. There had been no signs of Tom and Randi; no reports from any other teams in the other sectors—nor from the search helicopters. And no word as yet from Beale on the results of the SR-71 overflight. It *must* have been carried out by now, Paul thought. He was itching with impatience. He was growing increasingly worried. Were Tom and Randi still alive?

Two more Air Force scouts joined them, one with Ward and Wilson, and two Ranger vehicles, a jeep driven by Ranger Gordon and a pick-up. The men all looked dejected and grim. Paul gathered them around him, leaving Hays and Wilson with their scouts and radios.

Paul looked gravely at the men. "We've still got a few hours of daylight," he said, desperately trying not to sound discouraged. "Here's what I plan to do." He started to unfold his master map.

The radio in Paul's scout sputtered. Hays acknowledged. He turned toward Paul.

"Beale, sir!" he called.

Paul hurried over. He snatched the receiver from Hays and listened intently. He turned to the others.

"That was Beale Photo Analysis," he shouted. "They picked them up! The choppers are already looking for them. As of 1640 hours they were headed for the Devil's Golf Course."

He jumped into the scout. Hays was already behind the wheel and the vehicle took off in a spurt of desert dust.

The others followed. . . .

Hays brought the scout to a halt on a dirt road that skirted the forbidding area known as the Devil's Golf Course.

Paul dismounted and walked to the edge of the vast expanse. For a moment he stood looking out over the nightmarish landscape that lay before him. There was nothing to be seen. No movement. Only a vast sweep of hard, fantastically contorted, razor-sharp salt-and-mud crags and crusted pinnacles up to two feet high. It was the sun-baked bottom of an ancient ocean left by the primeval convulsions of a changing world; a hellish area that stretched before him, seemingly to the far mountains.

The other vehicles arrived and the men gathered around Paul, silently staring in dismay over the incredible expanse.

A sudden faint sound insinuated itself upon the oppressive quiet around them. They all looked up. Far out over the salt flats a helicopter wheeled low over the craggy expanse in a tight circle.

Hays called from the scout. "Sir! They've spotted them!"

At once Paul ran for the scout. The others followed.

"They're crossing the salt flats," Hays called. He picked up the binoculars.

Paul came up to him. "Where?"

"Almost across." Hays handed the field glasses to Paul. "It's too far to see good."

Paul looked.

The radio sputtered.

"Armadillo One . . . Armadillo One . . . This is Skybird Four. . . . Come in. . . . Come in. . . ."

Paul grabbed the mike. "Go ahead, Skybird Four."

"Returning to base. Repeat. Returning to base," the voice came tinnily over the radio. "Low on fuel. . . . Can't land on those damned crags. They're sharp as spikes. . . . Got 'em spotted for you, Armadillo One. . . . Hope you get to them. Out."

"Roger, Skybird . . . Out."

Paul put the mike down. Again he scanned the distant salt flats with the binoculars. Suddenly he started.

"There they are!" he cried.

In his field glasses he watched the two ant-like figures in the far distance stumbling across the treacherous, knife-edged salt-and-mud ridges. The image glimmered in the heat rising into the heavy air like a portentous mirage.

"Sergeant!" Paul snapped. "Get the other choppers."

Hays was already making contact.

Ward turned to Paul. "Can we get to them?" he asked anxiously.

Paul shook his head. "Not much of a chance. From here." He looked at the near-impassable salt flats. "We sure as hell can't drive across. We'll have to go around. By the time we get there, they'll be God-knows-where in the mountains."

Dismally he watched the helicopter flying off in the far distance. "And we've got no search teams over there," he added.

Wilson had gone down to the edge of the rugged salt-and-mud flats.

"Sir!" he called. "There's a path here! Across the flats! I can head them off!"

He ran for the nearest vehicle. It was Ranger Gordon's jeep. He jumped in, and, spurting gravel, he raced toward the salt flats.

Gordon shouted after him. "Hey! Wait! It's dangerous! It only goes a little way!"

"Wilson!" Paul shouted. "Wilson! *Come back!*"

But the words were drowned out by the roar of the jeep in low gear careening down the narrow, rugged path.

Aghast, the men watched the jeep bounce along the rocky, pot-holed trail, perilously close past the knife-sharp, distorted salt-and-mud formations. It was obvious that Wilson was having trouble keeping the vehicle under control; it lurched and bucked, skimming past the wicked spikes.

Wilson was hanging on to the wheel with a vise-like grip. It took all his strength to keep it from spinning out of control. He was sweating—the sweat of fear rather than heat. He regretted his hasty action. It had seemed the perfect thing to do. He could have reached the two fugitives before anyone else. Followed them. He wanted to stop his headlong rush—but now that he'd started, he couldn't chicken out.

The path narrowed. The jagged crags raced by, inches from his tires. Steel-hard salt-and-mud rocks littered the trail, making the going rougher and rougher and increasingly treacherous.

Violently he bounced in his seat. It seemed to him he'd been pitching over the bumpy path for an eternity. He knew it had been only seconds.

Ahead of him the trail made a sharp turn—the jagged spikes closed in across his view.

He took his foot from the accelerator and shifted it to the brake to slow down.

Suddenly he screamed. But the sound was knocked from his throat by the jarring impact as the jeep slammed into the misshapen crags.

The trail did not turn.

It ceased to exist.

Wilson was thrown from his seat. Its brake released, the jeep leaped forward out over the knife-edged crags. It bucked violently.

Wilson was hurled from the vehicle. His foot was caught and wedged between the seat and the metal skirt. In the split second before he hit the crags, he knew. He hung out over the side of the bucking jeep, dragged and raked across the razor-sharp salt-and-mud spikes baked steel-hard by the sun.

Almost at once the lancet peaks sliced into the heavy-duty tires, cutting them to ribbons. The four explosive blow-outs rang out as one. The vehicle's momentum carried it, caroming crazily, some twenty feet into the monstrous rock-salt mass.

Wedged among the spikes, it stalled—nose tilted up grotesquely, one wheel spinning, the mutilated rubber slapping a buckled fender.

Paul was the first to reach the mangled jeep. Ashen-faced, he stared at the grisly sight that met his eyes.

Wilson lay on the jagged salt crags, stretched out full length from the vehicle, his arms flung above his head, one foot wedged tightly at the driver's seat, his leg bent at an unnatural angle. His arms and face were horribly lacerated by the sharp spikes and still oozing blood—one hand impaled on a stiletto-pointed spur. Bunched around his shoulders, pushed upward as he was raked across the rock peaks, his shirt—soggy with blood—looked strangely bloated.

Paul swallowed. Hard. He stared at Wilson's exposed chest.

The bone of the ribs gleamed pallidly through the blood and the gashed and torn flesh. It was not just the boy's shirt bunched up high on his body. It was his skin—slashed and flayed from him as he was dragged along the path of death.

Ward came up to stand beside Paul. The two men did not look at one another. In silence Ward bent down to the maimed young man. Slowly he straightened up. There was no need for words.

Paul forced himself to look away. Without seeing, he gazed upon the men huddled together in shaken silence. His eyes met those of Sergeant Hays. The man's face was sickly gray.

Paul made his way slowly back toward the ill-fated trail. The path across the crusted salt ridges bespoke the violence of the plunge; crushed and broken spikes and pinnacles, chunks of mud-and-salt rocks marked the path of the runaway jeep. And closely paralleling it a gruesome trail of blood, bits of clothing and gore.

He stopped. He looked closer at the terrible trail. He bent down and picked up a small notebook lying hidden in the gory crags.

He turned it over in his hands. It was a cheap little date book, the kind that was available in any PX.

But it was torn and bloody.

He opened it. On the flyleaf a name had been hand-printed. He read it:

Wilson, Norbert A1C
U.S.A.F.
064 - 12 - 7313

For a moment he stood staring at it, a slight frown on his face.

Then he put it in his pocket.

Resolutely he stalked toward his scout.

The search operation through Death Valley had exacted its second life. . . .

6

The tortuous ordeal of the salt-and-mud flats had been left behind—but not the injuries and exhaustion it had inflicted. As she slowly and painfully followed her husband up into the foothills, Randi glanced down at her boots.

All of a sudden she felt an overwhelming gratitude toward them. They had saved her life! They were her friends. Old friends with whom she had shared many a hiking trip. And now she owed them her survival. She loved them. . . . Her fatigue-hazed mind allowed itself its euphorious extravagances of emotion.

Her thoughts grew bleak again. She stared dully at the boots as she agonizingly placed one before the other . . . one before the other. Reality returned.

They were badly scratched and cut by the sharp salt crags, and her feet were tender and sore from walking across the treacherous, uneven surface. On one knee a tear through her slacks exposed a blood-caked cut, suffered when she had brushed against a razor spike, and her right hand was gashed when she'd tripped and steadied herself on a spiny pinnacle to keep from falling. She had licked it clean.

Every step was agony for her.

But the worst agony was her thirst.

It burned in her. It robbed her of her strength. It seared her lips, her mouth, her throat—and parched her swollen tongue.

Had it not been for the deep blue-gray shadows cast by the late afternoon sun, she knew she could not have gone on.

Through sun-scorched eyes she peered at her husband laboriously making his way up into the craggy hills a little ahead of her. She knew he was as exhausted and thirst-ridden as she. She knew his fears were driving him on.

Perhaps to destruction.

And she knew she had no way of allaying those fears.

She twisted her foot on a loose rock and fell to one knee.

Suddenly she had no more energy. No more will. She let herself collapse. She could go on no more. No more . . .

Through a haze of utter fatigue she saw Tom stop and turn toward her as she lay on the ground. For a moment he stood gazing back at her. He seemed confused, hesitant. Unconsciously he touched the spot high on his head where the dried, caked blood formed a blackish cap. Slowly he walked back down to her. He grabbed her by the arms and raised her to her feet. She had no strength or will to resist. He urged her to go on, pushing her gently.

Spent, battered, without a will of her own, she walked on.

They crawled around a rock outcropping and came upon a little hollow in the mountainside. Suddenly Tom stiffened. He let go of Randi and half ran, half stumbled toward the cliffside across the hollow.

Out from the rock wall the water from a little spring, not much more than a trickle, ran down the stone to a small pool. It flowed a few feet, glistening in the last rays of the sun, running in a narrow stream to disappear into the ground.

Tom fell to his knees beside the little waterhole. He stared at the water. He put his hand into it and licked his fingers. He fell prostrate on the ground and buried his face in the water, drinking greedily.

Randi crawled up to him and he made room for her. Together they quenched their thirst.

Randi leaned back against the rocks and rested. She let every aching muscle relax. She was bone tired, but the cool water had refreshed her and restored some of her strength. She regarded her husband. The water had rinsed away the grime from his stubbled face and soothed his dehydrated lips. He, too, looked refreshed.

He returned her gaze. Then, abruptly, he broke off the eye contact and shifted to a spot from which he could look out over the salt flats below. He sat with his back to Randi, watching in wary silence, making sure the monsters had not followed.

Randi still felt hot. Her shirt was soaked with perspiration and clung uncomfortably to her skin. She pulled a handkerchief from her pocket, dipped it in the water and wiped her burning face. It felt good. The quickly evaporating wetness cooled her.

She glanced toward Tom, silently intent upon the flatland below. She unbuttoned her shirt and ran the cool, moist cloth around her sweat-sticky neck and shoulders.

She opened the shirt all the way and began to give herself a bracing sponge bath. She luxuriated. She could not remember anything at any time being as satisfying.

Again she glanced toward Tom. He was sitting on his haunches, watching her raptly. He reached a dirty hand to the buckshot wound on his shoulder and scratched it. He winced.

Randi observed the gesture with concern. The wound was getting infected, and Tom was making it worse. She dipped her handkerchief in the water and held it out to him.

"Here, Tom," she said, knowing he would not understand her words. "It'll feel good."

Deliberately she wiped her own shoulder with the wet cloth and again held it out to Tom.

"It'll feel good, Tom," she insisted gently. "Please . . ."

He watched her intently, but he did not move.

Her eyes searched his, but found no comprehension, no response. Tears welled—and smarted. Tom . . . Her thoughts rambled, confused. Tom. He was a man—and he was a wounded, troubled creature. He was vulnerable—and he was her husband.

It suddenly overwhelmed her. He had been all those things. All along.

But she had felt only her own wound. . . .

She crawled over to him.

"Here, Tom," she said softly. "Let me. Let me help. . . . It'll feel—good. Cool . . ."

She reached her hand toward his shoulder. He pulled away, his eyes never leaving her.

"Now, Tom," she said, gently reproving. "You know I won't hurt you. I didn't before. . . . Sit still, now. It'll be all right. . . ."

Again she reached for him.

He sat still. Wholly alert—but he let her touch him. Carefully she pulled the torn cloth of his suit aside. The injury beneath was still covered with the handkerchief she had placed there—stuck to the moist wound. Gently she peeled it away. He twitched, but did not move from her. The wound beneath the cloth was viscid, the raw edges angry red with irritation.

Gently she sponged it with the wet handkerchief.

"There," she murmured reassuringly. "Doesn't that feel better?" She leaned away from him, her open shirt falling from her shoulder. She rinsed the cloth in the little stream, turned back and began to sponge his sunburned neck and chest.

Tom was intent on her. Her caress felt cool and good. He liked it. He was fascinated with this being who made him feel good. He reached out his own hand—and touched one of her breasts visible through the open shirt.

With a startled little cry Randi drew back. Tom followed. The firm softness that met his hand excited him. He pressed his hand against it. He moved with her, both hands seeking the pleasure touch of her soft skin.

In growing alarm Randi tried to pull away from him. "No, Tom . . . No!" she whispered. "Please . . . Don't. . . . Don't. . . ."

He was not aware of her words. A new, unknown feeling swelled in him. Urgent. Demanding. Something was happening to him. Something he did not understand. Something that could not be denied. It enveloped him. He could think of nothing else. His hands grew totally insistent. It was no longer enough to feel, to experience the softness with his hands alone. His whole body strained to meet and enfold this other being, whose feel and smell excited and stimulated him.

Badly frightened, Randi shrank away from him, pleading with him—knowing she would not be understood.

"Please . . . Tom . . . Don't. Oh, God—don't. . . . Don't!"

Even the sound of her voice agitated him. His demanding hands tore at her open shirt, ripping it from her. Suddenly he pulled her to him and buried his face in the softness of her breasts. He breathed the woman scent of her. His open mouth tasted the moisture on her skin. It was like his own, like the bad water—but it intoxicated him.

They toppled to the ground. Tom was oblivious to anything but his needs, the fiery urge that possessed him. The impassioned desire to merge with the female being. He pressed himself down on her. He tore at her clothing—and his own. He raged against their obstruction. He felt a swelling of urgent pleasure and fought to free it, to fulfill it. A growing, droning sound surged in his ears.

The hook on Randi's pants snapped apart—the cloth ripped. Terrified, struggling under his urgent weight, she cried in bitter anguish: "Tom! . . . *No!* . . . Not like this . . . Oh, dear God! Not—like—this . . ."

Her cries beat against his ears, obliterating the steady drone—imflaming him even further. He arched against her, craving release.

The shock of a sudden, thundering roar slammed against them. A blast of unbridled force beat down on them as a terrifying demon shot over the mountain ridge and hurtled across the hollow only a few feet above them.

Instantly Tom reacted. Savagely he grabbed Randi and pulled her with him down among the rocks in the shadows close to the cliff wall. Terror and fury, vying for dominance, blazed hot in his eyes as he watched the fearful menace growl across the sky.

The helicopter slowly circled the craggy mountains, its rattling whirr reverberating among the barren rocks. Gradually it disappeared in the distance.

Tom searched the sky. His burning, broiling enemy above was not to be seen. But there were other enemies that came from the sky. He knew that now. He had seen and heard them before out in the open. Enemies even more frightening than the monsters that rumbled in pursuit on the ground.

Randi huddled against the rocks. She was deeply shaken. She gathered her clothing around her, fastening and tying the torn cloth together as best she could.

Wide-eyed, she stared at her husband as realization flooded her.

She had been aroused—as she had not been for such a long, long time. . . .

Tom was uneasy. He did not know if the monsters would come at him from below or from the sky. The little hollow with the waterhole was no place of safety. He must leave it.

He got up, cast a last, long glance toward the disappearing enemy, pulled Randi to her feet, and together they began to climb farther up into the desert mountains. . . .

It was dusk when Tom and Randi reached a little valley hidden in the mountains. None of their pursuers had been seen, either on the ground or in the air. They were quite high above the desert floor, and stunted trees grew scattered among the brush—scrub pine, Rocky Mountain maple, water birch.

Below, at the bottom of the valley, along a narrow, obviously seldom-used dirt road, stood a row of large, curious, cone-shaped stone structures—ten of them—looking like giant, rocky beehives. Randi recognized them from a picture on the wall in Stark's office. They were abandoned charcoal kilns from by-gone mining days, standing lifeless and deserted in the wilderness, robbed of their purpose.

Worn and haggard, every step a painful exertion, they made their way down the incline toward the kilns below.

They were climbing down around a rock formation on the hillside, its base covered with brush and scrub trees. Tom was passing close by a bush when suddenly a big black bird burst from the stunted branches and flew off, emitting a raucous croak of protest.

Tom started. Instinctively he crouched in an attitude of defense.

Randi followed the bird's flight to a rocky perch some distance away, where it sat scolding stridently. A raven? she thought. The bird of ill-omen . . . *Take heed that when a raven cries, misfortune soon it signifies.* . . . The old saw ran through her tired mind. It wasn't quite right. The remembered quotation. She prayed its prophecy would be even less so. But she felt chilled.

Tom watched the bird. Instinct told him it presented no danger to him, and his startled fright was replaced by curiosity. He looked at the bush from which the raven had flown. He parted the branches. In a sandy pocket on the cliff behind it a crude nest had been built. In it lay five good-sized eggs. He reached in, tore the nest loose and worked it out through the branches.

He picked up one of the eggs and examined it. He pressed on it—and it broke in his hand. The yolk and white ran out over his fingers along with a veined red spot. He sniffed it and began to lick the broken egg off his hand.

He put the nest on the ground and squatted down beside it. He picked up another egg, crushed it in his hand and began to lick it off.

Randi had joined him. She watched him eating the egg. She was suddenly aware of her own hunger pangs. She reached for one of the eggs.

Instantly Tom stopped eating. He sat stock still, watching her warily, stiffly.

Carefully she picked up one of the remaining eggs, her eyes firmly on Tom. She knew she, too, must have nourishment.

The muscles on Tom's face tensed—but he let her take the egg. Abruptly he returned to licking his fingers.

Randi broke a small twig from the bush. With it she poked a hole in each end of the egg. For a moment she sat looking at it in indecision. She had a flash vision of her husband eating the bloody lizard. She swallowed. Then she put the egg to her lips and sucked out the nourishment.

A sudden thought chilled her. She cast a quick glance toward the scolding raven. *She* was being robbed of *her* young—before they had a chance to come into the world. . . .

She gagged. With a conscious effort she willed herself to banish the thought. It was like trying *not* to think of a purple rhinoceros in the kitchen sink once someone had asked you not to do so.

Resolutely she swallowed. She *had* to. Her life—perhaps Tom's—depended on her preserving her strength.

Tom was licking yet another egg from his fingers. There was one more left in the nest.

She took it.

The kiln towered over them. At least thirty feet high, its massive, rough walls made of fitted stone were two feet thick.

It was quite dark inside. High on the back wall, facing the slope they had just come down, was a halfmoon-shaped opening. The gray light that spilled in through the six-foot-tall arched doorway revealed a few scorched timbers leaning against the far wall below the vent opening. It was a gloomy place, but a place that afforded refuge from the prying eyes of the whirling monsters from the sky.

They sank down on the sand and charcoal ashes that formed the floor. Randi leaned back against the hard wall. She watched her husband.

He investigated the whole rock kiln interior carefully. He sought out a spot close to her. He lay down and shifted around until he was comfortable. He pulled his knees up—and without a glance at her he fell asleep.

Randi closed her eyes. She was too fatigued to sleep. She sat quietly, resting against the stone.

When I close my eyes, she thought, the world still exists in my memory. What exists in Tom's?

Stray thoughts spun through her mind numbed with exhaustion. Tom was asleep. She could leave. Escape. He could not stop her. She could get help. And return . . . Would he be there? If she *could* find someone? Perhaps a camper? If he woke and went on without her, would he die? Before he could be found? . . . Had she enough strength left to venture out on her own? In the night? To look for help? To return? . . . It did not occur to her that she could simply try to save herself. . . . What should she do? What was best? She hadn't the strength to come to a decision.

She stayed. . . .

She did not know if she had dozed off, but something had alerted her. She opened her eyes wide. The kiln was almost totally dark. Only a faint bluish light seeped in to lie across the black floor and stab at the shadows under the timbers.

And she heard it.

A moan.

Her eyes sought and found Tom. Fitfully he tossed in his sleep, a small moaning sound escaping him. Suddenly he let out a little cry of anguish. He rolled over as if to escape some nightmare peril. His arm fell across Randi's thighs and his head came to rest in her lap.

She stiffened. She sat utterly still.

Then—slowly—she relaxed. She looked down at her sleeping husband, and with infinite tenderness she began to stroke his hair, consummately aware of the blood-caked wound high on the crown of his head.

Two large tears glistened in her eyes. Almost inaudibly she whispered:

"Please . . . Let them find us soon. . . . Someone . . ."

She sobbed; a small forlorn sound.

"Anyone . . ."

7

Colonel Gerhardt Scharff had an unconscious habit he had never been able to break. He doodled. Especially when under stress. In fact, special arrangements had had to be made to treat all paper scraps and trash from his office as highly classified material, to be burned under strict security supervision.

The doodle he at the moment was scribbling on the back of an envelope seemed to be a misshapen rocket or guided missile. Sitting at his desk, holding the telephone receiver to his ear, his face glistened with the sweat of acute discomfort. It was obvious from his obsequious tone of voice that there was a superior on the other end of the line. It was equally obvious that Scharff was not getting the better of the conversation.

"Yes, Comrade Minister," he said subserviently, "I—I fully understand. Fully. I—"

He stopped. He listened. He began to color, starting from the neck above his collar and slowly reaching the hairline.

"Yes. Of course I shall personally guarantee that the order is carried out." He licked his lips nervously. "But I should like respectfully to point out—"

There was a sudden click as the phone was disconnected. For a moment Scharff sat glowering at the dead instrument in his hand—even his doodle forgotten. Then he jiggled the cradle on the phone.

"Richter," he barked, "I want Blücher, OV III. In my office. At once!"

He slammed the receiver down. He stared at his doodle. He picked up the pencil and began to add angry black billows of smoke to the misshapen rocket.

He swore under his breath. *Verflucht!* In anger he pressed down on the black pencil. The point broke—just as there was a knock on the door.

"Herein!" he rasped.

The man who stepped into the room looked acutely apprehensive. He was in civilian clothes.

"Major Blücher," he said. *"Zu Befehl."* He stood stiffly before Scharff's desk.

The Colonel glared angrily at him. He did not put him at ease.

"Blücher," he said. He made the name sound like an insult. "The Minister and I are both highly dissatisfied with your performance." His eyes bored into the man before him. "With you. And your men."

"The California mission is highly unusual," Blücher demurred. He mustered his courage. "It probably should never have been attempted, *Herr Oberst.*"

Scharff glared at him. Damn the *Scheisskerl!* The man *knew* it had been his, Gerhardt Scharff's, decision to proceed. Hah! He would not be forgotten, *der Herr Major Blücher*, when heads were selected to roll!

Blücher went on. "It has been extremely difficult, as you may imagine. Extremely—delicate."

"Delicate!" Scharff exploded. He rose in anger. "The devil with it! The matter has been handled with stupidity. Stupidity, you hear? Blunders! Already your agents have been exposed to the risk of being blown. *Despite* my direct orders for strict secrecy. Utmost caution!"

"Their covers remain intact, Comrade," Blücher said tightly.

"As of your last report," Scharff countered acidly.

"As of my last report—*Herr Oberst.*"

Scharff glared at the man. He was building himself into a rage.

"*Verflucht nochmal!*" he shouted at him. "I demand results! Immediate results! *Verstanden?* Understood? The Minister is holding *me* personally responsible for the successful completion of this stinking affair." He took a deep breath of outrage. "*Me!* You understand? And *I* will hold *you* responsible. Totally responsible. Is *that* understood?"

Tight-lipped, Blücher nodded.

"You have failed in everything," Scharff lashed out at him. "Why has the pilot not been eliminated? Answer me. Why?"

"My original instructions, Comrade," Blücher said testily, "from you yourself, were to avoid raising undue suspicion. To make certain the—elimination looked like an accident—or to dispose of the body without the risk of discovery."

"To hell with instructions!" Scharff bellowed. He slammed his fist down on the doodle on his desk. "Eliminate him! Now! However it has to be done."

Flat-eyed, Blücher looked at his angry superior. Flat-voiced, he said: "He is—with the woman."

Scharff sat down. For a moment he fixed Blücher with a cold stare. He brought himself under control—back to his oily calm, so much more menacing than his rage. When he spoke, his voice was arctic.

"Then you will have to kill them both, will you not, my dear Major Blücher?"

DAY FIVE

1

Hayden slammed the receiver back on the hook—a little harder than he'd intended. For a moment he stood glowering at the telephone. Shit! L.A. control was losing his cool. What the hell! Did he expect him to step out of the damned phone booth in blue tights with a fucking S on his chest?

Angrily he pulled the door open and left the booth. He stalked toward his buggy parked nearby in the ranch area. His mind analyzed the situation.

The mission was turning into a God-damned frostbite operation, he thought with disgust. In the God-damned heat of the desert, yet. He'd heard about that kind of fucked-up case. Whispered about back at the training center at Eberswalde. Operations that somehow got all screwed up—and began "cooling" their operatives. Like in a case of frostbite. First the least important ones went—the fingers, toes and ears. Then the more significant ones, the field controls, the hands and feet—and the essential limbs, until finally the head of the whole fucking mess succumbed. He had no illusions. If a frostbite operation was in the making, they'd give *him* the finger.

He'd seen it coming, dammit. The constant changes in instructions. Getting more and more desperate. And now control had used the phrase "at any cost." Shit! He knew damned well what that meant. He had become expendable.

Should he ankle it? Defect? *Could* he?

Perhaps. But not for long. He had no desire to be "umbrella-jabbed." Like those Bulgarian turncoats a year or so ago. Those defectors who had broadcast attacks on the Communist regimes over Radio Free Europe, over the BBC and the West German station, Deutsche Welle. He wondered what KGB genius had come up with that little gem: injecting a tiny pellet of slow-acting but fatal poison with the jab of an umbrella tip or some other presumably harmless instrument. Sure was effective—both as a method of elimination that could be carried out on any up or down escalator, and as a deterrent against defection.

Those he knew about had been Bulgarians. Hell, it was too damned easy to read East German for Bulgarian. And the KGB didn't give a shit about literacy.

He reached his buggy, standing alone in the near-deserted parking area. He got in—and sat for a while. He was calming down. His best bet was to carry out his mission. Successfully. It was not impossible.

L.A. control had let another piece of information slip. His counterpart in Death Valley was on a flexible reporting schedule. He knew what that meant. The guy's cover was such that it would be impossible for him to report at specific times. It also meant that he was the primary operative on the mission. The head honcho. That made him, Jerry Hayden, the secondary one. He wondered idly who the man could be. A lot of "newcomers" had invaded the place in the last few days. New Rangers, Air Force people and, of course, a few tourists—no doubt in training for their expected hereafter. Could be anybody. As for him, Jerry Hayden, he'd better deliver or he'd be the first to turn black from frostbite while burning up in the fucking sun.

He started the buggy. It was beginning to run a little sluggish. He hoped the damned thing wouldn't conk out on him.

He looked at his watch. 0419 hours. It would be daylight soon. He had a couple of ideas how to come in out of the cold.

It was time he tried them out.

The monster was all around him—hard and shiny. He was surrounded by it. It was holding him tightly in its bowels. Its whining roar beat on his ears. And he was soaring in the sky toward the blinding disk that was his enemy. . . .

But he was not afraid. . . .

Other flying monsters were with him and they were not afraid either; but soon he was alone. Alone with the glaring ball in the sky. Suddenly it blazed up and rushed toward him. It let out a terrifying howl and hurtled down at him. His mind froze in fear. And the gleaming monster around him began to fall apart. A cacophony of grating, clanging, tearing sounds drowned out the monster's roar as chunks exploded from it and it disintegrated. He thrashed about in panic, held imprisoned. . . .

Suddenly he was alone. Floating in nothing. Silence all around him. And above him hovered a huge white egg. And the terror left him. . . .

The rocky ground came up to meet him and hit out at him in violent anger. The egg fell on him and enveloped him in white softness. It billowed around him. It covered him. It caressed him. It clung to him. It fastened itself to him and squeezed him until he could not breathe. And the terror returned. . . .

He tried to scream his torment—but no sound came from his throat. He tried to reach out, but he could not move. . . .

And he fell. Down. Down. Down into darkness—into something terrifying. Something unknown.

With a start and a sharp cry he woke up. He flailed his arms around him—but there was no enemy. Wild-eyed, snapping his head around, he stared at the walls of the kiln—dimly lit by the gray light of dawn. The huge white egg that had suffocated him was gone. The floor of the kiln was firm and whole. He knew it had not been so. He did not understand it. It made him uneasy.

He looked at Randi sitting against the wall, her legs drawn up, watching him with frightened eyes.

Had she brought his enemies upon him? He touched the wound on his head. It hurt. Perhaps she had made them go away.

Confused, disturbed by what had happened and unable to explain it, he crouched down on the sooty floor. He did not understand. Everything crowding in on him was frightening and not to be understood.

He sat quietly, watching the gray light outside slowly grow brighter. . . .

The kilns stood on the road below, silent, massive, looking eerily anachronistic in the early light.

He stood observing them in silence. They might be there,

he thought. If they had continued into the mountains in the direction they had been taking when they were last seen leaving the salt flats, this is where they might have ended up when darkness fell. If so, the kilns would have offered tempting shelter. One of them. Which one?

He'd have to investigate them all. One by one. He'd parked his vehicle far enough away so the noise of it would not have disturbed them if they were there.

He took a firmer grip on his gun and started down the hill, careful that his booted feet should make as little noise as possible.

Suddenly he froze.

In the distance, from the crest of the hill above, a shouted command floated down to him.

Damn! The search teams had arrived. He'd not been the only one to think.

He hesitated. Should he wait? See if they came out? He'd have a clean shot. He decided against it. He'd have no way of getting back to his vehicle and escaping. The sound of the shots would be heard for miles, and the searchers would be on him.

Cautiously, quietly, he ran back the way he'd come, squatted down—hidden from view by the brush and scrub trees. . . .

Tom crouched on the floor of the kiln, tense and alert. He, too, had heard the distant shout. He crept to the doorway and looked out. He hurried back and shinnied up the blackened timbers under the vent. He peered out through the opening.

Cresting the hill high above, he could make out several figures searching among the shrubs as they moved down the slope, strung out in a long line.

The enemies had come back.

He jumped down. He ran to Randi. Urgently he tugged at her. She got up. They turned to flee—and stopped.

The creature standing stiff-legged, threatening, in the doorway, blocking their way out, bared long yellow fangs and hissed in rage.

Involuntarily Randi let out a little cry. Tom pushed her out of the way. He faced the snarling cougar, never taking his eyes from it. His heart beat rapidly. Watchful and taut, he knew he had to fight the large beast. His only way of escape was barred by this new enemy. And he *had* to get out. His pursuers were closing in.

Petrified, Randi pressed against the wall, staring at the savage confrontation, convinced Tom would be torn to shreds. He could not know the big cat's strength. He could not know the danger that faced him.

Squarely, unflinchingly, Tom braved the growling mountain lion, its fetid breath hot in his face. He crouched down, coiled in readiness, his hands on the ground.

The big cat watched him, lynx-eyed, its menacing growl rumbling deep in its throat. Muscles rippling, it crouched—ears back, tail lashing.

Tom's whole being was intent upon the beast. He saw it tense to leap at him.

Suddenly he flung a handful of sand and ashes directly into the gaping maw and slit-pupiled eyes of the snarling cat. With a howl of surprise and rage the cougar jumped straight up into the air. It turned as it came down—and streaked away.

Instantly Tom grabbed Randi and they ran through the empty doorway, fleeing into the scrub trees. . . .

Paul made his way down the slope. To the right and to the left of him the others in his teams were searching among the shrubbery. He stopped. Below he could see the row of charcoal kilns Stark had told him about. He studied them. They would be just the place for Tom to hole up.

He did not know if his quarry had fled this way. The helicopters had not been able to spot them in the mountain rocks. He'd had little hope that they would. The shadows had been too dark; the hiding places too many.

He kept his eyes on the kilns as he made his way down the hillside. If Tom and Randi *were* there and were flushed, he'd spot them. He felt keyed up. His hunter's instinct told him he was close. The egg fragments had encouraged him. At least they were alive. . . .

Hidden by the shrubs and trees, Tom and Randi climbed over the summit of the far ridge. Below them lay a large, abandoned mine area. The hills surrounding it were pitted with adits and shaft holes. Several big pyramids of crushed ore tailings dotted the tract, and old timbers from mine entrances, stopes and box sluices were scattered about. Rusty ore carts lay overturned in a heap. On the slope Tom and Randi were climbing down stood a huge wooden ore ramp so massive that even the ravages of time had made little inroad.

The hills cupping the old mine area were almost devoid of vegetation and looked barren and stripped. Tom headed for the ore ramp, and he and Randi climbed past the sturdy, hand-hewn supporting beams bearing the immense structure and resembling the powerful, age-browned skeleton legs of some prehistoric behemoth. At the top of the ramp they sank down to rest. . . .

Paul fingered the eggshell fragments in Ward's hand. "They've been here, all right," he said. He looked toward the row of charcoal kilns a short distance below them. "Must have slept in one of the kilns overnight." He looked at Ward with encouraged excitement. "They can't be too damned far away."

From the far right flank of the line of searchers Sergeant Hays called out.

"Captain!" His booming voice carried through the stillness of the morning. "Captain Jarman! Over here!"

Paul and Ward both looked up. They began to run toward the big Sergeant.

Hays was standing on a narrow, overgrown trail that snaked along the hillside. He looked up as Paul and Ward joined him. He pointed to the ground. "Look, sir," he said.

Paul knelt down. On the ground was a small spot that glistened darkly. He touched it. He tested the substance with his fingers.

"It's oil, all right," Hays confirmed.

Paul nodded. "Someone's been parked here," he said. He glanced toward the kilns in the distance. "Within sight but not within earshot of the kilns down there."

"And it had to have been during the night," Hays added, "or early this morning. Or the sun would've dried out the spot."

Thoughtfully Paul felt the viscous oil on his fingers. "None of our vehicles," he said. "And this is our sector. And none of the others would've been in here or they'd have notified us." He turned to Hays. "Sergeant, signal the vehicles to pick us up here."

"Yes, sir." Hays took a Very flare pistol from his belt and fired one flare straight up. It soared high above the hills. . . .

Neither Tom nor Randi saw the flare that arched into the sky in the distance behind them. Tom was curled up in the shadow of the big ore ramp, resting. He licked the cuts on his hands, sustained while they were crossing the lacerating salt flats.

Randi watched him, desperate. The grueling ordeal was taking a heavy toll. Both she and Tom were badly dehydrated and deeply exhausted.

She tried to rally her fatigue-numbed mind. There had to be *something* she could do. Paul and his search teams could not be far behind them. She realized they had been seen. And they had left a trail.

A trail . . .

Mentally she shook herself. If only she could *think*. A trail . . .

Furtively she glanced at Tom. He would not know. She bent down. With small stones she spelled out TOM on the ground and an arrow pointing in the direction of the mine adits in the rocks.

She looked at her husband, torn by conflicting emotions. She felt guilty for betraying him, for violating his growing trust in her. Yet she knew that her betrayal was the only way to save him. To save them both. She knew with dreadful certainty that if she and Tom were not "caught" soon, they would die.

Suddenly Tom sat up in alarm. From far away the sound of laboring motors penetrated the quiet.

The relentless monsters were upon them again.

Like a big cat, Tom scampered up on the ore ramp. Warily he crouched down. He watched and waited.

Presently a line of vehicles, led by Paul's scout, rumbled into the mining compound below, rounding a huge pile of ore tailings. Scouts and Ranger vehicles drew up and came to a halt near some old, tumbledown shacks.

Quickly Tom scurried back down the ramp. He grabbed Randi and pulled her with him as he ran toward the mine excavations in the rocks nearby.

Randi threw a glance toward her pebble message. Please, God, she thought, let them see it. Let them find us. . . .

She and Tom were loping along a narrow path winding along the steep hillside, hidden from view from below. Abruptly Tom stopped. Randi gasped in shock. Mere inches before them gaped a tremendous hole. She stared down into it. The bottom was lost in the pitch blackness far below. It was an open mine shaft, a glory-hole, blasted straight down into the mountain rock. The trail ran around it along a narrow ledge to an abandoned mine tunnel and stopped a few feet farther on.

Dragging Randi behind him, Tom inched his way past the gaping shaft to the mine entrance. Half obstructed by debris and chunks of rock, the opening was just big enough for them to squeeze inside.

The tunnel beyond was a dead end. Barely ten feet in, an old cave-in sealed it off completely. Broken, rotted timbers lay wedged among the rocks. The remaining stretch was barely five feet to the ceiling; the floor was covered with rocks, and the support beams at the entrance were cracked and sagged askew.

Tom's eyes flew over the cramped refuge. At once he began to pile more rocks and stones on the debris already lying in the entrance, sealing the opening almost completely. Tensely he crouched inside. Waiting . . .

The men had left the vehicles at the old shacks and had begun to search the surrounding hillsides.

Hays and a Ranger were climbing up to the big ore ramp. They reached the top and Hays squinted at the sun, still low on the horizon but already hot. He walked along the ramp. He turned back to look for his companion.

The stones scattered by his boots as he walked on had spelled out TOM.

He did not know.

"There's nothing up here," the Ranger called to him. "I don't think they'll have come this way."

"There's an old mine entrance up there," Hays responded. "Let's check it out before we go back down. As long as we're here."

The Ranger shrugged. He joined Hays, and the two men started toward the adit.

They came to the deep glory-hole. Hays stared down into the black abyss. "Jeez!" he mumbled.

"Yeah," the Ranger said. "There're quite a few of these old shafts around here." He nodded at the hole. "That there hole's more than eighty feet deep. Straight down."

Hays carefully edged his way around the open shaft. The Ranger stayed behind. The ledge in front of the mine entrance was only wide enough for one.

Hays shook his head at the blocked mine entrance. "Looks pretty much caved in," he called. He tugged at the rocks.

"Watch your step, Sergeant," the Ranger cautioned. "One wrong move and you're gone. Permanent!"

Tom and Randi huddled against the tunnel wall behind the rock barricade. Tense and wary, Tom watched the light from outside as it stabbed through the cracks between the rocks, going from light to dark as the figure of Hays moved in front of the opening. One of the rocks tumbled away and pitched into the shaft outside. The sound of it hitting bottom did not reach him.

Randi raptly watched the figure in front of the mine entrance. Hope rose in her. The rescuers were just outside. They had been found.

It was over.

A few more rocks and they would be safe. She struggled to hold back the tears, her throat constricted. She could see the man outside trying to peer through the barrier into the gloom of the mine tunnel beyond. She was just about to call out to him when her eyes fell upon her husband.

And her cry died in her throat.

Tom was crouched on the tunnel floor facing the entrance. Tense and coiled to leap upon his hated enemy the instant he was exposed, he looked desperate and dangerous.

In bitter defeat Randi knew. She could not call out. She could in no way attract the attention of the men who would save them. The instant they were discovered Tom would throw himself at the man. And both he and his target would plunge to their death in the deep, open mine shaft just outside.

Another rock fell from the blocked opening, rolling out onto the tunnel floor.

Tom stiffened.

In another instant he would leap.

Urgently Randi touched him. He whirled on her. Quickly she clamped a hand over her own mouth. She reached out and placed her other hand over Tom's mouth. Her eyes, gazing at him over her hand, pleaded with him. Slowly she shook her head—and pulled him away from the opening.

Bewildered, Tom stared at her. He trembled with agitation and fear. His face, pale with desperation, loomed before her. She hardly dared breathe.

The voice of Sergeant Hays reached them. It sounded as if it were only inches away. Tom grew rigid under her hand.

"Must be quite a lot of holes like this one around," the Sergeant said to the Ranger. "How the hell are we ever going to find them if they're holed up in this kind of mess?"

Tom shook loose. He pushed Randi's hand from his mouth. In despair she knew she could hold him back no longer.

Another rock tumbled away.

Suddenly a distant voice rang out.

"Sergeant Hays!" Randi recognized Paul's voice. "Down here! On the double!"

Outside, Hays straightened up. "Okay, sir!" he shouted. "Coming!" He moved away from the opening.

Tom sat immobile, listening to the men withdraw. In silence he waited.

Randi felt desolate. It had been so close. But she'd had to stop Tom. Or he would surely have been killed. She suddenly realized what the men had talked about. If trapped, Tom *would* act in a way that might result in his own destruction. She shivered.

Quickly, carefully, Tom began to remove the rest of the rocks that obstructed the opening. He crept out. Randi started to follow. He pushed her back inside.

He moved to the edge of the ledge and looked down at the mining compound.

Paul had gathered all his men around him. He watched as Hays and the Ranger came running from the hillside. He was standing at a Ranger pick-up which had just driven up. He leaned into it and brought out a couple of flashlights.

"I want every one of these mine tunnels searched," he said to the men. He handed out the torches. "Use these. There are more in the pick-up." He looked at the men, his face earnest. "And remember. If you do find them, go easy. Don't rough him up, *whatever* happens." He paused for greater weight. "You could kill him."

He looked up as a jeep came driving into the area. It was Ranger Gordon. He dismounted and joined the group. He picked up a flashlight with the others and walked toward the old mine tunnels.

Hays joined him. "What happened to you?" he asked. "Coffee break?"

Gordon grinned. He nodded toward his vehicle. "Damned jeep overheated," he said. "Had to use my canteen water to cool it down. Took some time." He motioned toward the hills and the mine adits. "They holed up in there?"

Hays nodded. "Seems like it. We'll soon know."

On the ledge above, Tom crawled away. In his nostrils lingered the acrid stench of the fumes drifting up from the monsters below. He had come to hate it. He made his way back to the mine entrance and pulled Randi from it.

Together they inched around the glory-hole and skirted the big ore ramp.

Climbing down the rocky slope, they retraced their steps, doubling back the way they had come. . . .

2

For the first time in his life Colonel Gerhardt Scharff felt he'd painted himself into a corner, with no *Lehrlinge*—no apprentices—to put the blame on. Always before, whether serving the Third Reich or the D.D.R., if threatened with a mission failure he'd been able to come up with a scapegoat who— with a lesser or heavier amount of fabrication—was made to suffer the unpleasant consequences. This time he was unable to do so. This time the scapegoat had to be fat enough to satisfy both his own superiors and the KGB. And that tagged him, Gerhardt Scharff himself.

Again he mentally flipped through the other possibilities: The sleepers themselves, of course, or the L.A. control? Not nearly important enough. His aid, Richter? Too much would rub off on his, Scharff's, own skin. Blücher? While holding a responsible position, he was still not big enough. Besides— Scharff knew the man. He had undoubtedly worked up his own scapegoat scheme, one that most certainly would include one Colonel Gerhardt Scharff. Rejected. It still left *him* holding the shitty end of the stick.

He did not savor it.

And there was one more sizable problem.

Dr. Wilhelm Krebbs.

It was a problem of his own creation. The man knew too much. He was in possession of top-secret state information. Information given him by Scharff himself. Obviously the man had to be eliminated—before he could reveal his, Scharff's, indiscretion under interrogation during a subsequent investigation. But it did present a problem. The man could not be killed outright. Even in East Berlin the killing of a prominent scientist would raise questions. Questions he would rather not have to answer.

Yet he felt smug. It *was* a problem, but he strongly believed in turning problems around to work *for* you rather than *against* you. And he'd done just that with Krebbs. He had come up with a perfect safety valve, in case the Marcus affair should backfire—a contingency still far from certain, of course. . . . A perfect scheme.

It was time to set it in motion.

From his window in the State Security Building, Krebbs could see the slender, needle-like new TV tower, almost 400 meters tall. The bulbous polished-steel pod near the top as usual reflected the late-afternoon sun in a fiery cross. It was typical, he thought, that the Berliners should call the phenomenon "the Pope's Revenge."

It was his third day of detention in the room provided for him. He had been well treated, well fed—but he had not been allowed to leave nor to contact anyone. And there was a Vopo sentry on guard outside his door. He was getting increasingly apprehensive.

He started as there was a knock on the door.

"Herein!" he called.

The door opened, and Scharff entered. He looked grim—totally without his usual expansive charm.

"Krebbs," he said unceremoniously, "I want to have a talk with you."

"Of course." Krebbs indicated a chair. "Please sit down, Colonel."

Scharff did. Krebbs pulled a chair over to sit opposite him. With discomfort he noticed that his palms were sweaty. There was something disturbingly familiar and dreaded about the scene.

For a moment Scharff contemplated the scientist solemnly. "I shall be perfectly—perhaps brutally—frank with you, Dr. Krebbs," he said soberly. "The affair concerning your friend Marcus is not—eh, progressing as anticipated. It now seems doubtful that we shall be able to conclude it successfully."

Krebbs looked at him. He did not know what the Colonel was leading up to, but he was quite certain it would be something unpleasant. Or worse . . .

"Because of certain highly classified information I imparted to you in a spirit of cooperation," Scharff continued dispassionately, "you have become a liability to me, Krebbs. A—eh, danger." He pursed his lips thoughtfully. "My first inclination was to have you, eh—eliminated, of course. But—there are too many obstacles to such a simple solution."

Krebbs stared at the man, aghast.

Scharff smiled one of his cold, quick smiles at the scientist's obvious shock. It was an old trick of his. Shock a subject profoundly up front—then, when you backtrack, he's more willing to go along with whatever you want. "Therefore," he said, "I have decided on a different course of action. After all, you did not get involved in this matter entirely of your own volition. It should be considered, not so?"

"You can rely on my complete discretion, Colonel." Krebbs was aware that his voice was shaky. "What transpired shall remain entirely between us. You have my word."

"Of course, of course . . ." Scharff nodded. "However," he said, "the very nature of our—eh, arrangement here could become an embarrassment, should it become known."

Krebbs was about to protest.

Scharff stopped him. "There are too many others who are aware of the situation, Dr. Krebbs. It is not simply between you and me. And it would be an—eh, embarrassment to me that I cannot afford."

He leaned forward conspiratorially. "Instead," he said, automatically lowering his voice. "Instead, I have decided on a different way of—eh, getting rid of you!" He laughed, a quick little mirthless sound. "I have decided to make it possible for you to—to join your friend Professor Marcus abroad." He looked closely at the stunned scientist. "I am certain you will not mind. I do know of your past—eh, aspirations."

Krebbs stared at him. Somehow the promise frightened him even more than the threat.

"Join—Marcus?" he whispered.

Scharff grew coldly business-like. "Yes. This is what I have decided," he said. "You will be free to leave here as soon as we have finished our little talk. You will go home and you will continue to perform your usual tasks. To anyone who questions you, you will say you were on a short holiday. You will *not* try to leave Berlin. You will, needless to say, be under constant surveillance—and you would be prevented from doing so in any event. A—eh, prevention that would not be too pleasant. Are we in agreement so far, *Herr Doktor?*"

Mutely Krebbs nodded.

"Excellent. Now . . . Should we have need of your knowledge in connection with the Marcus device, we shall call on you. Nothing will have changed, in that case." He paused. He looked directly into the scientist's eyes. "But. Should the operation—eh, not be successful, you will be notified at once. You will then leave East Berlin and cross into West Berlin." He spread his hands. "There you will be on your own."

Unbelieving, Krebbs stared at the official. "West Berlin!" he exclaimed. "But—that is not possible. . . ."

Again Scharff flashed his switchcord smile. "Ah, but it is. Arrangements will be made for you to cross over at the Friedrichstrasse checkpoint."

"Checkpoint Charlie." Krebbs frowned. "But—that is open to foreigners only."

"Precisely. You will be given a—eh, temporary identity. As a Swiss national. You will be given a passport and the proper papers." He smiled thinly. "That will be no problem. For us. And you will be notified of the precise time to cross, and given exact instructions."

Krebbs sat staring at the State Security officer. His thoughts whirled. He had been totally unprepared for the turn of events.

"I need not impress upon you, Krebbs, that what has been said here stays between us," Scharff said impassively. "It is not that I put my trust in you, you must understand. That would indeed be foolhardy. But—you have no choice. Should you decide to go to the—eh, authorities with your story, it would be your word against mine. And *should* you be believed by virtue of revealing the confidential information you possess, *they* will—eh, eliminate you themselves."

He stood up. "And now, my dear *Herr Doktor* Krebbs," he said expansively, "get ready to go home!"

Shaken and uncertain, Krebbs watched Scharff leave. He went back to the window. For a moment he stood staring into space. The sun had extinguished the blazing cross on the tower globe. Dusk was falling over the city.

He tried to collect his thoughts. Not for a moment did he believe that Scharff was sincere in wanting to help him defect. He felt a leap in his chest. After so many years . . . Even the slim hope held out to him made his heart beat faster. So many years.

Ever since—Oberammergau . . .

He was bitter about it—but he blamed himself. He should have seen what was in store for the Communist-occupied part of the Fatherland. He should have left when he still had the chance—instead of one day waking up to the fact that he was a prisoner. Eighteen years ago. He still remembered looking in unbelieving horror at the ugly scar that suddenly ran across the face of his once beautiful city. A scar that was to be known as the Berlin Wall.

And still he had procrastinated, until the wall had become an insurmountable barrier.

For him.

He *had* often thought of joining Theo—but he had never found the courage to act. He had chuckled, in secret, with his friends over the *Witz*—the joke about the wall: What would you do if the barriers were suddenly removed? And the answer: Shin up the nearest tree. Why? To avoid getting trampled to death in the rush!

He had chuckled. But his heart had ached.

He knew that hundreds of men and women did manage to escape every year. Running the death strip—the *Todeslauf,* they called it. The Death Run . . . Digging tunnels or swimming icy waters in a hail of bullets; flying small planes; hijacking or crashing tank-like vehicles through the barriers; stuffed into converted gas tanks—or, as one family did, soaring across the hideous traps on a steel wire high in the air . . .

He also knew that most of the escape attempts were destined to be suicidal.

But he—he was too old to endure the exertion or perform the acrobatics necessary to flee to freedom. Too old to brave the alarm fence, the armed patrols, the minefields, the anti-

vehicle trench, the guard dogs, the trip wires and the auto-
matic-firing machine guns, the watchtowers—and the terrible
wall itself.

And now—after thirty-five years . . .

He suddenly drew in his breath. An idea had shot through
his mind. A preposterous, audacious idea. A way that he, Dr.
Wilhelm Krebbs, might turn the tables on the powerful State
Security Colonel and take advantage of the man's plot, whatever it was.

Perhaps he was no longer physically able to leap the wall.
But his mind was as agile as ever. . . .

Colonel Gerhardt Scharff felt pleased with himself. He
awarded his not inconsequential ingenuity with a glass of
brandy, savored in the privacy of his office.

He had devised a most clever solution to all his problems.

If the Marcus affair *should* go sour, it was, of course, imperative that he, Scharff, save face. And provide an acceptable
scapegoat.

It was childishly simple. And foolproof. He would let Krebbs
go now. That way, chances of his being connected with the
final part of the Marcus case, *should* it fail, would be minimized.
He would give the man his false papers—untraceable, of course.
He would let him get to the checkpoint unmolested. And he,
Scharff himself, would be there. On a routine inspection. He
would "discover" the defector—recognizing him from his prior
and still current investigation of the man when he became
suspicious of him and had him detained—and before Krebbs
could get across to the West, he'd kill him in a flagrant attempt
to defect! It would be simple to concoct some evidence connect-
ing the dead scientist with his friend in America. A connection
which might well have served to warn the U.S. military intelligence agencies. A perfect scapegoat—caught and eliminated
through the vigilance of a valuable security officer!

He savored his brandy. It was excellent.

So was his plan.

The brandy and his self-congratulatory exercise made him
feel almost mellow enough to put his latest confrontation with

his superior into perspective. Almost—but not quite. He still fumed inside at the supercilious attitude of the man, a pompous ass at best, lecturing him as if he were a minor bureaucratic minion on the fact that the D.D.R. government could not afford to create an international incident. That delicate negotiations were going on between the U.S.A. and the Russians. Negotiations that the U.S.S.R. wanted to conclude successfully. Negotiations that could in no way be disrupted—or wrecked—by Scharff's undertaking. The man had been insufferable. Even to the point of adding insult to injury by hinting at his own doubts that the *Unternehmen* should have been entered into at all! After he himself had given the go-ahead! The Minister quite obviously was setting up his own scapegoat.

And he, Scharff, was it.

So much more important that his own scheme was foolproof.

He was perfectly aware that there were holes in his presentation of his plan·to Krebbs. He did not care. Even if the scientist should get suspicious, there was nothing he could do but follow orders. And he was also perfectly aware that he was employing a cover-ass ploy. He always had. Always would. It was the only prudent procedure to follow.

He contemplated the half-full brandy snifter.

The Marcus mission was *still* far from *kaput*. There were still highly trained and dedicated agents on the case. The American pilot could still end up dead. If he could prove that *his* foresight, *his* actions, had set back the development of the Marcus device significantly, he could still come out smelling as sweet as a whorehouse customer.

Chances, he felt, were excellent that he would.

One way or another . . .

3

Stripped of past splendors, the gaunt brick skeletons of three- and four-story buildings stood silently brooding in the night as Tom and Randi slowly approached the mountain ghost town.

The invincible desert had won back its own and swallowed up the once great town of the lusty gold-bonanza days. Dead and deserted, the remaining ruins pointed huge, grotesque stone fingers reaching up from fists of rubble toward the night sky, where, high above, the moon still drenched the barren land with pale light.

Like some hollow-eyed desert beasts, the gutted walls stared down at the two exhausted creatures who sought refuge in their midst. It mattered not to Tom and Randi that once the imposing, silent stone-and-concrete ruins had formed a boisterous town proud of its name.

They crept down into the basement of a structure that looked like a classical ruin, standing forlornly under the stars. Among the rubble of decades they found a sheltered spot and sank down to rest.

A few withered weeds and shrubs grew among the ancient chunks of masonry. Tom ripped off some of the dry leaves. He sniffed them—and threw them away.

Leaden from fatigue, hunger and thirst, Randi gazed dully at her husband. Then she lowered her eyes. Hope was slowly dripping away. . . .

Tom got up and started to climb out across the wreckage littering their shelter. Tiredly, resignedly, Randi struggled to get up. Tom turned to her. He pushed her down. Again he moved away, stopping only to make certain she was staying.

Then he disappeared among the jagged stone shapes, leaving Randi behind, huddled miserably in the shadows of decay.

The strange, sustained sound came from a ramshackle hovel backed up against the rocky hillside just outside the ghost town and surrounded with heaps of old lumber and railroad ties, rusted drums and oil cans, a few pieces of broken furniture and other junk. It rose and fell and wailed in muted shrillness into the night.

Tom lay hidden in a clump of withered brush, listening. He cocked his head. The caterwauling sound frightened him. But not as much as the faint streaks of yellow light that seeped through a window hung with sacking and through the cracks in a crooked door.

He knew what danger that could mean.

But something else drew him inexorably to the place. A smell of food that drifted toward him from a bent pipe protruding from the roof of the shed.

Stealthily, overcoming his fear, he crept closer.

The tinny music blared lustily from the old wind-up phonograph, filled the cluttered little room with noise and washed over the ancient things that crowded it. The place was lit by a couple of kerosene lamps. On a pot-bellied stove a large stew pan of meat soup simmered, aromatic steam rising from it and drifting out through a vent in the ceiling. A massive wooden bunk heaped with crumpled blankets filled one end of the room; several crates and boxes served to hold a weird array of collected "art"—oddly gnarled, sun-bleached cactus skeletons and shrubbery trunks, curiously shaped rocks and a few yellowed coyote, bobcat and burro craniums.

Exuberantly keeping time with a big spoon, an old man sat at a crude table. Sparsely white-haired and white-bearded, clad in a faded red cotton shirt, patched trousers and broad suspenders, he would have looked decidedly anachronistic except where he was. His age could be between eighty and a hundred and eighty. It was impossible to tell.

At his feet an ancient dog, skinny and shaggy, lay fast asleep.

The old man—known to those who were aware of his existence at all as Op'ry Olaf, the crazy hermit—sang along with the raspy voice on the scratched old recording.

> "Nothung! Nothung! Conquering sword!
> What blow has served to break thee?"

Incongruously it was the Smithy Song from Wagner's opera *Siegfried*. Old Olaf was alternately either half a tone sharp or flat. But he enjoyed himself no less.

On the wall behind him was tacked up what was obviously one of his treasures: a faded and age-grimed poster from the New York Metropolitan Opera, dated March 10, 1926. A performance of *Siegfried*, conducted by Artur Bodanzky and with such illustrious bygone opera names as Friedrich Schorr and Mesdames Schumann-Heink and Larsen-Todsen among the long-forgotten cast, and marking the debut in the role of Siegfried of a new tenor named Lauritz Melchior.

The old phonograph started to run down. Not until it had almost stopped did Olaf notice. Annoyed, he got up.

"Dang-blasted contraption," he grumbled. "Never can trust them new-fangled gadgets."

He started to wind the handle. Suddenly there was a noise from outside. A can or metal object falling over. Olaf cocked an ear.

"Hear that, Siegfried?" He looked at the sleeping dog. The creature didn't stir.

"Siegfried!" Olaf shouted. *"Siegfried!"*

The dog showed no reaction whatsoever, only snored wheezily.

Olaf nudged him with his foot. "Get up!" he grumbled. The dog struggled to sit up. "You're getting as deaf as a doorpost, you old coyote."

Olaf rummaged up an old pan and broke some stale bread crusts into it. He kept up a steady conversation with the deaf dog.

"Mehitabel's out there. Come off her mountain to pay us a visit again. Smartest little ol' burro I ever knowed, and that's a true fact. Likes Wagner, too. . . . 'Ho, Ho! Ho, Ho! Ho, Hei!' " he bellowed.

He cackled. "Allus makes her come running, you bet."

He poured a little water over the bread. "Come on, Siegfried."

The dog didn't hear him.

"Siegfried!" The old man threw the spoon at the dog. Siegfried inspected it with mild interest—and struggled to his feet.

"Hell's bells, dog," Olaf complained. "Get that ol' bag o' bones rattling. You got nothin' else to do."

He started for the door.

The opening door sent a sudden shaft of yellow light spilling out into the darkness.

Tom was almost caught in it. Terrified, he leaped back into the deep shadows of the lean-to that protected the doorway, where a stack of rusty kerosene cans had been heaped. He pressed into the darkness.

Olaf put the pan of food on the ground outside the door. He peered out into the desert.

"Where's that critter at?" he asked of no one. "Where *is* that mangy mote?" He turned to the dog. "You see her, old boy?"

Siegfried nosed the pan of water-soaked bread crusts with obvious disinterest. He managed to wag his tail a couple of times. He sniffed the air tentatively—and slowly, stiff-legged, he ambled over toward the pile of kerosene cans.

Panic gripped Tom. He was trapped. Any moment he expected the roaring blast that came with the yellow light—and hurt. The only way out was directly toward the strange, incomprehensible creatures that always followed the monsters that pursued him.

The smaller one was almost upon him. He leaped from behind the cans, sending them tumbling with an ear-shattering clatter. He burst from his hiding place and lunged past the dumfounded Olaf into the darkness. Siegfried gave a startled yelp and fled, tail between his legs, into the shack.

Olaf stared into the blackness surrounding his hut. He scratched his beard.

"Jumping Jehosaphat!" he mumbled. "Did you see her hotfoot it outa here? Quicker'n hell could scorch a feather." He shook his head in wonder. "I never before seed that old donkey act like a dad-blasted jackass."

He went back into the shack, leaving the pan behind.

Swimming in it were the several crusts of water-soaked bread.

Tom slowed down. His heart pounded. He had escaped. But his enemies had been so close to him that he could smell the sour smell of them.

Something nagged at him. The frightening creatures that hunted him were like the one that was with him. The same— yet different. He could smell that one, too, but the smell pleased him and he was not afraid. He would flee from the enemy monsters, but he wanted the one with him to stay. He had come to think of them together. Fleeing together. Seeking safety together. Finding food and drink together . . .

He looked back toward the frightening place where he had almost been caught. The strange, compelling sound once again rang out from it.

He turned away and moved out into the night desert. He knew now. Where the strange, fearful creatures were to be found—so was food.

He would have to find others.

And be more careful . . .

JEROME McCABE

Born April 4, 1851
Died July 12, 1897

May he find more rest
in death than he found
in life.

The weathered inscription on the chipped tombstone meant little to most—Jerome had been gone a long time. To Tom, crouched warily behind it, it meant nothing. The stone, one of several markers in the old cemetery outside the ghost town, was merely another stone to hide behind while he watched a flat, nearly empty area in front of him. A row of the tall, slender plants he'd seen before stretched across the little plain to disappear into the darkness, but these had no tops of swaying leaves. Only long, thin lines strung between them.

At the foot of one of them stood the objects of his vigilance. Two squat shapes—one larger, the other smaller. He knew them for what they were. Monsters. At rest. In the larger one he could see faint yellow light shine behind square holes, and a short distance in front of it a pool of light glowed on the ground. He shifted his position uneasily.

There would be creatures there.

And food.

The camper trailer had a New Mexico plate, as did the '74 Chrysler hitched to it. They were the only vehicles in the out-of-the-way camping ground. The two aluminum-and-canvas folding chairs standing outside the door were red and green, and the embers of the dying campfire—prudently placed well away from the camper—glowed in the night. A short distance from the vehicles was a small cemented area with a low, squared-off, U-shaped stone wall around it. Inside stood half a dozen metal garbage cans with special, tightly fitting lids to keep the wild animals from foraging in the trash.

Furtively, silently, Tom crept up to the garbage-can enclosure, his eyes constantly flitting toward the quiet monsters nearby. The cans smelled of food. It excited him—and he salivated. He felt the cans. He groped them, frustrated because he could not find a way to get inside them. And he knew the food was there. He tugged at a handle. It would not give. He pulled at the screw-on lid. It would not budge.

He froze at a small, sharp sound from the larger monster. At once he crouched down among the cans, unwilling to leave his newfound source of food.

Suddenly a part of the large monster was thrown open and a shaft of light shot out from inside and reached a long finger toward him across the desert floor. Startled, he squeezed down into his hiding place, fear welling up in him, pressing in his throat.

From the light two creatures emerged. They looked dark and menacing to him, silhouetted by the light behind them. His eyes devoured them. One of them was a different one. Like the one who was with him. It carried a large brown lump in its arms. He watched them tensely. The creatures made noises at each other. The same kind of noises *his* creature made.

"I'll get the fire." One of them walked toward the pool of light on the ground.

"All right, dear."

"Watch your step over by the cans. There's a little ledge. Hard to see."

"I will."

The creature with the brown bulk in her arms was coming

straight at him. Terror rose in him. And rage. The creature was coming to take his food from him. The food *he* had found.

He threw a quick glance at the other creature not far away. It was kicking sand over the glowing pool of light. He whipped his eyes back to the approaching one, headed straight for him. And the food.

And fury swept away his terror.

He leaped from his hiding place. He stood defiant, trembling and menacing, before the woman, who stood frozen in shock. His eyes bloodshot and wild, his hair matted and blood-caked, his bristly face streaked with dirt, he looked wholly terrifying— and terrified. He drew his cracked lips back in a silent snarl.

The woman screamed. She dropped her bag of garbage and turned to flee in panic. She tripped and fell heavily to the ground.

Tom's attention was on the woman to the exclusion of all else. Desperate, intent only upon defending his food from the intruder, he growled deep in his throat as he slowly advanced on her. The woman stared up at the ferocious, unearthly apparition and whimpered in raw terror.

Like claws, Tom's hands came up before him. He was ready to pounce upon this enemy at his feet. He was wholly intent on his prey, oblivious to the man at the dying campfire.

Horrified, for a split second the man stared at the fearsome specter that threatened his wife. Then he was galvanized into action. He swooped down, grabbed a piece of firewood glowing in the embers and ran toward the brute, whirling it in the air. It burst into flame.

Tom was about to leap when suddenly the flaming firebrand was thrust at him, aimed straight at his face.

He howled in startled fear and jumped back. The blazing enemy was upon him! He could feel its scorching heat, and the blinding light seared his eyes. Lightning fast, memories surged through his mind . . . the blazing, broiling disk high above that burned his skin, come down to chase him in a thunder of sound and power; the blast of fire and smoke when he had fought the strident, tormenting creatures in the canyon; the sudden yellow light that roared and hurt, biting his flesh.

His enemies. Enemies of light and heat. Enemies he could not vanquish . . .

The man swung his fiery torch frantically back and forth before the terror-stricken Tom, screaming his rage at him. Sparks flew from the burning wood and bit Tom's face and hands. He stumbled back, retreating from the fiery enemy, staring at it in spellbound panic. He trampled on the garbage bag dropped by the woman and nearly lost his balance. The bag broke—and the smell of food reached him through his terror.

Unthinkingly, governed by an inborn need, never taking his eyes from the threatening creature whirling the dreaded firebrand at him, he scooped up the broken paper bag and fled into the protective darkness of the desert. . . .

Randi surveyed the feast spread out on the broken brown bag. Carrot tops with bits of vegetable still left on the greens; several pieces of melon rind, smelling sickly-sweet but with only the best part of the pulp scooped away; celery tops with many small stalks; a bread wrapper with a few stale slices of white bread; the empty tin of a canned ham, some of the fat still adhering to the inside; some wilted lettuce leaves; a couple of brown apple cores; and—best of all—a pile of fried chicken bones with substantial bits of meat still left on them, especially on the carcass and the wings. There were two cans of Coke with a sip or two of liquid still inside—and a carton half full of sour milk.

She looked at her husband, who had sat gnawing on a chicken bone, warily watching her lay out the food. She felt tender and proud. And a little ashamed. When he'd left her behind in the ruins, she had thought he'd gone for good, but she'd been too exhausted to try to stop him—or to follow.

And then—he had returned to her. With food.

She eyed the milk carton. She knew she—and Tom—desperately needed the liquid. Resolutely she picked it up and put it to her mouth. She gagged. She closed her nose and forced herself to drink. She heaved. But she kept it down.

She picked up a melon rind and broke it. Beads of moisture

formed in the break. She handed it to Tom. He took it and greedily raked the sweet, moist pulp into his mouth with his teeth. . . .

The food was all gone. Randi's hunger and thirst had quickly overcome her revulsion at eating the leavings of others. It was nourishment. She had eaten only enough to sustain her—and Tom had devoured the rest. She felt restored. Even her waning hope had brightened. Perhaps. Perhaps they would still survive. . . .

She wiped her hands on her clothing, vaguely amused at her gesture. She ran her fingers through her hair in an effort to untangle it a little. Tom was watching her.

She returned his earnest gaze. She felt herself in the grip of a deeply satisfying, primitive emotion. Her Tom. He had foraged for her. He had provided for her. And she loved him.

"Oh, Tom," she whispered. "I'm proud of you. I'm so very proud of you."

He was intent upon her. Unwittingly he touched the blood-caked wound high on his head. Her heart flooded with concern.

"Oh, darling," she said, speaking softly, her voice shaky and low, "I so wish I could make you know how I feel." She realized he would not understand her words, but she kept on talking to him. "I love you. And I feel so helpless. . . . I wish—I wish I could make up for all the times you needed me. For all the times things needed to be said between us . . . For the hurt—" Her voice broke. She gave a little sob. "And now . . . If only I could make you understand, we could be all right. If only I could make you understand how much I love you . . ."

The tears rolled down her cheeks. "Oh, please, Tom . . . Please understand me. . . . Please . . ."

Tom reached out toward her. With intense curiosity he touched the tears on her cheeks. He examined them—moist on his fingers. He sensed something was wrong. He wanted to help. But he did not know how. . . .

With tear-bright eyes Randi gazed at the man crouched before her. Her hair unkempt, her face and neck streaked with sweat and dirt, her clothing torn, she looked wholly beautiful, soft with love and tenderness.

Gently she reached out and caressed him, letting her fingers glide silkenly over his parched lips and stubbly cheeks—exploring his face as if truly discovering it for the first time. . . .

Tom sat still, letting the feeling of supple well-being, of growing excitement and want, swell in him. He responded in kind. With his hands he awkwardly stroked the face, the neck, the shoulders of the woman before him.

And once again he reached out and took her, pressed her to him, burying his face in her hair.

For an instant Randi grew rigid in his crushing embrace. She clamped her teeth together and squeezed her eyes tightly shut.

But Tom was not the controlled, considerate, civilized man. He was only—male. And he would not be denied. He strained against her.

Randi opened her eyes wide. Her feelings of guilt, injustice, of recrimination and frustration melted away. Reawakened emotions quickened within her and she found herself responding to Tom's absolute desire. She found herself wanting him as urgently as he wanted her.

Gently she pushed him away. Instinctively sensing that she did not rebuff him, he did not resist. With infinite tenderness she cupped his face in her hands and pulled it close to hers. She kissed his eyes, his cheeks, his lips. Softly she disengaged herself and loosened the knots holding together her torn shirt. She let it slip down her shoulders, down her arms. She reached out and opened his flying suit, exposing his chest. With tender, sensuous hands she caressed him, entwining the tufted hair in her fingers.

Excited, aroused, Tom let all the new and impassioning sensations possess him. His hands eagerly moved on Randi's body, enraptured by the softness of her.

Again she pulled away. She opened the fastener on her own pants, and she slid Tom's suit down his eager body.

And presently they stood, silent, naked to each other among the stark ruins.

Urgently he reached for her—and they came together, sinking down on the discarded clothing on the ground.

His grip on her yielding body tightened with the ferocity of animal want. The smell of her fired him; he pressed his open mouth to her salty skin and thrust his body against hers.

Randi cried out in a soft, involuntary moan—a woman taken by, and giving herself to, a male who was—and was not—her husband.

They clung to each other. They moved with each other, sharing and fulfilling the need that was all-consuming in them, straining to be consummated in a union at once savage and raw, tender and loving.

The dulling shroud of doubts and guilts was ripped from her—and her clarion scream of release rang out and echoed among the brooding night ruins as if reluctant to die away. . . .

They rested. Lying close in their retreat among the broken stones of long ago, languid arms and legs entwined, their bodies glistening with the sheen of afterlove.

Randi turned her eyes from her husband and gazed up into the starry night sky.

Her face was a study in love and loveliness. The serene, unequaled beauty of a woman fulfilled . . .

4

It was late when Colonel Jonathan Howell brought his car to a halt outside the Death Valley Ranger Headquarters, but the light was still on in Chief Ranger Stark's office. He had expected it. He strode toward the building. He was arriving unannounced—but he just couldn't sit on his ass back at Edwards while Paul and his men were running theirs ragged in the desert. He'd finished his work at the Base and driven up by himself. He'd made it in under three hours.

The door to Stark's office was open and Howell paused in the doorway before entering. At the big wall map, their backs to the door, stood Paul, Ward and the Chief Ranger.

"If we don't get them tomorrow," Ward was saying, his voice tired and discouraged, "I don't see how they can survive."

He looked up at the map. "It's been a hundred and twenty degrees out there."

Paul turned to Stark. "Chuck, can we reach the radio stations that serve this area?" he asked. He sounded determined, angry.

Stark nodded. "By phone."

"At this hour?"

Again Stark nodded. "Most of them have late shows."

"OK." There was a stubborn finality in Paul's voice. "We'll request that tomorrow they broadcast an alert. Throughout the day." Ward looked startled. "On *my* responsibility!" Paul said firmly. "And to hell with—routine! I want every camper, every hiker, every damned tourist looking for them!"

"Good evening, gentlemen!"

At the sound of Howell's arctic voice, the three men whirled on the door. Paul glared at the officer with ill-concealed animosity. "Colonel Howell," he said tightly. "We didn't expect you up here."

Howell looked coldly at the junior officer. "I hope my presence won't cramp your style, Captain."

He walked over to join the men at the map.

"We're planning tomorrow's search procedure," Paul said stiffly.

"So I heard." Howell confronted him angrily. "Didn't I tell you to keep Darby's condition confidential until *I* changed your orders?"

Paul looked stonily at his superior. He was obviously tired, under tremendous stress, and controlled himself only with difficulty. Dammit! Tom's life was at stake. And Randi's. And he had to wear a blasted blindfold looking for them! He made no reply.

"Well?" Howell snapped.

"*Yes*, sir." Paul's voice grated in the room.

"Is that all you have to say?"

Paul felt the hot anger rising in him threatening to break down his control. "No, sir, it is not. But I'm somewhat under a handicap, facing a—a *superior* officer!"

Howell turned red. He snapped his head toward Ward. "That's all, Major," he said with exaggerated calm. He turned

to Stark. "May I have the use of your office, Stark?" he asked.
"Of course."

The Chief Ranger and Ward left the room, closing the door behind them. Howell turned to face Paul squarely. For a moment the two men stood glaring at each other like fighting cocks getting ready for combat. When Howell spoke, his voice was glacial and ominously low.

"You may speak off the record," he said, "if you have anything to say."

Paul felt all the pent-up frustration well up in him. He could contain himself no longer. With his neck stuck out this far already, what the hell did another inch matter?

"I do," he said heatedly. "This entire operation has been hamstrung from the start. Mismanaged. By you! And—dammit!—I want to know why."

"I don't ever have to give you any reasons for my actions," Howell said coldly. "But I did. You know damned well why it's been necessary to—"

"Sure," Paul interrupted bitterly. "For Tom's own good. Let him kill himself out there. For his own damned good!"

"Captain!"

But there was no stopping him. "And Randi, too," he plowed on. "That ought to satisfy everybody."

Howell obviously had great trouble keeping his temper. "So you want to make this thing into a circus. A God-damned radio show!"

"Oh, hell! That's not where it's at and you damned well know it. We need help. And *they* can give it to us."

"You had your orders."

"Yes. Hunt Tom Darby down—like a wild beast!"

"Has it occurred to you that that's exactly what he is?"

Livid, Paul glared at the Wing Commander. Automatically he clenched his fists. "Tom Darby is the best damned test pilot the Air Force has," he growled. "Has *that* occurred to *you?*"

There was a moment's tense silence. With a conscious effort Howell collected himself.

"Every man on the Base who knows about Tom is rooting for us to get to him. To both of them," he said earnestly. "That includes you *and* me. For you it's a simple matter: Get everybody out looking. For me there are other important considerations."

"I can imagine," Paul said bitterly. "The latest directions to drop from the bowels of the Pentagon."

Howell ignored the interruption. "There's the safety of Tom himself—"

"We could have figured a way to keep him from harming himself. And from being harmed."

"And—primarily—security."

Paul stared at him. "Security!" he exclaimed. "What security? Sure, I know the F-15 is classified, but there's not one piece of classified hardware left on the damned wreck. It holds no secrets."

Howell looked straight at him. "No," he said quietly. "But Tom does."

Paul suddenly looked disturbed. He stood silent.

"Tom not only flies the F-15 enhancement tests," Howell continued. "He's involved in the XM-9 project as well. And that *is* a top-secret project."

Paul stared at him.

"The XM-9 was aboard Tom's plane. He was testing it. At maximum output," Howell went on soberly. "He was riding a God-damned missile!"

Paul looked shaken. "I—didn't know. . . ."

"You had no need to know. Tom did. Tom had very special knowledge. And may still have." He paused. He sounded urgent, grave. "But we can't afford to have *everyone* know. That's why we had to stick to routine. Or we'd be up to our asses in 'rescuers.' From the wrong side of the damned curtain."

Paul looked up quickly. He was about to say something, but Howell kept on talking.

"We know the Soviets are aware of the Marcus project. We know they're trying to get any information about it they can. We know they've been 'flagging' the Marcus name for many months. That's why he's been constantly guarded. Protected. His work—his knowledge—is of the utmost importance." He paused. "And so is Tom's." He looked straight at Paul. "I must conduct myself—and the search operation—as I think best."

"Sir. There's something I—"

Howell overrode him. "If you can't believe that as a human being I'm as anxious as you are to find and help Tom, think of it this way. That plane and that device took better than ten years to develop. Unless Tom can tell us exactly *what* went wrong up there, those ten years will have been wiped out in ten seconds!"

Paul looked grim. He spoke firmly. "Colonel," he said, "there's something you should know."

Howell gave him a sharp look, aware of the man's change of attitude. "Yes?"

"Until just a moment ago—until you told me about the XM-9—I didn't put it all together."

Howell was suddenly alert. "What is it?" he asked brusquely.

"Three things. First—there was the killing of Ranger Adams," Paul said. "I have a damned funny feeling that it, in some way, is connected with Tom."

Howell frowned. "I don't see how."

"And then this morning," Paul went on, "near a place where Tom and Randi had been holed up for the night, we found an oil stain on the ground. Fresh. And obviously not a camper. Someone had been parked there. Shortly before. And not one of ours. . . . Who? Why?"

Howell looked grim. "You said three things?"

"Yes." Paul fished Wilson's diary from his pocket. "There's also this. It's Airman Wilson's." He handed the little book to Howell. "Look at it, sir."

Howell took the diary.

"The front page. Where Wilson has written his name and service number."

Howell frowned at the diary page. He stared at the handwritten inscription.

Wilson, Norbert A1C
U.S.A.F.
064 - 12 - 7313

"Look at the numeral seven," Paul said. "It has a little dash through it. That's the European way of writing it. I learned that when I was stationed in Germany." He looked soberly at Howell. "Where did Wilson pick that up? He's been stationed only at Edwards. And his service record shows no trips abroad. I had it checked." He bit his lip. "I know it's damned thin, Colonel. But I have a gut feeling that won't quit. Someone outside our own rescue efforts is hunting Tom!"

Howell contemplated the younger man, his face cloudy. "And you suspect that Wilson was a—a foreign agent? He's dead."

"But not those behind him."

Howell suddenly felt chilled. An enemy "mole" in the Air Force? A spy? Penetration would be a hell of a difficult job. But—dammit!—not impossible. There *had* been cases. . . . He recalled two or three from the early seventies. That Air Force master sergeant—Perkins was his name—who'd been given a slap-on-the-wrist sentence of a lousy three years for attempting to smuggle secret documents to Russian agents in Mexico City . . . And that fellow Wood, an Air Force sergeant, arrested for treason when he was discovered with a whole damned car full of highly classified material to be handed over to a Soviet agent in New York . . .

"You're right," he said. "It *is* thin."

"I know," Paul agreed. "It's no neon sign proclaiming Foreign Intrigue! But is it ever?"

Howell nodded thoughtfully. "It *is* something to be considered, Paul. We can't overlook the possibility that foreign interests *are* involved."

"The question then becomes—how?"

Howell looked solemnly at him. "Perhaps," he said quietly. "Perhaps *they* are also aware that Tom is our only hope of saving the Marcus project years of work. Years of delay. Perhaps they figure that if the desert doesn't kill him off, they'll finish the job."

Paul stared at him. He felt suddenly cold.

"I'll start a top-priority internal investigation of Wilson at once," Howell continued. "Tonight. And I'll have the FBI run a check. In fact," he said tightly, "I'll give them a whole damned list of names. *Everyone* involved in this unholy mess, from Stark on down! And as far as *we* are concerned, we'd better keep our eyes open . . . wide." He glanced at Paul. He couldn't let it go. "It kind of puts the lid on your idea of an appeal to the public over the radio," he said.

Paul nodded bleakly. "Sure does. Be like an invitation to mayhem."

Howell turned to the wall map. "You realize, Paul," he said, "whether there are outside forces hunting Tom out there or not, it may already be too late. Tomorrow has got to be the deadline."

In more ways than one, he thought bitterly. That damned ultimatum by a handful of Congressmen would also reach its deadline then; the threat to blow the whistle. Hell, all those damned foreign spooks had to do was to wait—and what they wanted to know would be handed to them on a silver press release. Wouldn't be the first time. What the hell else could impact the damned operation? On top of everything, they now had to look under every blasted rock for a KGB hit-man.

He fixed his eyes on the map.

"They can't possibly last beyond that," he finished.

He turned back to Paul. "But you're right. We do need help. Dependable help. It *is* too late for—directives now. . . . I'll contact the National Guard. Get a task force up here. Two company strength should do it. We can spearhead the operation with your Emergency Service Teams from Edwards. We can have everybody up here first thing tomorrow morning. When we spot Tom and Randi, we can ring the entire area where they are and move in. The important thing now is to get to Tom before he kills himself—and his wife—with exposure and privation. And before anyone else gets to him." He grew wholly business-like. "Now—what's your plan?"

"We know that early today they were at an abandoned mine," Paul said. He picked up a key with a large plastic tag on it, lying on the desk. He showed it to Howell. "Randi left this for us to find near an old tunnel. We checked it. It's the key to her cabin."

"Clever girl."

"And this evening a camper's report puts them near that ghost town—here."

He poked a finger at the map.

"They seem to be traveling in the direction of this area here—the black desert. And we can make sure they go there by keeping that part of the valley clear and sending our choppers and search teams in behind them."

"Why that particular area?" Howell asked.

"Because of the old volcanic craters," Paul explained. "There's a small crater on the black desert. We know we have to corner Tom in a place where he can't hurt himself. The crater fills the bill."

He rummaged on the desk and came up with an aerial photograph. He handed it to Howell.

"The crater is a couple of hundred feet across and about one hundred feet deep," he explained. "The inside walls are very steep. Unscalable. Except here—" he pointed to the photograph—"where there's a natural break in the ridge. A shallow incline down to the bottom."

He turned to the wall map. He studied it for a moment.

"Go on," Howell said, caught up in the plan.

"The little crater is surrounded by a field of volcanic ash. The black desert. Once Tom and Randi are out on that field—using the ESTs and existing search teams, we can herd them toward the break in the crater rim. Like a big-game drive. And corner them in the crater itself—like in a giant trapping pit."

"As long as they don't slip through your cordon."

"We can't afford to let them do that," Paul said firmly. "They wouldn't survive."

Howell looked at the photograph in his hand. "You say the walls inside the crater are too dangerous to scale?"

"That's right."

Howell looked soberly at Paul. "What if Tom should try the impossible? Again?"

Paul returned his gaze. "Sir," he said solemnly, "a little while ago you reminded me that Tom's reactions are those of a wild animal."

Howell nodded.

"I think we've found a way to keep him from trying to scale those walls."

DAY SIX

1

Since before dawn trucks and personnel carriers had rumbled into Death Valley to disgorge National Guard troops in the marshaling area set up near Furnace Creek.

Howell himself had briefed the Guard officers on the plan of action worked out by Paul, while Paul had given the men of his Air Force Emergency Service Team their orders. The thirteen-man strong EST had come up from Edwards in three "six-packs" and a jeep. Rugged, expertly trained to cope with the dangerous and unusual, the men had listened to him eagerly and had grasped at once what was needed of them.

It had been a hectic night. Neither Howell nor Paul had slept.

Now all was ready for the crucial drive. Both men knew it would be their last effort.

The narrow dirt road snaking up into the hills was steep and bumpy. The two scouts groaning up the grade in four-wheel drive came to a halt below a small ridge. Paul, alone in his vehicle, dismounted and walked up to Ward, getting out of his scout. Already they had scoured ridge after ridge in the area. They had seen nothing.

Paul glanced up the hill. "We should get a pretty good view from up there," he said. He turned to the driver of Ward's scout. "Stay with the radio. Sing out if anyone spots them."

"Yes, sir."

The two men started to climb up the bluff.

From the crest they had a sweeping view of the barren and forbidding foothills stretched out before them. Below was the flat, cracked expanse of a dry lake, and in the distance—the black desert.

Paul lowered his field glasses. He wiped the eyepieces with a damp handkerchief. The sweat trickling down his brow had fouled the lenses. He glanced up at the broiling sun high above. The morning was already coming to an end and they had not as yet had any success. Time was running out.

Again he searched the hills with his binoculars. The ground shimmered, baking in the heat.

Suddenly he froze.

Movement! On that far slope.

He searched among the rocks.

Two figures.

Tom and Randi!

"I got them!" he cried, keeping his excitement in check. "Over there. Two o'clock."

Ward whipped his field glasses across. "I see them," he said.

He watched. Tom was kneeling on the ground, beating on something with a rock. Randi sat close by.

"He's cracking open a cactus," Paul said. He scanned the area. "OK," he said. "If we send in the choppers from over there, low, we can drive them down to the black desert." Without looking at Ward, he issued his orders. "Get Howell on the radio. Fill him in. I'll stay here. Keep them in sight."

"Right!"

Ward quickly started down from the ridge. Paul fixed his field glasses on the two figures on the far slope. Tom and Randi had scooped the crushed cactus pulp into their hands and were sucking out the moisture.

Suddenly Tom spun around. He clutched his side and fell to the ground. Almost at once a faint, sharp crack reached Paul's ears. Two little geysers of dust erupted close to the supine Tom—and two more cracks sounded from the distant hills.

Paul was frozen in shock.

"Jesus!" The exclamation was wrenched from his throat. "He's been shot!"

Randi threw herself over Tom's body, even as Paul whipped his binoculars to a distant hill across from her and Tom.

There was the glint of sun on metal, a fire flash-point—and another faint crack.

Paul leaped to his feet. He rushed headlong down the steep

slope. He shouted at the startled Ward: "Tom's been hit! Someone's shooting at him! Get help!"

He ran for his scout.

"Get to him, Quent. Fast! Do what you can for him."

He tumbled into his scout. In a cloud of sand and dust he
slewed it around and roared off, whamming down the washboard road. . . .

Scrambling across the rugged ground, Randi helped Tom
painfully drag himself behind a big rock. He leaned against
it. He touched his hand to his side. It came away wet with
blood. Uncomprehendingly he stared at it. Randi watched him,
wide-eyed.

"Oh, dear God!" she cried out, incredulous horror making
her voice hoarse. "They *are* hunting you! They *are* shooting
at you! . . . *Oh, dear God!*"

Without thought for her own safety she reached out and
peeled the blood-soaked cloth from Tom's wound. He stiffened,
but he did not stop her. The bullet had grazed him, leaving
a long, shallow gash in his skin. It bled profusely.

Randi turned to glare hatefully out over the dead and desolate hills. Her eyes blazed with anger.

"Damn you!" she whispered tightly. "God damn you!"

Hayden shifted his eye from the rifle scope. He peered at
the distant hill. Hell! He couldn't see them. He'd winged the
guy. He was certain of it. He'd seen him spin around at the
impact. But he knew it hadn't been a clean kill. And the fucking
girl was still alive.

Shit!

The range had been too far, the shimmering heat deceiving.
But—dammit all to hell!—they were forcing him to take
chances. And all because someone, somewhere wanted to give
some big-shot's ego a hickey!

He stood up from his ridge-crest blind and began to slide
down the precipitous drop to his buggy parked below, his rifle
held high.

Fuck it all! He'd have to get over there.

Finish the job. . . .

Paul was racing along a trail running along the foothills, paralleling the dry lake. The little scout pitched and bucked over the rugged path. His thoughts were awhirl. Someone *was* out to kill Tom. Who?

A flash memory shot through his mind. Of a time before— when he had raced to Tom's aid. When, together, they had been lying supine on the ground. When all around them the air had been hideous with the staccato clangor of enemy fire. He had read the prayer in the eyes of his companion. He'd known it had been there in his own.

He knew it was there now.

He was headed for the canyon that he calculated would take him to the row of hills from where the shots had come. He prayed there'd be a road going in—or a trail the scout could negotiate.

Almost there . . .

The scout hurtled along the trail. Ahead he could see a dirt road leading into the foothills.

Suddenly a dune buggy came shooting out of the ravine. The driver spotted Paul's scout. At once he veered sharply away and careened off the trail, racing out onto the flat, cracked bed of the dry lake.

Paul was startled. He knew instantly and with absolute certainty who the man was. The rifleman from the hills! The killer who had shot Tom! Immediately he raced in pursuit. His powerful little vehicle flew across the hard, arid surface of the dry lake. He was gaining on the buggy ahead of him.

Hayden watched the pursuing Air Force vehicle in his rearview mirror. Dammit! Another couple of minutes and he'd have been out of the area. Even as he had the thought, he knew it was invalid. He had obviously been spotted. Had he headed for his wounded target, he'd have run into a horde of eager fly-boys. Perhaps what had happened was for the best. This way he had only one adversary to contend with. One man.

He should not be too difficult to eliminate. . . .

Paul kept the accelerator pressed against the floorboard. He was within a couple of hundred feet of the fleeing dune buggy.

And he was gaining rapidly. He glanced at the speedometer. Close to seventy.

Suddenly he saw the vehicle ahead of him slew to a halt, raising a cloud of fine, powdery dust. As quickly as it happened, he registered the actions of the driver of the buggy. The man leaned into the back of the buggy. When he straightened up, he had a rifle in his hands. Without breaking the momentum of his motion, he brought it up into firing position—aimed straight at Paul.

The bullet shattered the windshield on the passenger side of the scout. The report ripped the distant silence, washing in waves out over the empty expanse. Even as the glass splinters showered the scout, Paul made his decision. The next one would very likely hit its mark.

In the split moment it took for the marksman in the buggy to resight and squeeze off a second round, Paul acted.

He wrenched the steering wheel sharply to one side. The little scout reacted instantly, turning sideways in a violent skid that shot billows of powder dust into the air, completely obscuring him. At once he backed off behind the cloud of dust. He gunned his scout and roared straight for the protective dust screen.

He shot through it and emerged on the other side headed at full speed directly for the dune buggy halted ahead of him. . . .

Hayden saw him roaring down on him. There was time to squeeze off one more round. It was the last. It went wild. He had no time to reload . . . and the scout came hurtling on.

He threw the rifle into the back of the buggy and stomped on the accelerator.

The buggy shot forward and sped across the lake.

Hayden sat hunched over the wheel. He knew he could not outspeed the damned Air Force scout, but he might be able to outmaneuver it, reach an area where the rugged buggy would leave the scout behind.

He glanced into the mirror.

The scout was closing in. . . .

Paul urged the last ounce of speed from the scout. He was

close enough to make out the driver of the buggy. The man's long hair whipped wildly in the wind. His face looked tense and hard. Paul's anger spurred him on. This was the man who wanted to kill Tom.

He hated him.

He was only feet behind the buggy. How the hell could he stop him? By ramming him? Perhaps he could make the bastard lose control.

He steered his scout a touch to the left and came up on the driver's side of the buggy. The man threw him a cold-eyed glance. The two vehicles were racing side by side across the cracked expanse of the dry lake.

Now!

With a short jerk on the steering wheel Paul crashed his scout into the side of the buggy. The vehicle lurched violently and fishtailed, on the verge of going out of control. Paul, too, fought the wheel of his own vehicle, barely avoiding turning over. He swore. Ramming the bastard was not the way. It was equally dangerous for himself. The little buggy was too damned sturdy.

There was another way.

Again he urged his scout forward until once more the two vehicles were careening along side by side, metal grating against metal. This time Paul was on the passenger side of the buggy.

He was just about to act when the buggy driver turned away and raced off at an angle.

Paul roared after him. He felt coldly confident. He'd get the bastard. Tense with the imminence of violent action, he clutched the wheel. He knew the buggy could not elude him.

Once again he brought his scout up at the side of the buggy—touching, scraping. He more sensed than saw the driver getting ready to veer away.

Now!

Without warning Paul rose in his seat and leaped from the scout into the buggy next to him. He landed awkwardly. He struggled to keep his balance. Startled, Hayden fought to keep his vehicle under control. The driverless scout continued its wild ride for a moment, then turned sideways, rolled over—bouncing into the air again and again in a spray of dust, to explode in a gigantic ball of fire.

Hayden fought to steer clear of the fire blast. In the same instant, clinging to the buggy, Paul kicked across him. With one leg he stomped down on the brake.

Taken unprepared, Hayden rammed his head against the windshield. Paul grabbed the wheel and yanked it vehemently around. The buggy turned sharply, lifting two wheels off the ground, and Hayden was flung from the careening vehicle.

His scream of terror was cut short as he hit the ground. Limbs flailing grotesquely, he tumbled violently across the hard surface—to a final, dead stop.

Paul brought the buggy to a halt. He turned it around and headed back toward the still figure of the man sprawled in a twisted heap of broken bones on the dry lake bed.

He was dead.

From the foothills two scouts came racing toward him, raising long plumes of dust behind them. They came to a stop and Ward jumped from one of them. He ran up to Paul.

"We lost them, Paul," he panted. "When we got there—they were gone."

Paul felt a surge of relief. "He's alive," he said.

"He's alive."

Paul's relief suddenly turned to misgiving. "Alive," he said bleakly, "but for how long?" He gazed desolately toward the foothills. "They slipped through our lines."

He scowled at the broken body lying on the sun-baked ground. At least the outside threat to Tom was now eliminated, he thought.

Or—was it?

From the other scout an airman called out: "Captain! . . . Sir!"

Paul looked toward him. The man was listening on his radio earphones.

"They've spotted them!" he called. "From a chopper. They're headed out on the black desert!"

Paul's spirit soared. They had 'em! It was only a matter of

time, now. Time and patience. And a little luck. He glanced at his watch. There would be time enough. It was just past noon. . . .

Half way across the globe on this, the sixth day of Operation Marcus, darkness had already fallen over East Berlin. . . .

2

Berlin

Time was running out.

He could hear their heavy, hobnailed boots pounding down the cobblestones in pursuit. There must be at least six of them, he thought.

He heard a gruff voice shout, *"Halt!"*

He stopped his bicycle, put one foot on the ground and waited. His heart beat wildly. It was a few minutes before 2300—the hour Scharff had instructed him to arrive at Checkpoint Charlie.

The papers given him suddenly felt heavy in his inside coat pocket. What was the name again? For an instant he was blank. Kramer! He must remember. His name was *not* Krebbs. Kramer. Wilhelm *Kramer.* Scharff had explained that a cover name was best if it was close to the real one. Less chance of making a mistake. And a mistake easier to explain away. Involuntarily he touched his jacket. Any second the effectiveness of his false papers would be proved.

Or disproved. . . .

The border guards caught up with him. A roving patrol. He was surprised to see there were only three of them. They scowled at him from under their toadstool helmets.

"What are you doing here?" one of the soldiers asked him. "At this hour?"

Krebbs swallowed. He knew he looked and acted nervous. He also knew it would be normal to do so.

"I—I am on my way to the international transit point at Friedrich-Zimmerstrasse," he said. "I wish to cross before midnight."

"Your passport!"

A chill shot through him. It would be now. . . .

He pulled the passport from his pocket. Folded in it was his visitor's permit.

The soldier took the document. In the light of a flashlight he examined it.

"Swiss?" he asked unnecessarily.

Krebbs nodded. "Yes." He was about to add that he'd been visiting friends, their names, their addresses—all the facts Scharff had provided him with. He caught himself. He also remembered the admonition: Volunteer no information. Answer only questions asked.

The soldier unfolded the visitor's permit. He checked it. Carefully he refolded it and replaced it.

"Schon gut, Herr Kramer," he said. He gave back the passport.

Without another word the soldiers turned away and left.

Krebbs looked after them. He was suddenly aware that he was trembling. He pushed off and started to pedal down the street.

There were seven blocks to the checkpoint.

And it was almost 2300 hours.

He was pedaling down Friedrichstrasse between the rows of six- and seven-story buildings lining the street. He knew that some of the ones closest to the wall had observation posts on the upper floors, constantly manned by armed troops of the *Volksarmee*—the People's Army. Ahead of him he could see the checkpoint buildings and watchtower clearly. The street and the checkpoint area were brightly lit by the double rows of tall, slender, swan-neck lampposts gracefully bending out over the roadway. Traffic was moderate, both vehicular and pedestrian. He was not the only one wishing to cross over before the curfew, but neither was the checkpoint crowded.

It was a pleasant, cool evening with a gentle breeze drifting down the street—yet he could feel the sweat collect in his armpits and trickle stickily down his sides as he approached the checkpoint.

He glanced at his watch. Two minutes. He was exactly on time.

He arrived at the first checkpoint building. He dismounted and pushed his bicycle to the rack placed outside. He locked it. He started to remove a package wrapped in brown paper and tied to the bicycle luggage-carrier—but thought better of it. He left it on the bicycle and entered the building. . . .

From the guard tower Colonel Gerhardt Scharff watched his man arrive. He felt smugly gratified. The *Herr Doktor* Krebbs had followed instructions implicitly. Everything would work out exactly as planned. He checked his automatic rifle. Ready . . .

He could almost hear the scenario played out. That man! he'd shout, pointing to Krebbs as he was starting to cross. I know him. He's not an *Ausländer*. He's German! An important scientist. Defecting! He'd whip the guards to a full alert. Create as much of an uproar as he could. Pin Krebbs in the beam of the searchlight. The poor *Tropf*—the poor fool—was bound to be startled out of his wits. Whatever he did would be wrong. And—he'd shoot him. Make certain he was dead. Another would-be defector—a traitor—shot in his attempt to betray his country. His falsified papers and the abortive attempt to defect under an assumed nationality and name would prove his guilt. There could be no doubt. And he, Gerhardt Scharff, would be credited with the vigilance and decisive action that stopped him. It would be perfect. He savored the anticipated moment.

He hoped, of course, that even now in the eleventh hour the Death Valley operation would be as successful. At last report the elusive pilot was still being hunted. *His* men might still beat the American Air Force to it. . . .

He resumed his watch of the door to the checkpoint building. It would be several minutes before Krebbs would emerge. Then—the customs check in another building, and the man would begin to cross, pushing his bicycle along the pedestrian lane running next to the barricaded street. He rubbed his hands. He found himself growing impatient with anticipation. . . .

Krebbs joined a short line waiting for the first passport-and-permit check. Ahead of him stood a young man. Dark hair.

Dark eyes. Turkish worker, he thought, returning from a visit to his East German girl friend. The young man looked relaxed. It would be a routine procedure for him. Krebbs shifted uneasily. He felt clammy with anxiety. Did he stand out from the others?

His eyes were drawn to a large clock on the wall. The seconds were ticking away.

Next to it a poster proclaiming OUR REPUBLIC—HONORED, RESPECTED, RECOGNIZED shared space on the wall with a large color reproduction of Gerassimov's *Lenin at the Rostrum*, printed in the U.S.S.R.

Again his eyes sought the big clock. He had been standing in the line almost a full minute.

And the seconds ticked on. . . .

Suddenly there was an explosion outside. He had known it would come, but he started violently.

He was committed.

He resisted the urge to rush outside.

Wait!

Ten seconds. Count. *One thousand—two thousand—three thousand* . . . He tried to shut out the shouts of alarm ringing out all around him, the sudden sirens and horns.

Ten thousand. He sprang for the door and rushed outside.

The entire area was covered with a dense white smoke which still billowed from the shattered package on his bicycle. His formula had been correct. His timing device exact. Sixty seconds.

The solid white phosphorus had exploded from its airtight container, catapulted into the air by the explosive charge; broken into a myriad tiny, powdery fragments that instantly, spontaneously ignited as they were exposed to the air, turning into thick smoke that obscured everything. Phosphorus pentoxide, he thought automatically. The densest smoke known to science. Larger fragments scattered through the street burned furiously, adding more heavy white smoke to the already impenetrable screen.

He resisted the compelling impulse to run. Follow the plan, he admonished himself. The breeze was starting to waft the smoke down the street toward the west. He had calculated he'd have five minutes.

He pressed himself against the building next to the door. Before his eyes he saw the detailed layout of the entire checkpoint area he'd drawn, from photographs, maps, descriptions. Every feature charted and measured—and memorized.

He stepped off. He counted his steps—deliberately, evenly taken. Each step the exact length of his stride scale.

Eight—nine—ten. He stopped. He would be in the middle of the street. He made a quarter-turn to his right and stepped off again.

He collided with a man. A soldier? He could not see.

"To the left!" he shouted, glad that he had anticipated the situation and decided how to deal with it. "To the left, you idiot! He's over there!" The man rushed off into the obscuring smoke.

Krebbs went on. *Six—seven—eight* . . . All around him the air and smoke reverberated with the shouts and sounds of confusion. Sirens screamed, horns blared, the noise of soldiers and travelers blindly milling about was everywhere.

Suddenly two powerful searchlights blazed on. Unable to penetrate the dense white smoke, the intense beams of light were reflected back at the guards, blinding them. As he had known they would. He knew they would not fire, not knowing what to fire at.

Unable to see, himself, he stepped off his calculated paces. Deliberately. Accurately. Resisting the urge to hurry. To run.

He stopped. He reached forward. It was there. The first barrier boom. He ducked under it. Again he started off, counting his measured steps. Ahead of him, he knew, lay three massive concrete barriers placed so that a car was forced to zigzag a slalom course through them.

Three—four—five. The dense smoke enveloped him, clung to him, concealed him. Through his mind ran the phrases used to describe this warfare smokescreen: To blind hostile observation. Cause confusion. Minimize firepower. Conceal activities . . .

It did all of that and more. The chaotic din around him bore irrefutable witness.

And he went on. *Ten—eleven—twelve* . . .

Colonel Gerhardt Scharff was furious. Livid. He fumbled his way down the steps from the guard tower. He raged at the thickly billowing smoke.

Krebbs had tricked him!

The white smoke blinded him. He turned and screamed up the stairs. "Turn off the *verdammte* searchlight, you idiots! Turn it off!"

The light went off. A few seconds later the other beam also died.

Scharff was on the ground. In his hands he clutched his automatic rifle. His mind whirled. What was Krebbs planning to do? How could he stop him?

How could he kill him?

The man would have only a short time to negotiate the obstacles of the checkpoint. The smoke would soon dissipate—at least become lighter. It had been a single explosive discharge. The smoke was not being replenished from a continuous source. That was in his favor. He took heart. He was not beaten yet.

Where would Krebbs try to cross? *He* could not see either. The most direct—the fastest—way was down the pedestrian path along the street. He tried to orient himself. As fast as he could, he began to grope his way toward the lane leading into the forbidden area. . . .

Krebbs took the last step before reaching the first concrete barrier. He stuck out his arm to feel it.

Nothing.

A chill went through him. Had he gone wrong? Miscalculated? Angled off from the straight line? Was he lost? With his hand stretched searchingly before him, he quickly took another step forward. At once his fingers bent against the cold, rough concrete. He had been only inches off.

Immediately he began to run along the wall, letting his hand scrape across it, not wanting to lose it, oblivious to the burning abrasion of his skin.

He reached the end. Quickly he turned the corner and, carefully positioning himself, started out toward the second barrier—counting to himself:

One—two—three . . .

Scharff located the beginning of the pedestrian path. He began to run as fast as he dared in the heavy fog. Almost at once he collided with a guard.

"Halt!" the man shouted. "Halt or I shoot!"

"Out of my way!" Scharff barked at him. "I am Colonel Gerhardt Scharff. State Security. *Ausweichen! Los!"*

"You will have to prove your identity, *Herr Oberst,"* the guard said firmly. "Emergency orders are in effect. No one passes here!"

Scharff thought furiously. While he was arguing with that voice in the fog, his quarry would get away. The smoke was thinning out a little. He peered into it. Faintly he could make out the figure of the guard barring his way.

"Understood," he snapped.

He stepped closer to the man. Suddenly he jabbed his rifle butt up and struck the guard a crushing blow on his jaw. He could hear the crunch of shattering bone. As the man collapsed at his feet, he jumped over him and ran down the path. . . .

Krebbs felt the tension as a physical thing straining to erupt from his chest. The final concrete barrier lay ahead. The smoke was still too dense for him to see it. He stepped out, counting his strides toward it:

Seven—eight—nine—

His shin hit a sharp obstacle, sending waves of pain up his leg and his side. A car. Halted between barriers. Trapped by the smoke—unable to see. Desperately he groped his way around it, trying to estimate his steps. He was clear—*thirteen— fourteen—*

He stopped counting. Ahead, faintly visible through the slowly dissipating smoke, lay the last barricade.

He ran to it. Around it. A few more steps to the final barrier boom. He reached it, ducked under it. Visibility was returning. Before him stretched the empty no-man's-land. Fifty meters. Fifty meters to freedom.

He raced down the street.

The flesh crawled on his back—exposed to his enemies. Any second he expected to feel the bullets slam into him.

Or—feel nothing at all.

He ran on. . . .

Scharff was beginning to be able to distinguish objects as he sped down the pedestrian path. The smoke was rapidly blowing away.

He neared the final barrier across the lane. Beyond lay the buffer zone. He hoped he was in time. . . .

On the watchtower the guard peered into the dissipating smoke. He thought he could see movement far out toward the forbidden zone.

The defector!

He grabbed his fog binoculars. He searched the area. There! He spotted him. Running. On the pedestrian path.

Scharff raced out into the no-man's-zone. Suddenly he tensed. Ahead he could see a man running toward the black-and-white-striped barrier boom to the west.

Krebbs!

He was almost there.

Scharff stopped. He brought his rifle up. He found his prey in his scope. . . .

On the watchtower the guard steadied his submachine gun on the parapet.

And opened fire. . . .

3

Death Valley

The scorching black sand and ash of the gently sloping volcanic field stretched unrelieved before them to the mountains on the far horizon. A peculiar rash of bleached-yellow bushweeds grew sparsely all over the smooth black expanse, giving the desert a strange, unreal appearance—like a huge photographic negative.

Side by side, Tom and Randi trudged across the black sand in the blistering heat. Breathing scalded their lungs; motion was agony; but they moved on in unremitting flight. Tom knew nothing else to do. Fleeing was all he had done as long as he had existed. . . .

Her eyes smarting, Randi peered ahead. The ground was becoming gradually steeper. A short distance directly before them the desert pouted up in a circular ridge—as if its white-pimpled black face had been scarred by a gigantic pockmark. A saddle broke the near rim.

Exhausted, wanting to avoid the climb to the ridge ahead, Tom angled away from the rise.

He stopped.

He listened, staring dully out over the emptiness.

From the distance in the direction he was headed, the faint droning sound of motor vehicles toiling through the soft sand and ash in low gear came rolling ominously across the desert.

The monsters were coming for him.

Fright and anger and dismay darkened his sun-tortured face. He turned and started off in the opposite direction, quickening his steps.

They had gone only a short distance—away from the oncoming demon growls—when Tom again stopped dead.

Ahead of him the muffled noise of more engines laboring across the sand rose with the shimmering heat.

For a moment he stood frozen in indecision, his mind numbed with fatigue. He touched the fresh wound in his side. It pained him with every step he took. In his mind the torment was conclusively associated with the grating, growling monsters and the creatures with their lightning flashes of roaring sound.

With growing alarm he looked back, aware of the motor sounds behind him. And now in front of him as well. The monsters were closing in on him from both sides, persisting in their relentless pursuit.

He glanced at the ridge ahead and turned away. He grabbed Randi by the arm and urged her on—back toward the foothills from which they'd come. . . .

They had gone only a few steps when Randi sank to her knees. She turned up her face to look at Tom, beseeching him with tear-misted eyes. "Please, Tom," she whispered. "No more . . . Please let them get to us . . . help us . . . Please."

He watched her. He did not know what she was saying, but he knew her anguish. He thought that fear of the terrible demons after them had taken her.

With deep anxiety he listened to the droning clatter of the monsters moving in from both sides, and his own dread grew. Doggedly he yanked Randi to her feet. He pushed her on. They must flee. Flee from the creatures that roared terror and hurled out pain.

And he heard it.

The deep-throated rumble of still more demons bearing down on them—this time from straight ahead.

Desperately he looked around, straining to see his enemies.

And he saw them. Steadily crawling toward him across the black expanse. More than he had ever seen before—the growling menace of unrelenting encirclement from all sides. Except one.

The ridge rising from the black desert floor.

Suddenly a new, piercing sound shocked remembered terror in his mind. The strident, raucous blast of a horn rang out sharply over the sand. As if in answer, eager for the hunt, the blaring horn was taken up by others all around him, blowing discordantly, filling the air with a penetrating din that reverberated through the world.

In terror, he turned away. Dragging Randi along, he began a stumbling, shuffling half-run toward the only way left free to them by the threatening monsters.

The crater ridge.

They hobbled on.

A sudden fear chilled him.

With icy dread he gazed up at his old enemy—the searing, incandescent disk high above. Was it, too, hurtling down to chase him? As before? Would it reach him this time? Engulf him with agony? He increased his effort to run. His feet were leaden. They scuffed little grooves in the black sand as he dragged them forward, unable to lift them free.

The ridge was rising under his feet. Pulling Randi along, he headed for the break that stood out on the crater rim like a giant's thumbprint in a pie crust.

Slowly the ring of vehicles lumbering across the desert herded the two fugitives toward the saddle in the rim of the little crater. Air Force scouts, EST "six-packs," National Guard trucks, Ranger pick-ups and jeeps converged on the slope.

Paul stood in his scout in the center group of vehicles approaching from the foothills. He raised his arm and pumped it up and down.

Gradually his scout, driven by Hays, pulled ahead of the group—followed by a second.

From each of the groups on his left and right two vehicles pulled out. The six of them formed a semicircle, steadily driving Tom and Randi toward the break in the crater rim. . . .

The shrill ring of the telephone standing next to her elbow made her jump. She picked it up.

"Chief Ranger Stark's office," she said. "Debbi speaking."

The voice on the phone made her sit up.

"This is FBI Agent-in-Charge Irwin Buter," it said crisply. "May I speak to Colonel Jonathan Howell? It's important."

"I'm sorry, sir," she said. "Colonel Howell is not here."

"Is Captain Jarman available? Captain Paul Jarman?"

"No, sir," she said regretfully. "Everyone's gone. Chief Ranger Stark, too. There's nobody here right now."

"How soon can you contact Colonel Howell?" Buter asked. "It's extremely urgent."

"I—I don't know." She bit her lip. "I think radio communication *is* possible. I'll try to find out."

"Please. Contact him as soon as possible. Tell him to call me at once. At the FBI office in Los Angeles. Agent-in-Charge Irwin Buter. It's vitally urgent. Have him ask for Operator 77."

"Yes, sir," she said. "Operator 77." She was getting excited. "Is there any message I may give Colonel Howell?"

There was a moment's pause. "Tell him we checked the list of names he gave us," Buter said. "Tell him my men are on their way up there." He paused again. He continued tightly. "Tell him I have some urgent information about one of the names on his list."

Debbi ran from the office to the Visitors Center. What she had said was true. Everyone—or nearly everyone—was away from the Headquarters Building. It was out of season and the center was all but deserted. Only one Ranger was on duty. Perhaps he could be of help. He would know how to operate the radio transmitter. She knew there was a transmitter somewhere around, but she wasn't familiar with it—didn't, in fact, even know where it was. After all, she was only filling in for two weeks while the Chief Ranger's regular secretary was away on vacation.

The ranger station in the Visitors Center was deserted. There was no one around.

She glanced at her watch. Lunchtime. The man would be eating somewhere. Should she run out and try to find him? No. She might easily miss him. And she would be gone if he returned. She'd wait for him right here at his station. . . . No. That way she'd miss any possible telephone communications coming into the office. She looked around. She found a crayon under the Ranger-station counter. She pulled a large poster from the wall and in big letters wrote on the back of it: COME

SEE ME IN CHIEF RANGER STARK'S OFFICE. *URGENT!* She signed it: DEBBI, and propped it up on the Ranger's chair. She ran back to the office.

She wondered what it was the FBI agent so urgently wanted to tell Colonel Howell.

Whatever it was, she loved being part of it. . . .

Stumbling with exertion, Tom and Randi crested the saddle and started down the slope into the crater itself. Slipping, sliding, they staggered down the incline until, utterly spent, they reached the hard, flat bottom.

Through a tormenting haze of pain and exhaustion Tom stared at the forbidding, unscalable walls towering tall and precipitous around him.

The realization knifed through him.

They were trapped.

Swaying, he whirled toward the break slope—even as the vehicles arrived at the crest and—motors laboring, grating and growling—began to creep down the incline.

He was frantic. Like a caged wild animal, he turned and turned and turned around in the trap, desperately seeking a way to escape.

There was none.

For a moment he stood immobile in the middle of the flat, circular crater bottom, ringed with dead and withered brush tumbled down from above, his hand holding on to Randi in a vise-like grip.

All around him loomed the tall, steep crater walls. Below them a small fan of rocks broken off the hard volcanic cliffs formed a short incline up to the near-perpendicular palisades— and on the only way out, the gentle slope of the break in this formidable, insurmountable barrier, the monsters that had hunted him all his life were inching down toward him and his mate. Squat, threatening and noisy, they lumbered on, striking terror into his mind. . . .

Paul didn't move his eyes from Tom. Sergeant Hays was at the wheel of his scout, coaxing it down the slope. A few more feet and the vehicles would reach the crater bottom. The moment of truth was close at hand. What would Tom do?

He threw a quick glance at the vehicles around him. Of the six, two were Ranger jeeps, each with three men—Stark in one of them. The remaining four were Air Force scouts. Howell was on his right, Ward on his left. The rest of the three-man vehicle complements were his EST troops. Eighteen men in all. He had thought it all out carefully. Yet—he ached with tension.

He stood up in his scout, gripping the windshield, his knuckles showing white. Below, Tom turned to stare at him. He returned the gaze. He thought he could see the hate, the rage, the terror that distorted his friend's face. He knew it was there. . . .

Suddenly Tom whirled around. Never letting go his grip on Randi, he struggled in a stumbling run toward the towering crater wall, away from the pursuing creatures, away from the enemies closing in on him—bent on doing the impossible. If it cost them their lives . . .

At once Paul's arm shot up over his head, a flare pistol gripped in his hand. The brilliant red flare exploded from the muzzle and arched up out of the crater like a long-delayed cinder from a primordial volcanic eruption.

Immediately, from evenly spaced points all along the crater rim, flames shot up and columns of black smoke billowed into the air. Blazing balls of fire at once started to tumble down the sheer crater walls, pushed and kicked over the edge by the Guardsmen ringing the rim. The flaming, kerosene-soaked tumbleweeds hurtled down, trailing long tails of glowing embers and sooty smoke, bouncing off the volcanic rock all along the inside of the crater in an avalanche of fire and sparks. Rolling out on the bottom, the burning missiles crashed into the circle of withered brush, instantly igniting the dry clumps to form a horseshoe ring of blazing, crackling flames—open only toward the break slope, blocked by the oncoming vehicles.

The long-dead volcano had suddenly borrowed violent, fiery life. . . .

Terrified, Tom stood rooted to the ground, staring at the sheet of roaring fire barring his way. Panic ripped at the raw edges of his mind. He whirled toward the lone opening in the ring of flames. The monsters were closing the gap. One of them suddenly slipped, lurched and threatened to overturn on the slope. Angrily it grated and whined and spun its wheels in roaring fury, digging in and spewing ash and sand. The fearful uproar of the crackling flames and the roaring, clanging monsters assailed him.

His terror broke through to the last reservoir of strength still in him and set it surging through his pain-racked body— the final flare-up before the burn-out.

Turning away from the terrifying monsters, he tugged at Randi. Exhausted to the marrow of her bones, she sank to the ground. The limits of her endurance reached—and passed—she buried her face in her hands.

Frantically Tom tried to lift her up. He could not. The monsters were almost upon them; the frightening creatures clinging to them were jumping out. He stared at them, eyes wild with terror. In primeval fear he looked at the leaping flames. Then— abruptly—he spun around and raced away from the monsters straight for the crackling, blazing wall, belching fire and smoke, barring him from his escape attempt up the sheer crater wall.

His mouth stretched open in a frenzied scream, drowned by the roar of the flames, he leaped through the inferno and raced for the cliff.

Suddenly he stopped. He turned. His hand went to the crusted, matted spot high on the crown of his head. He stared through the smoke and flame toward Randi lying on the ground, helpless, imprisoned within the hellfire. And from the monsters the menacing creatures were running toward her. He saw her raise her head and gaze toward him. Through the haze of smoke and heat their eyes spanned the distance and met. Total, unreasoning fury born of utter despair gripped him. Snarling his hate, his rage and his torment, he hurled himself back through the fiery wall. He raced to Randi's side— to crouch in desperate defiance over her.

And the fearful creatures, his enemies, his pursuers, his tormentors were upon him.

With a savage snarl, half growl, half scream, he threw himself on the nearest foe.

With the instant, automatic reaction of deep-seated training,

Paul tensed to deliver a lethal blow to his attacker. His hands flew up. In the last possible moment he checked himself. He clenched his fists at his side and turned to parry Tom's savage attack with his shoulder. He spun around. He tried to get a grip on his enraged assailant. He failed.

Tom whirled to face his enemy, snarling his fury and hatred, totally absorbed in his rage. Paul's body grew taut to meet the onslaught of the maddened creature that was Tom. He knew he could not fight back. Not as he had been trained to do. His senses were wholly alert. He was aware of Hays and Howell racing to join him and Ward running toward them with his medical kit. He saw Stark and his Rangers take up their positions, ringing them, to prevent Tom from escaping, should he break away. He sensed that his emergency-team members were fanning out and speeding toward the ring of blazing brush, their Indian backpack extinguishers bouncing on their backs.

And Tom attacked.

He hurled himself at Paul, oblivious of the two men racing toward them. Together the three tried to subdue him, warding him off, careful not to inflict any further physical injury, knowing that an accidental blow to Tom's head could be fatal. But no restraint hampered the infuriated Tom. He fought with blind, black fury. It was man-beast against mere man. Howell's face was raked by Tom's nails as Howell deliberately refrained from striking him. Paul was scratched and kicked; Hays' arm was gashed by Tom's teeth. And still Tom eluded them. . . .

The crater seethed with activity. To Stark's shouted orders the Rangers paced around them, containing the fight. On the break slope National Guardsmen were pouring down into the crater pit to help the emergency team battle the crackling flames, the fire-fighters pumping the hand cylinders on the extinguishers, shooting heavy streams of water onto the fire. The steam and smoke rising from the burning brush, washed red by the flames, obscured the air. It was a scene from hell itself.

In the affray of sound and action no one heard or paid attention to the urgent sputtering of the radio in Colonel Howell's scout. . . .

Randi watched the fight in horror—and yet with the awed realization that Tom was fighting to protect her. Her mind, assailed by the pervasive din, registered the frantic action through a mist of fatigue. Her eyes fell on one of the Rangers moving closer to the struggling men.

And she stiffened.

In the man's hand, furtively held out of sight, was a steel-blue tire-iron!

Uncomprehendingly, but instinctively alarmed, she rose to her feet. She cried out to the man—but no one heard her.

And suddenly the Ranger made his move. He ran toward Tom and his adversaries locked in their unequal struggle. He started to lift his weapon.

Somewhere deep beneath her exhaustion Randi found a surge of strength. She was not consciously aware of it. She only knew that she had to protect her mate. With a choked cry of fury she lunged at the Ranger, leaping on his back, clawing his face with her nails, tearing at his ear with her teeth and kicking her heels into his groin. Tom's fight was hers.

The deadly tire-iron flew from Ranger Gordon's hand as he fell to his knees under Randi's explosive assault. Clawing and scratching, biting and kicking with the ferocity of a wildcat, she bloodied the man savagely before Stark and his men pulled her off and restrained her victim. The Chief Ranger stared at the man in shocked astonishment and outrage. "Hold on to the bastard," he growled at his Rangers.

Tom was totally spent—near collapse. He stood swaying, battered and bloody, the blazing fury in his eyes dying with exhaustion, as the big Sergeant encircled him from behind, pinning his arms in a powerful grip. At once Paul and Howell rushed in and grabbed him, holding him securely. Ward was ready. The needle of the hypodermic bit into Tom's arm—and the men gently lowered him to the sandy ground.

Howell turned to Hays. "Get the chopper!" he snapped. "Move!"

Hays took off for the scouts.

With gentle hands and anxious eyes Ward examined the barely conscious Tom: the wound high on the crown of his head; his festering shoulder; the bleeding gash in his side, opened up in the violence of the fight. He looked up at Paul, tensely hovering over his friend. He nodded.

Randi fell to her knees beside her husband. She looked searchingly up at Paul, her eyes mirroring her fears and her prayers.

"He'll be okay, Randi," Paul said, his voice gravelly. "He'll be okay."

Gently Randi put her husband's head in her lap.

From the scout Hays shouted. "Colonel Howell, sir!" he called. "They want to speak to you. Urgent!"

Howell hurried to the scout.

Paul picked up the tire-iron dropped by Gordon. He held it in his hand as he stalked up to the man, held by two Rangers.

"You bastard!" he growled. "What the hell were you going to do?" It was not a question. It was an accusation.

Gordon scowled at him. He said nothing.

Howell came striding up to them. He glared at the captive Ranger.

"I don't know who the devil you are, Mister," he grated. "But I'll sure as hell find out!" He fixed the man with cold and baleful eyes. "They found the real Gordon."

He looked up as the whirring noise of a helicopter beat down from above.

The chopper carefully descended into the crater, sending clouds of ash and the remnants of the smoke and steam whirling in the air. As soon as the aircraft touched down, medics—carrying two stretchers—jumped from it and hurried toward the group. Immediately, at Paul's direction, they began to load Tom onto one of the stretchers while Randi was led to the other.

Tom was fighting to stay conscious. He could not move. But his eyes, filled with fear and anguish, sought out Randi. In shattering desperation he gazed at her. She reached out a hand toward him.

"Medic!" Paul called. He motioned toward the two litters. "Keep them together."

The rotor of the chopper whirled and bit into the air. The

craft swayed, lifted and slowly soared up and out of the crater.

Below, like ants, the men remaining behind scurried about, extinguishing the last of the flames, while the tiny, squat vehicles began to labor up the sandy slope from the crater pit—like beetles from an ant-lion's trap.

High in the sky above, his troubled eyes firmly resting on his mate beside him, Tom finally slipped into blackness.

His flight had come to an end. He had been vanquished by his enemies.

And saved. . . .

PHASE IV

Edwards Air Force Base

The twin palm trees outside the window on Hospital Drive lazily waved huge, lush fronds in a gentle breeze. Randi watched them with a feeling of pleasure. The trees, the lawns, the fresh green gardens at Edwards had never looked better to her.

The air-conditioned corridor at the Base hospital was cool, Randi's sunburned skin had healed and she felt comfortable. She glanced at Paul and Major Trafford standing near the door to Tom's room. They were talking to each other in subdued voices, but they were really waiting. They were all waiting. . . .

Her ordeal was a nightmare already fading in the light of day. Jonathan Howell had explained to her as much as he felt she should know, and he had asked for and received her pledge to keep everything confidential. No use rocking this particular boat, he'd said. It's hard enough to keep the damned thing from foundering as it is. Measures will be taken by the proper authorities.

He had told her of her husband's knowledge of top-secret information—without divulging what it was. He had told her of the attempt by a foreign power to wrest that knowledge from him—or destroy him. It was they who had tried to shoot him.

There had been two men, he'd said. Two men in the employ of a foreign intelligence service. One was a man going under the name of Jerry Hayden, a sometime artist. He'd been a known agent and under FBI surveillance; but he had given them the slip when he suddenly had taken off for Death Valley. The other was an impostor. A foreign agent who had taken the identity of a reserve Park Ranger named Gordon. He was the man she had jumped in the crater. She only dimly remembered. The real Gordon had been found dead. In the basement of his home in Barstow.

She shivered. Death had been close throughout the entire ordeal—even closer and more violent than she'd known. Close to Tom and to her; and finite to a young Ranger and a young airman named Wilson. Jonathan had told her of Paul's suspicions of the young Wilson when he deduced that outside forces were hunting Tom. They had been groundless, but Paul's resourcefulness and action had ultimately saved both Tom and her. . . .

The door to Tom's hospital room opened and Colonel Howell and Dr. Marcus came out. Marcus was carrying a sheaf of papers in his arms. His face literally shone with satisfaction. Paul and Trafford turned to him.

"Did you get what you wanted, Dr. Marcus?" Trafford asked.

Marcus bobbed his head. "Yes. Thank you. Indeed." He beamed. "Major Darby was most helpful."

"Was he able to pinpoint what went wrong?" Paul asked.

Marcus smiled at him. "As a matter of fact—"

"I think we'd better let Dr. Marcus get to work," Howell interrupted firmly. He looked at the men.

"Yes. Ah—yes, of course," Marcus said. He hefted his papers, taking a firmer grip on them.

An airman came down the corridor and stopped before him.

"Dr. Marcus?" he inquired.

Marcus looked startled. "Yes?"

"General Ryan would like you to come to his office, sir. Right away."

"Oh?"

"He has a gentleman on the line who wants to talk to you, sir. I have a car downstairs."

"To me?" Marcus looked surprised.

"Yes, sir. It's an overseas call. From West Berlin. A Dr. Wilhelm Krebbs."

Marcus looked thunderstruck. *"Gott im Himmel!"* he exclaimed. "Willi!" He stared at the airman as if seeing a ghost from the past. Perhaps he was. Without another word he almost ran down the corridor.

Randi turned to Trafford. "Is it my turn now?" she asked.

Trafford smiled at her. "Of course," he said. "Of course. Go on in."

Tom was sitting up in bed. His head and one shoulder were bandaged, the skin on his face looked new and tender—but his grin went from ear to ear.

"Hi, honey!" he said.

"Hi, yourself." She walked over and sat on the edge of his bed. For a moment they just sat. Together. Looking at each other.

"Randi," Tom said quietly. "What—what really went down? I have to know."

Randi bit her lip. She made no immediate reply.

"I don't remember a damned thing," he complained. "From the moment I came down like a sack of bricks and hit the ground . . . until I woke up here, smelling of disinfectant and wearing this turban."

"You look cute in it." Randi tried to change the subject. He would have none of it.

"What did happen, Randi?"

She looked concerned. "They—they told me not to discuss it with you. Not yet."

"I want to know," he said quietly.

She sighed. "You were—running," she said.

"Running?"

"Yes. Running away. From everyone. From the fears you built up in your own mind. From the demons that existed only in your own head." She looked at her husband. "We—we all do that. Sometimes. Flee from the demons in our own minds."

He took her hand. "I'm back, Rand."

She looked into his eyes. She needed to say nothing—but she did.

"I am—too. . . ."

Paul came into the room.

"Hey," he called. "You're famous, old cock!" He tossed a

newspaper onto Tom's bed. "Friend of mine sent me this."

Tom picked up the paper. *The Berkeley Questioner.* On the front page was a photograph of him standing before an F-15 Eagle. An old PR shot. The headline read:

DOWNED PILOT HUNTED IN DESERT WAR GAMES

IS THE USAF PREPARING FOR MILITARY INTERVENTION IN THE MIDDLE EAST?

By

"Questioner" Staff Reporter
David Rosenfeld, Jr.

Tom threw the newspaper on the floor. He looked at Randi. "I've got better things to do than being famous," he said.

He did not see the story on the below-fold front page:

TOP EAST GERMAN INTELLIGENCE OFFICER KILLED AT BERLIN WALL

COL. GERHARDT SCHARFF SHOT
IN ATTEMPT TO DEFECT
TO THE WEST

He did not see it.

If he had, it would have meant nothing to him.